The
Favour
Laura Vaughan

CORVUS

Published in hardback in Great Britain in 2021 by Corvus,
an imprint of Atlantic Books Ltd.

This paperback edition published in 2022.

Copyright © Laura Vaughan, 2021

10 9 8 7 6 5 4 3 2 1

A CIP catalogue record for this book is available from the British
Library.

Paperback ISBN: 978 1 83895 204 4
E-book ISBN: 978 1 83895 203 7

Printed and bound by CPI Group (UK) Ltd, Croydon, CR0 4YY

Corvus
An imprint of Atlantic Books Ltd
Ormond House
26–27 Boswell Street
London
WC1N 3JZ

www.corvus-books.co.uk

The Favour

To my parents, who have given me
a life filled with treasures.

'One sees as one wants to see; this is false;
and this falsity constitutes art.'
– Edgar Degas

On my return, I found the city bleached of all colour, shimmering dully in an August heatwave. The water was almost as full of glare as the sky. Once again, I had miscalculated. Once more, I was unprepared. Ancient treasure gleamed within dark doorways, shopfronts winked with made-in-China trash, and their competing glister seemed one and the same. My armpits were swampy, my mouth sour. My hands shook. So when I realised it was him, my first thought, absurdly, was *I don't want him to see me like this.* After all those years, he still had that effect on me.

Cheer up, Ada, he said. You look like you're going to a funeral.

His mouth crooked. And then, of course, we laughed.

PART ONE

Trompe l'Oeil

CHAPTER ONE

Inevitably, I blame my mother.

I am aware that this is unreasonable of me. Perhaps entirely so. But when all's said and done, things would have turned out differently if she hadn't sold the house.

Garreg Las was what people generally think of as a 'country house'. While very far from being a stately home, it was still large and dignified enough to be the seat of landed gentry, which is what my father's family had always been. Our particular branch – the Howells – hailed from an overlooked corner of Carmarthenshire. It was there, in 1807, that my great-great-great-grandfather Edwin built the house. His design was almost aggressively plain. The roughcast façade didn't boast so much as a pair of pillars, let alone a portico. Yet the entrance hall, with its sweeping staircase and arcaded gallery, was pared-down classical perfection. The cornicing was delicately moulded, the windows tall, the rooms brimming with pale light.

'It's rather awful to admit,' I heard my mother saying on the phone to one of her friends, 'but I never liked the house. With Anthony gone, it's even more of a millstone.'

I was thirteen years old at the time and my father had only been dead three weeks. But even before his diagnosis, and the cancer's ferociously swift assault, the house had always seemed an extension of his best self. Although my father was gone, the spirit of the place did not leave with him. It lived and breathed within our walls.

If one was going to be unkind, one could say that both the house and my father had seen better days. Once a well-regarded novelist, Daddy's career had petered away into self-published volumes of unintelligible poetry. Garreg Las, too, was not what it was. A lot of the rooms didn't have quite enough furniture, their walls sporting sad bleached squares where paintings had once hung. The roofs were a catalogue of leaking valleys and blocked drains. There was a perpetual chill, even in summer, and the bathwater was never more than lukewarm.

Those memories are distant. I have others which carry with them the sheen of a fairy tale. I remember the mossy smell of apples softening on the larder's shelves. The faded gold of the drawing room walls, the same colour as the roses that foamed by the rotting entrance gates. And the narrow valley in which the house lay, its hills as rain-sodden as the sky and the heavy yet tender colour of a bruise.

I accept that my mother may have seen things differently.

My mother had been a self-avowed city girl the moment she escaped her provincial Midlands town for university in London, and then a job as a publisher's PA. That's how she met my father. Our move to the country was meant to be a temporary break, intended to cure Daddy of a bout of writer's block. But although the block came and went, the three of us stayed put – in a valley that seemed to spend three-quarters of the year under cloud. My parents' circle was chiefly composed of the old county set Daddy had grown up with and a handful of raddled hippies.

Meanwhile, I went to the village primary along with the local farmers' kids, who, though they quaintly referred to Garreg Las as 'the Big House', rather pitied me for the lack of hay bales and quad bikes in my life. Other gatherings involved the children of my father's own childhood friends. They too grew up in large draughty houses with shabby portraits on the walls and damp stains on the ceilings – yet by the age of eleven, vast sums of money were mysteriously found to send them away to public school. By contrast, I was sent to the only independent college in the area, a cheerful but rackety establishment under constant threat of closure. I was dimly aware that this, together with my lack of trust fund or wealthy older relation, was a source of parental concern. But then Daddy fell ill, and everything changed.

'Garreg Las's always been too big for us, darling,' was how my mother broke the news. 'And it *eats* money. If we try and stay the house will literally fall apart around us. That's why we need to pass it on to people who can give it the care it needs.'

The estate agent sucked his teeth as he was shown around and looked doubtful. 'Big old houses like these ... there's not much call for them round here. Nowadays, people want the mod cons. Shame you aren't any closer to the motorway. And just the garden, you say? No real land?'

Hearing this, a rush of hope scalded my heart. Perhaps the house would never sell. However, against the odds, Garreg Las was snapped up by a Manchester businessman with Welsh roots, whose younger wife 'fell in love with the place'. There was an illustrated feature about them in the local paper once they'd finished their renovations. One of our old neighbours sent it to us, perhaps to commiserate, or else out of some private spite:

The substantial 6,000 square foot country home now oozes period elegance, combined with modern additions all done to the highest of standards.

'Oh, it was a real wreck when we bought it,' laughs Tania Price, the glamorous new lady of the manor. 'The fittings were hopelessly dated, and nothing worked. All our friends thought we were crazy! But I saw the potential straight away.'

The old stables now contained a hot-tub and gym. There were gold taps in the bathrooms and feature walls papered in whimsical designs of palm trees and pagodas. The final photo showed one of the Prices' lumpish teenage daughters posing on the stairs in a fish-tail sequinned ball-gown. When I saw this, I cried so hard I was sick.

Should it have made a difference that Daddy was not my biological parent? I suspect my mother thought so. There were times when I sensed the words coiling in her mouth: *He was not your real father. And it was* his *family home, not ours.* She never said them out loud, though. I'll give her that.

I was conceived during one of my mother's rare visits home, when she ran into an old schoolmate in her parents' local. Two weeks later he was killed in a car accident. I was a year old when my parents met; Daddy always said he didn't know which of the two of us he fell in love with first. He was close to fifty at the time and had assumed he would be childless.

I can't remember a time when I was not vaguely aware of the facts of my birth, so my mother must have followed the conventional wisdom to be open about such matters from the start. The couple of photos she provided showed a blandly cheerful twenty-something with sandy hair and broad shoulders. Tim Franks, I was told, had been sporty at school. Good at maths. He became the manager of a regional sales office. His parents and younger sister had emigrated to Australia; he enjoyed Korean food and Formula One. But my mother's efforts were tepid at best; I could tell that the man was essentially forgettable. That made it easy for me, too, to shrug off the idea of him.

I only remember one conversation with Daddy about this. It was some weeks before his diagnosis; though he was already ill, we didn't yet know how badly. I was helping him to clean the frame of one of the portraits. It was of great-great-great-aunt Laetitia, young and roguish in pink satin. She had always been a favourite of mine, partly because the painting was overlaid by an ironic melancholy: poor, beautiful Laetitia had died of TB two weeks after her wedding day. 'Do you think I look like her?' I had asked.

'I think you do,' Daddy replied gravely. 'It's in the eyes. You have the Howell eyes.'

'But how can I? If I'm … if I'm not really a Howell?'

Everyone in Wales, and therefore everyone we knew, assumed I was Daddy's biological child. Nobody ever said anything to correct this. I think this was the first time I openly acknowledged it myself.

Daddy looked surprised. 'Of course you're a Howell. The last of a long line of 'em.'

I nodded. I knew the stories: our branch of the Howells could be traced back to the ninth century and a Welsh prince named Rhydian.

My father must have guessed something more needed to be said. 'You think there haven't been love-children or foundlings before? Every family has its share, if you look hard enough. That's because a so-called family line is actually a series of links. Think of a long chain of different metals, forged together. It's the variation that makes it beautiful. Strong.' He cleared his throat. 'I might not have made you, Ada, but I chose you. You're my legacy, *cariad*.'

The Welsh endearment sounded odd in his public school tones. I think Daddy must have guessed he was dying. Perhaps he was convincing himself as much as me. Perhaps he sensed that his books and his poems were not enough, that any kind of heir was better than none. But he loved me. Of that I was sure. He gave me his name. He left us his house.

The house was proof of everything.

The sale of my father's ancestral home and the auction of most of its contents bought us a three-bedroom Edwardian terrace house in Brockley, London. It had an Ikea kitchen, waxed pine floors and a small garden bright with geraniums. At least the portraits came with us. Aunt Laetitia, of course. Uncle Jacob, the

East India Company colonel. Grandfather Edwin, who had built the house. But I could tell my mother was embarrassed by her dead husband's entourage of ancestors. All those cracked faces and dusty smiles.

Although Daddy's family might not have changed history (no great rebels or reformers or potentates), his ancestors were still a visible part of it. You could pin their individual stories next to the timeline of the national one, and the symbiosis was plain to see. They were people who had always had a tangible stake in the world. Without Daddy, and far from everything he loved, how was I to find mine?

The few bits of furniture we'd kept looked as cramped by the new house as I felt. I stood in the boxy living room, listening to the traffic grind up and down the high street at the end of our road, and assured myself that this exile was temporary. I did not belong here. This was not my life.

For good or ill, our lost house was no longer just the stand-in for what I loved and remembered about my father. It had become the talisman for everything I wanted to be. Austere, yet romantic. Picturesque. Patrician.

Mine is a familiar story, I suppose. The lonely outsider who craves the status and glamour of a privileged elite. But, so I told myself, *my* trajectory was different. I wasn't trying to break in, you see. I was trying to get back.

I really believed that.

CHAPTER TWO

'I'm having trouble with the meaning of three words: lie, deceive, mislead. They seem to mean something similar, but not exactly the same. Can you help me to sort them out from each other?'

To study English Literature at Oxford, at the same college as my father, had gradually supplanted my impossible ambition to reclaim Garreg Las. Various teachers had remarked on my facility with words; I had begun to hope I might even share Daddy's gift for storytelling.

And like hundreds, thousands, of misty-eyed hopefuls before me, I was convinced that Oxford's hallowed ground would provide both rescue and reinvention.

Until I faced the three little words that struck my dream dead. Lie. Deceive. Mislead.

I was moderately happy with my performance in the first interview and my analysis of a poem that I guessed, correctly, to be a Seamus Heaney. In fact, when I took my seat before the second panel, I thought I was on my game. I knew the point of these so-called 'trick questions' was to show that you were capable of thinking creatively, and on your feet. Enjoy it, I'd been told. There is no one right answer.

In this particular case, my best strategy would have been to contrast the words in pairs or, like a good dictionary, give examples of sentences in which they could be used. Instead, I plunged into lengthy definitions of each word, which proved impossible to do without pulling the other treacherous simulacrums into the fray. I blundered about in search of similes, lurched after delineations, piled clarifications on top of qualifiers in such a headlong rush that the whole tottering heap of verbiage threatened to crash around my head. A hot pulsing blush began to spread from my damp armpits up my neck and over my face. It was a mercy for all involved when I finally ground to a stop.

Even then, all might not have been lost. I could have recovered. I was dimly aware that my interviewers were trying to be encouraging. And yet – unaccountably, disastrously – I retreated into a wounded *froideur*. My expression grew haughty, my words clipped. In the final moments I think I even attempted a smirk.

Somehow, the rejection letter still came as a surprise. I'd managed to tell myself that the second interview couldn't possibly have gone as badly as I imagined. That's what my mother and teachers kept saying. I was apt to catastrophise, wasn't I?

I don't remember much about the day Daddy died or when we left Garreg Las. I'd blacked them out. The end of Oxford was not of the same magnitude, but the physicality of my loss was still extreme. Long blank hours would pass, heavy with nothingness. And then, out of nowhere, I'd be hit by a jolt of cold sick energy that left me shaking. I was rancid with shame.

For of course, everyone I knew assumed that I was Oxford bound, especially at school, where I was the designated posh swot.

On first moving to London, I'd been a natural target for derision. My clothes were practical, bought to withstand bad weather and a draughty house. My voice was plummy, with an occasional and inconsistent Welsh lilt. My parents did not own a television. I had only encountered department stores and public transport once or twice a year, on our rare excursions to Swansea. I worked hard to compensate for these deficiencies. But while I was not actively unpopular, I was only ever tolerated, never liked.

Thanks to its catchment area as much as its OFSTED rating, my comprehensive was entirely respectable. It was also hopelessly middle-of-the-road. And so, I was beginning to fear, was I. *What if*, whispered my secret, only part-acknowledged dread, *I took after my real father, after all?*

It was my godmother who came to my rescue. Delilah Grant, an old family friend of Daddy's, was the affluent bohemian type, who painted a little and travelled a lot. The sale of Garreg Las was something she bitterly lamented – 'The place was dear Anthony's muse, after all.'

My mother bit back a laugh. 'Better a house than a mistress, I suppose. And only marginally more expensive.'

My parents had always been an unlikely couple, age-gap notwithstanding. Daddy had had a melancholy stoop and a quizzical manner. My mother was plumpish, prettyish and as direct as my father was (charmingly) elusive. And while I felt that everything about our move to London had devalued me, my mother had come into her own.

Quite quickly, she found a job as office manager at a small architectural firm. She cut her hair short and started wearing make-up. On the weekends, she attended a supper club and repainted the house in seaside shades: whites, blues, sandy beige. When I embarked on my A levels, she started dating a divorced surveyor called Brian, who was as kindly as he was dull. I didn't want my mother to be lonely. But why did everything about her new life have to be so relentlessly conventional? Whenever I tried to talk about our past she looked at me with a kind of polite incomprehension.

Delilah found this as baffling as I did. Whether she had volunteered or Daddy had appointed her to the job, she was an attentive godparent and had been a frequent visitor at Garreg Las. There, she would turn up at very short notice, bringing champagne, impractical shoes and implausible but always entertaining anecdotes. She professed herself to be 'scraping by' but lived in a large flat overlooking Hampstead Heath, and she favoured embroidered kaftans from vintage boutiques. We saw less of her in London than we had in Wales, presumably because Brockley was provincial in a way the wilds of Carmarthenshire were not.

However, Delilah's indignation at the Oxford debacle was too excessive to be of much comfort. 'Didn't they know who you are?' she demanded, when she came over for a post-mortem tea. 'Your father's *name* should have been enough.'

I felt embarrassed for both of us. Anthony Howell's moment of literary acclaim seemed all the more fleeting in light of his later disappointments. Delilah, however, had kept the faith right to the end. We suspected she was responsible for most of the sales of his privately published poetry.

'Now listen,' she said, 'I have just the thing to cheer you up. University's all well and good but honestly, darling, there are so many other exciting ways to expand one's horizon.'

'Ada is still going to university,' said my mother. 'She got offers from everywhere else she applied. In fact, UCL is probably a better fit–'

'Ah, but *this* is something special.' Delilah thrust a couple of thick brochures into our hands. 'A friend's grandson went on one of these courses last year and is still *raving* about it. He'd been one of those hulking, monosyllabic types, you know. But after two months in Italy, he was positively Byronic! Not that there's anything unprepossessing about *you*, Ada darling. *You've* always been adorable. But Italy is transformative. You've read *A Room with a View*, haven't you?'

The brochure's colour scheme was turquoise and plum, with the name of the company – Dilettanti Discoveries – printed in dull gold. Its strap-line was 'The Grand Tour Reimagined for the Modern Age'. I read on breathlessly.

Three hundred years ago, wealthy young Englishmen celebrated coming of age by touring Europe in search of art, culture and the roots of Western civilisation. They commissioned art, collected antiquities and mingled with the elite of continental society.

Here at Dilettanti Discoveries, we believe that this is a tradition worth reinventing. Our gap-year courses follow in the footsteps of the Grand Tourists, travelling the length of Italy in search of its greatest treasures, inspiring a passion for art and intellectual discovery in new generations of young people.

'The company does various tours around Europe but the Italian gap-year course is what they're really known for,' Delilah explained. 'It's been running for fifteen years but they don't tend to advertise much; it's mostly word of mouth. And their connections mean they have all sorts of privileged access. That's what you pay for.'

'I'll say.' My mother was looking at the small print. 'Eight weeks in Italy is twelve grand. Not including flights! Or –' disbelieving snort '– food. Lordy.'

I barely heard her. I was looking at a photograph of a handsome, floppy-haired youth gazing intently at a Raphael Madonna. For so long – and exhaustively – my dreams had been filled with quadrangles and spires and wood-panelled studies. Here was a different set of clichés, no less seductive. In the next picture, a trio of laughing girls drank prosecco on the steps of an amphitheatre. The light, the wine, their glowing faces seemed equally sun-doused.

Who are our students?
Our courses seem tailor-made for those interested in pursuing a career in the arts, but in fact our students come from a range of disciplines. To enjoy the Dilettanti experience, all you need is an open mind, a love of beauty

and curiosity about the world. And it's not just about learning, of course – we're known for inspiring life-long friendships, as well as a passion for art.

Who are our tutors?
Whether they're artists, academics or curators, all our 'Cicerones' are experts in their fields. Young and friendly, they're also keen enthusiasts of *la bella vita*! Our teaching style is lively and informal, with debate encouraged. There are no notes to take or final exams, so students are free to learn at their own pace.

Who were the Dilettanti?
The Society of Dilettanti was a club founded in 1734 by a group of British aristocrats who had shared the transformative experience of having made the Grand Tour of Italy. But as the name Dilettanti (from the Latin word *dilettare*, to 'take delight') suggests, its members took the enjoyment of life as seriously as they did their fascination with the ancient world.

These original Dilettanti were proud to be amateur enthusiasts, not dusty scholars. We hope their exuberant spirit lives on in our tours.

'It's not cheap, I'll grant you,' said Delilah, 'but that's where I come in. Not the whole amount,' she added hastily, 'but I'd like to make a significant contribution.' She gave a self-conscious laugh. 'I was planning to leave Ada a little something once I shuffle off this mortal coil, but then I thought, why wait? At least this way I'll be around to see you enjoy the spoils.'

'Goodness, Delilah. This is – extraordinary of you. Extraordinarily generous, I mean.' My mother sat up even straighter. 'I'm not sure we can in all conscience accept.' She cleared her throat. 'No. Thank you for your great kindness, but it's altogether too much. Ada's expectations have a way of getting out of hand; it would be better to keep to the existing plan–'

I flung down the brochure and burst into tears.

'Nonsense! *Nonsense*. I absolutely *insist*.' Delilah's eyes, too, were watering as she pulled me into an embrace. 'It's what dear Anthony would have wanted.'

I assumed Delilah was right and that my father would have been delighted with her gift, but it was not something I could be certain of. It troubled me that my memories of Daddy were becoming much less vivid than those of Garreg Las. Like a benign ghost, he seemed to have been absorbed into its remembered shadows. If I closed my eyes, I could see one of his hands resting on the lid of the piano, tracing the storm clouds of its polished wood. If I dreamed of the lime trees in the avenue, then I would glimpse his smile in their shivering, silver-green light. I had his books, of course, but they were paradoxical and wilfully abstruse. They might as well have been written by a stranger. I fretted that my own attempts at fiction felt like a stranger's too. How did a writer find their voice? And what if they were too fragmented or adrift to recognise it?

And, yes, I blamed my mother. As time wore on, and my restlessness only increased, my mother's lack of interest in her marriage, and my childhood, began to feel a deliberate betrayal. There was a certain ruthlessness in how easily she'd shrugged off our former lives. Our old neighbours didn't get so much as a Christmas card. The one time I tentatively suggested we go back to visit, she looked at me in surprise. 'What would be the point of that? You'd only wallow.'

Generally overlooked at school, I wondered how different my experience could have been if the people there had understood where I came from. I wasn't stupid; I knew that bragging about past Howell glories would have been met with incomprehension or ridicule. But if there was a boy I liked, or a girl I wanted to befriend, I'd have these embarrassing fantasies of taking them back home, to my *real* home, where I would teach them the geography of a house with wings (*gun room, bell room, butler's pantry*) and the language of its furniture (*credenza, settle, armoire*). I wouldn't be pompous or snobby. Yet they would be impressed and beguiled nonetheless: first by the house and then by me.

This was not going to happen in Brockley.

Then there was the day I came back from school to find the portraits and the few bits of furniture we'd brought with us from Wales had been packed up and sent to storage. Even Daddy's books had been cleared from the shelves. The only photographs of Garreg Las that remained were the ones in my bedroom. 'Let's not be *morbid*,' my mother said briskly, when I questioned the purge.

It was as if everything my father represented had been stripped away and sanded down, then painted over. Shades of beige.

I didn't want to turn into my mother. I didn't want to end up like Delilah, either. With her greying mane of hair, her kaftans and kohl-smudged eyes, she was costumed for a part in a play she hadn't been cast in. Delilah was nobody's muse. She was picturesque, but also pitiable.

No, I thought, resting my palm on the gilt-edged brochure, I am going to be one of these kinds of people. A Dilettante.

CHAPTER THREE

I was able to defer my place at UCL without undue trouble; the real challenge of my last-minute gap year was funding my share of the Dilettanti costs. Generous as Delilah's contribution was, I still had several thousand pounds to raise.

The Dilettanti course ran for two months, from mid-March until mid-May. In the meantime, I found a part-time job at a local bar and took an online secretarial course. Brian, my mother's paramour (as Delilah insisted on calling him), had a friend who worked for a company that ran English language schools and helped get me temp work at their head office in Holborn. Most of my time was spent doing data-entry in the basement, but I decided to look upon this drudgery as just another aspect of the émigré experience. It gave me a measure of satisfaction to think my co-workers would never guess the mantra that got me through our desultory chats by the water-cooler: *This is not my place, these are not my people. This is not my real life.*

We may lose faith in many things over the course of our lives, but belief in one's own exceptionalism is generally the last to go.

My mother's lack of enthusiasm for the trip was a continued thorn in my side. 'I'm very grateful to Delilah, of course, but I can't help thinking that a contribution to your tuition fees would have been a more appropriate gift. Goodness – if you want a holiday, you could always go for a week or two to Italy with a couple of friends.' How, I wondered, had my mother failed to notice I didn't *have* any friends? 'I mean, you've never shown any particular interest in art before.' Then the final stab: 'You know you've a tendency to build things up, or else blow them out of proportion. I just don't want you to be disappointed.'

To prove her wrong, I spent as much time as I could in museums and galleries. Here I was free to strike the attitude of an insouciantly sexy bluestocking. (My expression was pensive, my skirts were short.) And I accessorised my commute with pickings from the Dilettanti Discoveries suggested reading list: *A Room with a View*, *The Wings of the Dove*, Ovid's *Metamorphoses*, Dante's *Divine Comedy* … '*Do not be afraid,*' I recited to myself, while taking orders for the tea run or trudging back from the copy-shop with a stack full of binders, '*our fate cannot be taken from us; it is a gift.*'

The most compelling piece of Dilettanti paperwork was the list of my fellow students. Rocco Carrington, Petra Deane, Annabelle Gilani, Melissa Harrison, Kitty Henshaw, Lorcan Holt, Jonathon Jolf-Stratton, Mallory Kaplan, Willa Murray, Oliver Seaton-Bryce. Saying these names aloud, I should have been uplifted by their cut-glass chime; instead, my mother's words rang in my ears, and I felt the first intimation of unease.

Melissa ('Missy') took charge of communications, converting an introductory email into an instant messaging group. The ensuing banter revealed that Missy and Kitty were already besties, and that Lorcan and Willa were school friends who'd likely enjoyed past benefits. Annabelle and Lorcan were step-siblings (or half-siblings; it wasn't clear). They and Kitty shared an acquaintance with Oliver. It was beginning to feel as if the in-crowd had already been formed.

I kept my own introduction brief and breezy. Better to hold back until we met in Italy, I reasoned. In a foreign country, far from home, prior alliances were bound to fall away.

To this end, I blew off the introductory drinks Missy organised for those living in or near London. Only a couple of people could make it in any case; most were busy with alternate adventures. If they had a job, it was working the ski season as a chalet girl or volunteering on a Kenyan game reserve or doing an internship at Christie's or *Tatler*. For them, Dilettanti Discoveries was just one of several stops along a luxuriant gap-year path.

I think it was this realisation that shook my confidence most of all. How would these people know I was supposed to be one of them?

Although I wasn't alone in having a marginal online presence, I was still able to scroll through a seemingly endless montage of shiny, pretty people partying on ski slopes and beaches and the aforementioned game reserves. Minor-league celebrity and aristocracy were both represented: Oliver was the younger son of a baron; Petra Deane had been a child actor. I recognised her winsome pout from a BBC costume drama of five years before. Meanwhile, the lone American, Mallory, clogged her social media feeds with quotes about Unleashing the Inner Goddess and Loving the Power of You. Rocco had an upended fedora with vomit in it as a profile picture.

I widened my online investigations to include our so-called

'Cicerones'. Assorted specialists would come and go during the course of the trip, but three tutors were set to accompany us from start to finish. Dr Nathaniel Harper was on research leave from the Classics department of a red-brick university, Ben Ainsworth was an art history teacher at one of the big public schools, and Yolanda Franks was a professional artist, as well as Learning Consultant at the V&A. These were serious people, I reassured myself; they would run a serious course.

The final flurry of packing and repacking, research and rehearsal, passed in a blur. I felt simultaneously over- and under-prepared. And all of a sudden it was a chilly March night, and I was disembarking from a bus onto Piazzale Roma, Venice.

This utilitarian square, with its parking garages and bus bays, was not the introduction to La Serenissima that I had imagined. Indeed, the guidebook I'd bought had waxed lyrical on the joys of arriving at Venice by boat over the lagoon, and thus 'seeing the city as it was meant to be seen: a jewel rising from the waves'. The water-taxi approach was what the rest of my course-mates had opted for. But since it was up to individual students to arrange their travel, my mother and I had gone for the cheapest offering of a budget airline. I had, therefore, landed at Treviso, a town sixteen miles outside of Venice, three hours after the rest of the group, instead of the lagoon-side airport of Marco Polo. Flight delays had held me up by a further hour.

Ben Ainsworth, the lead tutor, had supplied instructions on how to find the party. I tried to take heart from the fact I wasn't the last to arrive; Lorcan Holt was staying the first night with friends in the city and would not be joining us until the morning. But this was the first time I'd really travelled on my own; by the end of my somewhat flustered transit through airports and bus stations, I felt both dingy and diminished.

My first full view of the Grand Canal restored the magic. Or so I told myself – like all the best conjuring tricks, Venice's beauty depends in part on one's willingness to accept the illusion. The Disney strip of palazzos, with their faded pastels and spun-sugar trimmings, was lit up like a stage-set. The water's surface was satiny, with ruffles of black and gold. Once I had boarded the vaporetto, I leaned over the side of the boat, straining to catch, beneath the exhaust fumes, the city's fabled mermaid whiff. My stop, San Stae, was dominated by a towering baroque slab of pillars and pedestals and writhing saints.

But then the city performed another sleight of hand. Leaving the Grand Canal was to turn away from the Disney palaces and their tinsel glitter; almost immediately, I was in a maze of dank alleys and dead campos shuttered up against the night. At only half-past ten, the city seemed deserted. The trundle of my suitcase was embarrassingly loud. Street lamps pooled sour light on peeling stucco and powdery bricks hollowed by age.

After only one wrong turn, I came to a narrow canal with the trattoria on the left. The windows' spill of buttery light should have been inviting; instead, I held back. *Just don't fall over your suitcase*, I told myself, before squaring my shoulders and attempting to saunter confidently through the door. Seconds later, the maître d' tripped over my bags instead.

Amidst the resultant apologies and confusion, somebody was calling my name. There was no need to shout: the place was mostly empty except for the large table at the back, which, of course, had fallen silent the moment I'd made my chaotic entrance. 'Here you are, here you are!' exclaimed the man who had now taken my hand in both of his and was pumping it up and down vigorously. '*Benvenuto in Venezia!*' He had round childish cheeks, tufts of gingery hair and a polka-dot cravat knotted jauntily around his throat. Ben Ainsworth, I presumed. I recognised the cravat from his photograph on the Dilettanti Discoveries website.

'What a time you've had, poor duck. Come on, sit down, let's get you settled. Have you eaten?' Garlic gusted from his breath. 'Of course you haven't. Plane food is pap. Let's get some pasta in you. And wine. Lots of it! *Dell'altro vino, per l'amore di Dio,*' he shouted cheerfully at the waiter, before launching into an animated chat in what appeared to be fluent but excruciatingly accented Italian.

'Hello there,' said another man, rising to shake my hand. He was tall and fair, with a long bony face that shouldn't have been attractive but kept you looking. 'I'm Nate,' he said, with a slightly stiff courtliness. 'It's lovely to have you with us.'

Indistinct sounds of agreement and welcome came from the rest of the party. Coffee had just been served; they had the flushed, hazy look of people who had been drinking and talking just a little too long to hold their focus. The table was littered with the remnants of the meal – bloody stipples of wine, the ticker tape of breadstick wrappers, whiskery bones of fish lying in a nimbus of green oil.

27

'Scootch up, sistas,' said an American voice. The girl – Mallory – was shifting her bottom about and gesturing to the bit of bench next to her. Her wide snub face was redder and shinier than anyone else's; the eagerness of her smile suggested she was a bit too relieved to see me. Had she, in her own seconds-swift appraisal, decided that we were in some sense on the same level? Was this because of the clumsiness of my entrance or had she picked up on some other, deeper insecurity? And was it apparent to the others too?

But since nobody else was making space for me, I was obliged to sit next to her. This was the cue for other people to lean forward and introduce themselves.

Jonathon ('JJ') was the first to say hello, a big sloppy boy with an acne-roughened complexion and comically overgrown thatch of hair. Rocco sported grimy silver rings and even grimier-looking tattoos. By contrast, Oliver, the baron's son, was slight and elfin.

Of the girls, Annabelle was slim and dark with a cool smile. Willa was a blonde with the coarse, sensual features of a saloon-bar madam. Petra put me in mind of a younger version of Delilah: self-consciously bohemian, determinedly artless, with a tangle of improbably red curls. Two Sloane-y girls with identikit giggles, one button-nosed and blonde (Missy), the other a diminutive brunette (Kitty), completed the group.

A plate of cured meats was put in front of me, followed by a glistening coil of spaghetti and clams. I tasted oil and salt and gristle. Sweat and brine. The trattoria's scuffed white walls and heavy wood furnishings were softened by candlelight. Through the fog of the wine and my own tiredness, I felt as if I was looking at a memory, as if hindsight had already gilded the scene with bittersweet significance. *The night my life began.*

'I like your pearls,' said the dark girl, Annabelle, out of nowhere. From her surname, Gilani, I'd assumed she was part Italian, and her colouring suggested the same, though I later discovered her mother was in fact Iranian. Annabelle had been one of those with no accessible online presence and I thought she might be shy, for she was sitting in a corner and had been quieter than most. Now I saw that she was beautiful, and that this reticence was self-possession.

'Thanks. They were my grandmother's.'

Previously kept for special occasions, the pearls would now be my signature accessory, I had decided. After long and anxious thought, I had attempted to reinvent my personal style as country-house nostalgic. I pictured dreamy floral tea-dresses and homespun knitwear, prim blouses with a sexy edge. Sourcing this vision proved tricky: in the event, the dresses' prints were too brash for vintage charm, the knitwear was scratchy and the blouses were made of a polyester blend that made me sweat. But the necklace, at least, was authentic.

'Gorgeous,' Petra conceded. 'Lucky you.'

I touched the rounded warmth of the pearls and felt a surge of well-being.

Afterwards, as we wound our raucous way back to the hotel, the night-time streets revealed themselves in different ways. The dark waterways and empty campos swirling with sepia shadows and dead leaves now seemed mysterious rather than sinister. For this time, they were graced with glimpses of loveliness – a wellhead garlanded with pockmarked cherubs, a loop of embedded arches, an iron grille as fine as filigree.

Or maybe this memory is a composite one, gleaned from the course of many such nights. Maybe I have only imagined the hints of what was to come and invented the portents we brushed past so blithely. Here, an angel's wing. There, a fanged lion.

CHAPTER FOUR

The pursuit of beauty was an abiding theme of our two months in Italy. We were told that artists of the past believed beauty was virtuous because it redeemed suffering and showed life to be worthwhile. Earnestly, we debated the merits of this view and whether beauty deserved to be seen as one of the foundations of art, along with goodness and truth. Art that pursued beauty above everything else was, we laboriously agreed, no more than decorative.

The question of our own decorativeness was, of course, equally vital, at least for us girls.

When I was six or seven, I had a favourite navy dress with a lace collar, which Daddy said gave me the look of a Victorian governess. It was an image that stuck with me. On good days, I am pale and dainty. On bad ones, mousey and wan. I used to wear my hair pulled back in a rather severe knot, Jane Eyre style, so that I could shake it out at the end of the day and admire its ripple. *But Miss Howell … you're beautiful.*

My last year at university, I asked a passing fling if he thought I was pretty. He was regular-guy handsome, which was something that made me more, not less, insecure. I asked him late at night, when we were both drunk. 'Tell me honestly,' I said, dishonestly.

'I'm just curious. It's not a big deal.' 'OK,' he said. 'You're almost hot. But you can be almost kind of ugly too.' And then he went on to say, 'I guess that's true of most girls I've dated.'

Almost hot. Almost ugly. At the time, and for a long while afterwards, this boy's assessment stung. But I think he was right, both about me (specifically) and other women (in general). It still surprises me, the consistency of men's looks, when contrasted with women's capacity for transformation. Simply by darkening her eyelashes, rearranging her hair and putting on a particular bra or slick of gloss, a woman can completely reinvent herself. It is as destabilising as it is liberating.

That year, the year of Italy, I was more almost-ugly than not. I had yet to fully grow into my looks, such as they were, nor did I know how to best exploit them. Still, I was starting to trust that, yes, I could be hot – almost – in the right light, in the right clothes, with the right people. But I had also accepted the fact that there was to be no final, dramatic metamorphosis. I was not and never would be beautiful.

Beauty is, at its simplest, the gift of being chosen – by heroes and villains, for good or ill. And this is why the beautiful tend to play more interesting roles and have bigger stories than the rest of us. They are chosen for blessings, chosen for curses.

Mostly for blessings, obviously.

Willa, the bosomy saloon-bar blonde, was the girl who attracted the most attention. Whistles and cat-calls accompanied her wherever she went, and she accepted these tributes with complacency.

While Petra did not have Willa's flagrant sex appeal, her air of bohemian sophistication put her in the same league within our group. Since she and Willa were different enough not to be in direct competition, they were able to put on a fairly convincing show of sisterhood.

Annabelle was the girl who could have been alpha if she wanted to, and was all the more intriguing because she did not. Without being aloof, she managed to keep a certain distance. She had the classic Persian features – a delicately hooked nose, high arched brows, wide cheekbones – but her mixed-race parentage meant her eyes and hair were a dark mahogany, rather than black. In spite of having a place to read Classics at Oxford, her contributions to our over-heated discussions of history and culture were quiet as well as astute.

I felt a secret affinity with Annabelle because she was the only other person in the group who appeared to be operating under a budget. Like me, she rationed her coffee stops, never ordered a starter and frequently skipped wine with lunch; she made no impulse purchases from markets or souvenir stands. She had also packed very light. One pair of jeans, one pair of black cigarette pants. One knitted skirt. One draped blouse, one lace tank. Two plain T-shirts. Two cardigans. Three pairs of shoes: ankle boots, plimsolls, ballet pumps. One coat, one handbag, one scarf. The only jewellery she wore was a thin beaten-gold chain that she never took off. Her face was bare.

It was not that Annabelle didn't give thought to her appearance (her clothes were of quality; their muted colours had been chosen with care) but her lack of conspicuous effort only confirmed her superiority. On the rare occasions she had a pimple, she didn't even bother using concealer to cover it up. I would have welcomed a sign, however small, of personal vanity. I think all the girls would. By contrast, our over-stuffed suitcases bore witness to what really drove our acquisitiveness: indecision, impulse, insecurity.

That first morning, I woke up just after six, my head buzzing from the cheap wine. Our hotel, which was a little way off the campo of San Giacomo dell'Orio, did not look any more prepossessing in the light of day than it had at night. The room I was sharing with Mallory, Kitty and Missy was crowded with pine furniture and painted a sickly pink. But I could hear the slop and slosh of the canal outside the window, and this was enough to propel me out of bed.

The other girls were deeply asleep. Kitty was snoring, her soft little pout bubbling over with sighs. I crept out to the tiny shower stall along the corridor and got dressed as quickly and quietly as possible. The day officially began with meeting in the lobby at eight, and I wanted a moment to myself in the city beforehand.

Nate the tutor was standing by reception, tapping away at his phone. I felt a little shy. Unlike Ben, the garrulous bon viveur, Nate seemed entirely adult. His bony face wore a scowl of concentration. But when he saw me, he smiled. 'An early riser. How novel. If you're on the hunt for coffee, I can recommend the bar on the far side of the campo.'

The campo was flooded with a watery primrose light. Sparrows skittered and chittered underfoot, their plumage the same mottled dun colour as the buildings around the square. I went to the bar and ordered a cappuccino, carefully counting out the coins. I'd spent months of office work drinking instant in order to provide for just such an occasion.

I sat down outside, hunched deeper into my scarf and opened my copy of *The Passion*.

'Hi. Hello. Sorry to intrude, but are you by any chance a Dilettante?'

I looked up. A boy was standing in front of me, battered hold-all in one hand. His navy pullover and jeans were similarly worn around the edges. I recognised this shabbiness; it was the kind I had known in my childhood. The gentrified kind. The boy was slim and brown with heavy, slightly wavy hair the colour of old gilt. It was not a conventionally handsome face – his grey eyes were a little too pale, his features a little too beaky. But his mouth was curling in an ironic smile, and his voice was rich as brandy butter.

'A dilettante?' I heard myself saying, my voice plumped by the same richness. 'Not where coffee's concerned.'

I knew from the very beginning that Lorcan Holt was out of my league. But when he grinned and asked if I could direct him to the hotel, I also knew there had been a moment between us, however fleeting. A frisson. Something about me – the line of my brow, the light in my eye – had caught his attention. I was not going to be chosen by Lorcan Holt. But I had been noticed by him.

So although I pointed Lorcan towards the hotel, I didn't offer to accompany him. This would be something else he'd notice. A boy like Lorcan would be all too used to girls tagging along, eager to be seen at his side.

Although he and Annabelle shared a certain glamour, there was no familial resemblance between them. Annabelle's presence was still and self-contained. Lorcan, by contrast, had a glinting restlessness. He could be sullen, his face suddenly growing narrow and shadowed, but this occasional darkening only enhanced the swoop and glitter of his charm.

'They didn't really know each other growing up,' I overheard Willa tell Petra. 'Lorcan's father left his mother for Annabelle's. He knocked up both women at pretty much the same time. And then moved on to someone else less than two years later ... Mr Holt's a reformed character these days, but he used to be *quite* the ladies' man. Anyway, sending the two of them on the Discoveries course is part of his belated attempt to make amends.'

Petra looked thoughtful. 'Like father like son, do you think?'

'Oh, Lorcan's not so bad,' said Willa tolerantly. 'All the nicest boys were rascals at school. But I'm not convinced by Miss Butter-Wouldn't-Melt. I mean –' significant glance in Annabelle's direction '– think of the daddy issues.'

My own paternal issues proved something of an asset. Once the opening night's mist of candlelight and wine had cleared, I realised I had underestimated the scale of the task ahead of me. I had to re-learn the ways of these people. The drawl of their voices. The flick of their hair. The pearly lustre of their confidence. And I only had two months to establish myself in a way that would carry our friendship through university and beyond. Lorcan, I knew from the message threads, was going to Oxford. So was Annabelle. Oliver was Cambridge bound. I was glad not to be saddled with a bunch of dim Sloanes. But this sense of relief was complicated, tied up as it was with my own Oxford rejection.

I had a lucky break that first morning. Our day began with an Italian culture and conversation lesson. When we stopped for a break, the chat moved to books and I managed to drop in that Daddy had been a writer.

'No way!' said Mallory. 'Amazing. That's incredible.'

'Anyone we'd have heard of?' Rocco asked.

'Probably not. His name was Anthony Howell, but he fell out of fashion a few years back.'

'Anthony Howell?' Nate repeated. 'You're kidding. I read him my first year at college. *The Mechanist's Knot.* I thought it was hugely impressive, in a tricksy, post-modern sort of way.'

'Well, I'm obviously biased … but I agree.' *Mechanist* was a heady concoction of Celtic fabulism and cyberpunk, laced with paranoia. In truth, I found it almost impenetrable.

'Funny, I didn't know Anthony Howell had a daughter. The couple of profiles I read portrayed him as something of a lone wolf.'

'Yet here I am,' I said lightly.

Everyone was looking at me with new interest.

Missy wrinkled her snub nose. 'You said your dad "was" a writer. Is he, like, retired?'

'He died when I was thirteen,' I said bravely. 'But I suppose I'm lucky in some ways. A part of him will always be with me because of his books.'

There was a respectful pause.

Then, 'Do you write?' asked Lorcan, in the same way one might ask 'Do you ski?'

'Sure.' Guiltily, I thought of the twenty-odd false starts of my 'novel', most of which were barely a few paragraphs long. 'I mean, yeah, it's something I'm definitely exploring. I suspect I'll end up working with books one way or another.' I shrugged. 'After all, it's in my DNA.'

That first day was enough to establish our hierarchy and coalitions. Once again, I had a nagging suspicion that Mallory was operating on the assumption that we were going to be allies. Although a wealthy New Yorker, she was hardly the Park Avenue princess I'd imagined. Everything about her was stolid and sensible, including her uniform of loose slacks and pastel crew necks. I found it hard to reconcile her appearance with the social media aphorisms of which she was so fond. *Fire Needs Air – Desire Needs Space … Never change to be accepted by others: stay weird! … In a world where everyone wears a MASK, it's a privilege to see a SOUL … I Dream of You in Colours That Don't Exist.*

Meanwhile, I was waiting to see which of the girls Lorcan would go for. Willa was the obvious choice, but whatever they might have got up to at school, she and Lorcan shared a matey camaraderie that appeared devoid of sexual tension. This left

Petra the front-runner. I was relieved by this. Willa was too much of a bruiser for me to make any headway with her. Petra, however, had potential. I thought I detected a thread of anxiety in the theatricality of her gestures and the outrageousness of her anecdotes.

I had an opportunity to watch her and Lorcan together at dinner on the second night because I was on the same table as them, together with Mallory and Yolanda, the last of our three tutors to arrive. Yolanda was thin and freckled, with a watchful manner. She was asking us for our first impressions of Venice. Mallory confessed to finding it 'beautiful, but kinda poky'.

I knew what she meant. The pale light of morning had given way to darkness and drizzle; without sunshine to make the waterways sparkle, the maze of ancient streets had seemed to close around us, more cramped, cluttered and crowded than I had thought possible. But I was not going to admit this. 'Maybe she should've stuck to the Venetian hotel in Vegas,' I murmured to Lorcan. 'I hear most Americans rate it more highly than the real thing.'

I was gratified to see him smirk. But Yolanda had overheard me.

'You know,' she said, 'American cash has helped prop this city up over the years. The Save Venice foundation alone has raised over twenty-five million dollars for restoration projects.'

Her tone was placid, but I felt rebuked. Yolanda was someone I had wanted to impress. Her mother was Ghanaian, and she drew on this heritage for her artworks. I knew from her website that these were intricate embroideries in which vignettes of modern

British life were sewn in black thread onto traditional kente cloth. I'd been planning to ask her about them. Now I fretted that we'd already got off on the wrong foot.

But when she turned back to Mallory, Lorcan rolled his eyes at me and I knew it had been worth it.

Later that night, I was on my way to the bathroom when I overheard Yolanda speaking on the phone in the darkened stairwell. From the hushed intimacy of her voice, I guessed she was talking to a partner. 'All present and correct.' She sounded tired. 'Oh, it's fine. It's fine. I'll be fine. Really. Just ...' Small, rueful laugh. 'Yeah. The usual.'

I frowned. Our tutors were supposed to be more mentors than authority figures. I had believed the marketing material when it suggested we were to be comrades – co-conspirators! – in the same great adventure. It stung to think that for the adults in charge it was just another job. Perhaps Yolanda and I even took solace from the same mantra: *These are not my people, this is not my life.*

CHAPTER FIVE

I had not expected to be so cold.

Even in early spring, I'd assumed Italy would be balmier than Britain. But I had failed to anticipate the effect of hours spent standing on stone floors in churches and crypts. I had also forgotten how to dress for bad weather. My thin jackets and acrylic-mix jumpers proved woefully inadequate.

Meanwhile, we gazed upon parched plains and blue hills basking in the sun: all those *pietàs* or *sacra conversazioni* in which the assembled figures were sombre yet languid, robed in cool silks. The scenes of martyrdom – flayings, roastings, disembowellings – had a dark heat of their own. In the majestic murk of the Scuola Grande di San Rocco, whose chill beat an icy pulse through my body, the Tintorettos seemed roiled in blood and sweat and tar.

The visit to the Scuola occupied the morning of our fourth day in Venice. The afternoon was free and so the girls elected to go shopping, with the exception of Annabelle, who said she was going to take some photos on the Zattere. I'd been looking forward to browsing glass trinkets and papier mâché masks. But my course-mates only had time for the designer shops on the Salizada San Moisè.

Outside the warmth of the boutiques, our breath puffed like dragons'. The iron lid of the sky gave everything beneath a monochromatic tint. Old ladies trudged over the bridges, squat and burly in their furs. I envied their snugness as I jammed my fists in my pockets and stamped my frozen feet. I envied the other girls, too, cocooned in cashmere and virgin wool. Their cheeks looked rosy. Mine, I was sure, were merely raw.

Afterwards, we retired to Campo Santo Stefano and drank hot chocolate in a café. The boys had spent their afternoon at a gondola workshop but Lorcan rejoined us ahead of the rest. From my window seat I watched Petra, nestled into a creamy fox-fur collar that I coveted beyond all things, flirt with him on the steps of a monument. Although nothing definitive had yet happened between them, it was clearly only a matter of time.

'Aren't they cute together?' said Mallory. 'Petra's so … artistic. And Lorcan's a real gentleman.'

'She can have him. Personally, I'd take his cousin,' said Missy, nudging Kitty, who nodded and giggled. 'Mm-*hm*.'

'What cousin?' Mallory asked.

'Teacher Nate. What, you didn't realise?' Willa looked scornful and I was grateful not to have betrayed my own ignorance. Nate and Lorcan shared the same build and colouring, as well as fondness for battered tweed, but I had assumed the joshing informality between them was because they knew each other socially.

'Huh,' said Mallory. 'Guess I hadn't realised Dilettanti Discoveries was such a family affair.'

'Nate's mother and Lorcan's are sisters,' Willa condescended to explain. 'He's no relation to Annabelle.'

I was surprised to find Nate so admired. I thought the fact I'd seen something attractive in our tutor, despite – or because of – the things that should have made him ugly, was a mark of my discernment. Perhaps it was his manner that people found intriguing. He was formal, even a little stiff, in contrast to Ben's exuberance.

On our second night in the city, we had had a private after-hours tour of St Mark's, and Ben had read aloud from Ruskin:

'… and in the midst of it, the solemn forms of angels, sceptred, and robed to the feet, and leaning to each other across the gates, their figures indistinct among the gleaming of the golden ground through the leaves beside them, interrupted and dim, like the morning light as it faded back among the branches of Eden, when first its gates were angel-guarded long ago …'

Ben had worked for Dilettanti Discoveries for several years and taken many tours to Venice. He must have recreated this moment many times. He looked a little ridiculous standing there under a golden dome with his chubby child's face and voluminous cravat. Yet he read beautifully, and as he did so his eyes had filled with tears. So had Mallory's. Even JJ, the most outwardly stolid of the boys, was blinking furtively.

One of Ben's favourite anecdotes was about how the French writer Stendhal had collapsed one day while visiting Florence, overwhelmed by the splendour of the art, and so giving his name to 'Stendhal syndrome'. Ruskin had suffered similarly in Venice.

Surrounded by the basilica's half-pagan glitter, its incense-spiced shadows, I too wanted to feel transported, overcome. It was the same in the Scuola. I had shivered before the Tintorettos, but I couldn't tell if this was because of the cold or the shock of those vast canvases of contorted flesh. The more art I saw, the less I knew how to respond to it. I was constantly distracted by not only how I might look or sound but by my own thought processes and how inadequate – inauthentic – I feared them to be.

My one transcendent moment had come in the church of San Giovanni e Paolo. Its size made it seem more severe than most, yet the rosy brick walls gave its expanse the illusion of warmth. Lines of giant pillars soared up to where slender wooden beams sprang and arched, and as I gazed upwards I thought, not of the next world, but of the avenue at Garreg Las and the spreading wings of lime trees above my head. And then I found there were tears in my eyes, and Ben was there, squeezing my arm and saying proudly, 'It does *get* to you, doesn't it?'

I wondered then if Garreg Las had spoiled all other beauty for me.

Thinking of this, it was a few moments before I realised the conversation had moved to Nate's wife, Clemency. Again, it was Willa who was our informant. 'She's a couple of years older than him, thirty-six at least,' she was saying, with the careless privilege of an insider. 'And she's had these health problems that mean she can't get knocked up.'

Mallory looked stricken. 'That's so sad.'

It was true this information imbued Nate with an appealing air of sorrow.

'My sister and her husband tried for three years before she got pregnant,' said Kitty. 'It was shagging to a fertility schedule that killed their sex life. Not the baby.'

For some reason, this made us laugh. We were still snorting when Annabelle came through the door. 'What's the joke?'

'There isn't one,' said Willa, already bored. 'They're just mooning over the Cousins Charming … Are you seeing anyone, Bels?'

I got the impression that Annabelle did not appreciate being known as Bels, and that Willa knew this. 'In a manner of speaking. It's complicated.'

'How exciting.'

'Quite the opposite, sadly.' Annabelle tilted her head towards Petra and Lorcan. 'Not like love's young dream over there.'

We all contemplated the enviable cliché of a holiday flirtation in the most romantic city in the world. Shortly afterwards, the other three boys arrived at the campo, heading towards us in a noisy scuffle.

'Such darlings,' said Missy indulgently.

Mallory beamed – too eager, as always. 'I already feel they could be like brothers, almost?'

Fraternal affection was realistically the most I could hope for. The shortfall of boys on the course was disappointing, though not surprising, given art history's unfortunate reputation as a hobby for well-heeled girls.

At night, we girls leaned across our beds and exchanged

confidences in the tipsy dark. From this we learned that Kitty's relationship with her high school boyfriend was serious and Willa's fling with a South African rugby player was not. That Petra had lost her virginity to her French pen pal the summer she turned sixteen. That Missy preferred giving blow jobs to actual sex. And that Mallory had been in love with a boy from Hebrew camp who used to send her pressed flowers by the mail. I wasn't sure how much of this last story I believed, but kept my counsel. After all, I'd spun a desultory hook-up with the assistant manager of the bar I'd worked at into a bona fide relationship.

The atmosphere was reminiscent of childhood sleepovers and, as such, our confessions had a kind of innocence, despite ourselves. A few of us speculated as to what admissions the boys might exchange. How they talked about us, how they rated us. Whether they, too, were more open and vulnerable in the forgiving dark, or if they became the opposite once released from the gentlemanly confines of the day.

Of the boys, I found JJ the easiest to get along with. He was shambling and cheerful and liked pretty much everything we saw ('nice!'), though he owned up to finding 'all the religious stuff' somewhat heavy going. He would be happiest when we reached Florence. 'This is more like it,' he would say in the Uffizi, bounding between *The Birth of Venus* and that little painting of a cherub strumming a lute.

By contrast, Rocco fancied himself an expert on everything. Fresh from an internship in Christie's Post-War and Contemporary Art Department, he could crowbar 'radical alterity', 'ontological' and 'Lacanian' into a discussion of a Titian nude. I wasted a lot of time being intimidated by the jargon and the punk-pirate aesthetic.

Oliver I was wary of. His apparent girlishness – the limpid blue eyes, the slight frame – was belied by his laugh, which was a dirty old man's snigger. When he was drunk, which was most nights, he acquired a goblin leer. The other girls seemed to find this contradiction hilarious. He'd grab and paw at them shamelessly and they'd bat him away, shrieking with glee. Except for Mallory, I noticed. She would turn an unflattering red, which he enjoyed, but her acquiescing grin was more of a grimace.

Oliver did not, however, play these games with Annabelle or with me. I knew that the reason he respected Annabelle's space was different to the reason I was spared his attentions, and though I found him repellent on a number of levels, I still resented this keenly.

He had shown his teeth relatively early on. We were on a day trip to Verona from Venice, swigging prosecco on the steps of the amphitheatre, just like in the photograph in the brochure. I was describing my encounter with a creepy security guard in the Museo, when I realised Oliver was watching me with an expression of excessive puzzlement. I broke off.

'What?'

'Your voice. You sound different to when you first arrived.'

'How do you mean?'

He smiled winsomely. 'Like you've swallowed a few more plums.'

Willa let out a barely suppressed snort. Even Kitty, usually so amenable, exchanged a mischievous look with Missy. I felt hot with rage. I understood where Oliver got his sense of blue-blooded entitlement from. I didn't see why the others – raised amid prosperous Home Counties dullness, the children of bankers and lawyers – should feel so superior.

Even Mallory had a natural advantage over me, simply by being a New Yorker and rich. Her life experiences were enviable and mine were not. It was becoming clear my personality wasn't big enough to capitalise on the novelty of being the daughter of a writer; I needed to establish myself in other ways. Oliver had unwittingly provided me with a now or never moment.

'Oh, I'm sure my accent's all over the place,' I said carelessly. 'Most of my classmates spent their time trying to kick the RP out of me.'

'Lordy, where were you at?' asked Petra.

It was a question I'd previously done my best to evade. 'Where were you at?' was shorthand for 'Which public school did you attend, and what connections did you make there?' Now it struck me that I could turn my unconventional answer to my advantage.

'The local shithole. Look, it could've been worse – at least I wasn't knifed for failing to drop my aitches.'

I saw Yolanda look up from her spot a few steps down. I remembered we'd put our educational history in our application forms. A South Londoner herself, Yolanda presumably knew the wholly respectable status of my comp. But I wasn't going to worry about that. As far as my course-mates were concerned, all state schools were slums.

'Was this after your dad died?' Mallory asked, in hushed tones.

'Yeah.' (*Yuh.*) 'We had to sell up afterwards.' Then, as casually as I could make it: 'It was Daddy's family place, so it held a lot of memories. History. Coming to London … well. There were some big adjustments.'

'Selling up' is a phrase that means a very particular kind of loss for a very particular kind of family. Families for whom even an SW1 townhouse stuffed with heirlooms will never compensate for having had to give up the mouldering old mansion in the arse-end of nowhere that was their original home.

Oliver blinked. For the first time, he looked a little unsure of himself. Even better, Lorcan was leaning towards me, his face bright with sympathy. Although the conversation was almost immediately broken up by an official coming over to tell us to put our booze away, I didn't mind. The groundwork had been laid.

Sure enough, Lorcan came and sat next to me for the train trip back to Venice, folding himself into the seat in a way that was somehow both awkward and elegant. His elbows looked about to poke out of his ancient tweed jacket but his cheekbones were as moneyed as his tan. He gave me a sleepy smile. 'So you had to sell up, huh? That must have been tough.'

'It was a bit, yes.' The tremor in my voice was genuine, though it came from relief as much as regret, because I knew Lorcan would understand.

'What was it like?'

This was my chance. At last. 'Well, the original family place was in Ireland, actually. That's long gone. Garreg Las was just a country house.' Hinting at an older, grander ancestral pile was a bit of a stretch – the Irish landowners in question had belonged to a very distant branch of Daddy's family tree. Still, I knew the suggestion of past glories would be far more effective than exaggerating those of Garreg Las. 'It was early Regency. Kind of falling apart, to be honest; not much land. But lovely all the same.' My voice caught. 'Lovely to me.'

'Sounds a bit like the house my grandparents had to sell up. Greenmount Lodge. I was too small to remember much about it, but maybe it's better that way.'

I cleared my throat. 'The Welsh have a word: *hiraeth*. It's basically untranslatable, but it means the grief you feel for the lost places of your past. And something more: a longing for a home or time that may have never been.'

I had nursed these words for a long time, imagining the soulmate I might one day share them with. Lorcan was not my soulmate. But the moment felt so significant he might as well have been.

I couldn't afford to fall in love with Lorcan. I have always been as much a pragmatist as a romantic, and I knew, almost from the start, that even a mild crush would be more trouble than it was worth. It would make me weak, distracted. And if the impossible happened and the spark between us was kindled, the light it gave would be fleeting … and the fallout disastrous. No. I needed our bond to be something more. Even in those early days, I planned for Lorcan to be my lodestone for everything else.

Still, when he looked at me seriously, my breath caught. 'That's beautiful. *Hiraeth* … I must remember it.'

We smiled at each other.

'Do you speak Welsh, then?'

'My family used to – I mean, the Howells have been in Wales since forever. Daddy taught me odd bits, like the Lord's Prayer and the national anthem. But the rest of it's gone.' I looked down at my hands. 'Along with everything else.'

'Ah, but heritage isn't just about bricks and mortar, or even memory. You can't erase a bloodline. That's why the wisdom of the Celts still runs in your veins.'

Talk of bloodlines made me a little uncomfortable. In any case, it was time to move the focus back to Lorcan. I couldn't afford for him to grow restless. 'Was Greenmount your mum's family home? Or your dad's?'

'My mother's. Pa could have easily held on to it, if he felt like it. He had the money. But he wasn't to the manor born. Self-made and all that. He married up, and the old bastard's always resented her for it … Still, at least my parents can be civil in public. Apparently Annabelle's mother makes the sign of the devil whenever she hears his name.'

'I'm sorry.' I was immensely flattered that he was telling me this. The bitterness in his tone was oddly intimate. I wondered what it must be like to negotiate this kind of family dysfunction with a sibling you hardly knew. He and Annabelle were amicable, but seemed a little circumspect around each other.

'Pa's moved on to wifelet number three now. Some bimbo he met at rehab, of all the clichés.' Lorcan laughed; now he looked merely mischievous. 'She's common as muck, but they live in state in Kensington. All the mod cons.'

Lorcan, I knew, lived in a rambling Wiltshire vicarage. Both that and a Kensington town house were a world apart from the Brockley terrace. It didn't matter. By evoking the spirit of Garreg Las, I had joined a new class.

And, like Nate, I now bore an appealing hint of past sorrows. *Austere, yet romantic. Picturesque. Patrician.*

CHAPTER SIX

Shortly after our trip to Verona came a tour of the villas of the Veneto. Its plains were pockmarked by industrial estates and suburban sprawl; the day was milk-pale and chilly. Yolanda was the lead tutor for the trip, but she struggled to bring energy to her talk on how Palladian architecture expressed the humanist values of the Renaissance.

'The humanists believed the universe to be perfectly ordered, symmetrical. Remember Plato's Theory of Forms? Well, Palladio's architecture was based upon the circle, the square and the principle of harmonic proportion because Palladio believed them to represent the Forms – the ideals of the Good, of Justice and of Harmony.'

'So,' piped up Ben, who was accompanying us, his cravat as jaunty as ever, 'you might say his buildings are designed to reflect the lines of heaven!'

I was unmoved by the cool rationalism of the Villa Rotunda. But later, gazing up a dark green lane towards the sunburned heights of the Villa Barbarigo, Yolanda told us the approach to the house was designed to be an allegory of man's spiritual journey towards salvation. Here, the arrangements of stone and hedgerow had a gentler, dreamier geometry. I couldn't help but think, again, of the avenue at Garreg Las.

So many porticos. So many frescos and fountains and statues of gods. But however grandiose the facades looked, many of the houses were only one room deep. They were summer palaces but also working farms, with agricultural land coming up almost to their doors.

Used to the National Trust properties where every room is furnished and curated within an inch of its life, it was a surprise to find most of these villas were empty shells. 'I wish there was more actual *stuff*,' said Kitty to Missy or perhaps it was Missy to Kitty. (They would have been virtually indistinguishable if it wasn't for the colour of their hair.) At the time, we were strolling past a trompe l'oeil of a palace-within-a-palace, complete with peeping servants and marble balustrades overlooking a fantasy view.

'Many frescos were done to save money,' Yolanda told us. 'After all, it's much cheaper to paint a fancy door frame or pair of pillars than commission the real thing.' She cleared her throat and we braced ourselves for the rhetorical flourish that would inevitably follow. Ben and Nate integrated this sort of thing seamlessly into conversation; Yolanda's contributions always sounded a little studied. 'So, is this obsession with illusion – this "deception of the eye" – a delightful game or just a fraud?'

'Isn't most beauty a con?' Oliver smirked at Willa, who was reapplying lip gloss with a liberal hand. 'A trick *and* a treat?'

'Piss off,' she said amiably.

In one of the privately owned villas, the count, a ruddy-cheeked man with a straggling comb-over, took us round to admire the Tiepolos himself. This house, too, was sparsely furnished, except for sideboards crammed with photographs of the kind of people you find in *Hello!* royal-wedding spreads.

Oliver, I noticed, made a point of seeming entirely at home. Touring these places, there was something a little too casual, almost proprietorial, about his admiration. 'Those were the days. When people had real ambition, vision, about what it meant to be a man of the world.' He meant the patrons, not the artists, I was sure. Oliver was eyeing up the genius of Palladio (a miller's son) or Veronese (raised by a stonemason) and thinking, *If it wasn't for the likes of me, there would never have been the likes of you.*

'Of course,' Yolanda had said to us at the Rotunda, 'Palladio's style was much imitated, all over Europe and America too.'

Mallory dipped her head in that annoying way she did when she was attempting to articulate something important. 'Like the Capitol. And also Thomas Jefferson's house? Monticello, in Virginia? It's kinda ironic how it was built in a style that you're saying was all about liberty and the Enlightenment and suchlike. Because Jefferson's house was, like, in the middle of this huge plantation worked by slaves.'

'Thank you,' said Yolanda, her face brightening. 'Yes. That's a very important point, Mallory, and something it's all too easy to lose sight of. So many of the great houses of England, too, were built on fortunes made in the colonies.'

Mallory was practically squirming with pleasure.

'Suck-up,' muttered Lorcan as we moved on. Mallory was only just ahead, and I saw her back stiffen.

'What do you mean?' Petra asked.

Lorcan lowered his voice further. 'Mal only brought up that slavery stuff because Yolanda's black.'

'So? She was still right to say it. Good for her.'

'Yes. Sorry. That was shitty of me,' he said, so ingratiatingly and promptly that I wished I'd been bold enough to call him out myself. But Petra, now his confirmed paramour, had special privileges. 'Thanks.'

'For what?'

'For telling me to stop being a dick. It's something I occasionally need to hear.'

Petra did not squirm with pleasure, but I could tell her level of satisfaction was the same.

As we continued our tour, I noticed the other visitors, mostly well-heeled and middle-aged or older, were eyeing us approvingly. At the ticket office, an elderly American had a brief exchange with Rocco that clearly left her aflutter. Even Rocco, with his grungy tattoos, his pseudo-intellectualism and stale fag breath, could be impressive if he chose. Truly, there's nothing quite like the public school kid's alacrity in holding open doors or offering seats, their firm handshakes and ready smiles. The respectful ease with which they converse with their seniors. The happy confidence with which they enter a room. Knowing how to apologise and keep one's dignity, like Lorcan with Petra, was a part of this.

Of course such polish is impressive. And frighteningly effective, when you think of its powers of distraction.

I was paired with Rocco for the day's final activity: navigating the Villa Pisani maze. Yolanda and Ben sent us in two-by-two, promising a prize for the first pair to make it to the tower in the middle.

Unlike the American at the ticket office, I did not find Rocco particularly appealing. The box-hedge labyrinth was yet another symbol, this time of love. In days of old, masked ladies would position themselves on the tower as the prize for the ardent knights who had to untangle the maze to get to them. As dusk approached, the washed-out light grew softer, prettier. I tried not to imagine what it would be like getting lost in such a setting with a lover. After only a few minutes of wandering about, Rocco sat down in a dank dead end, skinny-jean-encased legs crossed at the ankle, trilby tilted low, and set about fixing a roll-up.

'Sod this for a game of soldiers.'

I wasn't sure if this was an invitation to join him but I squatted down beside him nonetheless. It would be humiliating to have to navigate the place on my own. Everyone else seemed to be having a high old time, if the happy shouts and laughter coming from all directions were to be believed.

'Don't you want to win?' I faltered.

'I'll tell you a secret: pick a hedge, left or right, and follow it till you get to the end. Piece of piss. Works in every maze, every time.' He scowled at his roll-up. 'You know, if we were going to do this on acid or something it *might* be fun. Trippy. Otherwise it's just *lame*. I mean, running around gardens for prizes? Sometimes I think these people reckon we're just a bunch of dumb kids.'

He scowled some more. Rocco was working hard to position himself as an intellectual maverick, and thus the true brains of the course. But Yolanda was less tolerant than Ben and Nate and had shown little interest in his theory on how, since Plato was 'basically a proto-Fascist', Palladio's embrace of Neoplatonism 'ironically foreshadowed' the architectural legacy of the Mussolini years.

He hadn't offered me a cigarette. Even though I didn't smoke, this irked me. I tried to visualise the sort of girl Rocco might go for: some posh emo blonde with smudgy black eyelids and nipple piercings.

We watched as Oliver and Annabelle passed by the open end of our cul-de-sac. Annabelle looked preoccupied, not really listening to whatever Oliver was saying as he trotted at her heels.

'You think he's got a chance with her?' Rocco asked unexpectedly.

I laughed. Oliver, so fair and small and finicky, with his too long eyelashes and goblin grin ... The idea of him seducing Annabelle was grotesque. But no wonder Oliver was arrogant enough to think he was entitled to a girl like Annabelle. He was arrogant enough to think he'd be on equal terms with a man like Palladio.

'The day Oliver pulls Annabelle is the day Mallory pulls Lorcan.'

'Huh.'

From Rocco's expression, I could tell I'd crossed a line. He wasn't like Lorcan. Most boys don't like bitchy girls.

Too late, it occurred to me that Rocco might be nursing a secret passion for Annabelle too. She didn't seem his type, but what did I know? Maybe his question wasn't idle speculation; he might really want to know if Oliver was a rival. Rocco could have been about to unburden himself, and I'd just blown my chance to become his confidante. I wasn't yet established enough within the group to be too picky about my alliances. However, the day had been a long and tiring one, and at that moment the effort of repairing things with Rocco felt beyond me. Laboriously, I got to my feet. 'OK. I'm going to put this maze-busting theory of yours to the test. See you later.'

The hedges were not particularly high at first, so you could more or less orientate yourself. Quite quickly, however, they rose in height and one lost all sense of direction. The tower in the middle had a double spiral staircase up to the viewing platform, which was presided over by a statue of Minerva. Its looming presence was first tantalising, then taunting.

Shortly after leaving Rocco, I heard a shout of triumph and looked up to see that Lorcan, Petra and Annabelle had already won the game. Lorcan had originally been paired with Mallory, Annabelle with Oliver, and Petra with JJ, but all three had clearly managed to ditch their original partners. Lorcan and Petra were now kissing each other on top of the tower, with the ravenous gusto of a Hollywood film. Annabelle stood with her back to them, surveying the labyrinth. In profile, I thought she wouldn't have been a bad fit for Minerva herself.

I wandered on, feeling no great impetus to join the lovebirds. The day had become a disappointing one, so being aimless and alone felt gloomily appropriate. I wasn't the only one, however. 'Ada – hey, Ada! Wait up!'

It was Mallory, looking sweaty despite the chill and waving far too vigorously. I increased my pace. 'Sorry, Mal. I've lost Rocco.

Need to catch up with him –' I looked back at her crestfallen face, just before speeding around a corner. 'Good luck, yeah?'

A little way along I found another stray. Oliver, this time, also looking somewhat disconsolate.

'I see Annabelle managed to give you the slip.' This sounded a little more snide than I intended. Then again, I still felt resentful about Oliver's attempt to embarrass me in Verona.

'Hardly,' he said coldly. 'I thought I'd dropped some cash so had to retrace my steps. I told her to go on without me. What's your excuse?'

'Rocco thinks mazes are lame unless you're off your face.'

'Mazes? Are you sure he didn't mean *you*?'

'Har, har.' I put my right hand on the hedge and marched grimly onwards, past a trio of giggling Japanese, a couple of bickering Germans and Willa, taking tits-'n'-teeth selfies with Kitty 'n' Missy.

Thanks to Rocco's ruse, I was the fourth of our party to arrive at the tower. Lorcan clapped me on the back and Petra gave me a victory hug. JJ was next, in high spirits and clearly bearing no ill will for being ditched by Petra. The threesome of Kitty, Missy and Willa followed a little while later. Rocco and Oliver sauntered along afterwards. Uneasily, I wondered if they had been discussing me.

Mallory, inevitably, was still hopelessly lost, and for a while Willa and Oliver amused themselves by shouting out misdirections. The rest of us were soon doubled up with laughter. She looked up, trusting and confused, as they sent her down a succession of dead ends, then circling back towards the exit, until JJ and Petra took pity on her and intervened. At long last, Mallory was guided to the foot of the stairs, to ironic applause from us, and more genuine congratulations from the other tourists who'd made it.

Afterwards, of course, it was tempting to see our time in the maze as an allegory for so much else. Wrong turns, dead ends. The lost and the saved. But real life isn't a labyrinth, with patterns to unlock. There isn't a trick, like Rocco's, to guide you to the prize. And even if you do kill your minotaur, there's no way of following the thread back home.

We arrived at our hotel in Vicenza late and footsore. I'd have welcomed an early night, but Lorcan, Annabelle and Petra's prize for beating the maze was a bottle of prosecco from the private estate we'd visited, and once we'd started drinking it was, everyone agreed, pointless to stop.

'How you doing?' said Yolanda, coming to sit next to me in the between-courses shuffle at the restaurant.

'Good, thanks. Great. Tired.'

'Frescoed out, huh?' Her voice was hoarse after a day of tour-guiding.

'A bit. I mean, it's all amazing. But I'm looking forward to our visit to the Guggenheim once we get back to Venice. It'll be nice to mix things up a little.'

'The palate cleanser of modern art.'

'I'd love to hear about your own art some time,' I said shyly.

'That's very kind of you.' But she didn't follow up. 'Actually, I wondered if I could have a word with you about something else?' Her voice lowered to a scratchy rasp. 'Is Mallory having a good time, do you think?'

I had a guilty flashback to Mallory's face when she escaped the maze: conscious of being played, pathetically grateful for finally being rescued. Her too wide smile as she tried to pretend she'd been in on the joke. I'd been glad when Petra and JJ had intervened – but they could afford to. Petra was desirable and JJ was popular. I wasn't, not yet.

Ben and Yolanda hadn't gone into the maze; now I wondered how much they had witnessed of our game.

'Um, sure. She might be a little homesick, I suppose?'

'Well, if that's all it is …' Yolanda took a swig of water. 'This course asks a lot of you; I know it can get emotionally as well as intellectually intense. And we've got some big personalities here. So I sometimes think the, uh, quieter personalities can struggle to be heard. Or find their place.'

'We're all great friends.' I resented the implication that I was one of these quieter personalities or – worse – that I could particularly relate to Mallory's position.

'Well, that's lovely to hear. Just … keep an eye on Mal, would you?'

Mallory was at an adjoining table, boring Willa stiff with some anecdote about Hebrew camp. I gritted my teeth. 'No problem.'

CHAPTER SEVEN

There was an unspoken agreement among us that loving Venice was a little unsophisticated. There were just too many clichés to navigate. Florence, on the other hand, was a proper working city. Its streets had an unexpected amount of dog shit and litter and exhaust fumes, but none of Venice's tired melancholy. The locals were surly rather than long-suffering.

Our hotel was a run-down fifteenth-century palazzo, overlooking a scruffy square in which youths revved their motorbikes throughout the night. The beds were rickety and floors none too clean. This was a cue for low-level outrage: 'It's hardly better than camping, is it?' 'I wasn't expecting a bloody youth hostel.' 'What exactly are we paying for?' et cetera.

There were compensations, however. The rooms had creaking wooden shutters and spotted mirrors that cast everyone in a flattering light; the *salone* was stalked by tortoiseshell cats as haughty as they were decorative. Even better, I was sharing a room with Annabelle, Willa and Petra. Although this was pure luck – room-share selections were drawn out of a hat, just like our tutor groups – it seemed like a good omen. Our arrival in Florence meant that we were a third of the way through the course, and I was already thinking ahead to when we scattered at the end. Which alliances would last and what could be made of them.

I had a setback on our first night. My room-mates and I were getting ready for bed, layering lotions onto our faces with the solemn care of ancient dowagers. (Except for Annabelle, inevitably, who applied her moisturiser as briskly as she brushed her teeth.) We were talking, as we often did, of the boys, employing the vague fondness girls use towards men they have no intention of sleeping with. The chat moved to Oliver.

'Brideshead regurgitated,' I said.

It was not an original line – I'd read or heard it somewhere. But they all laughed. Annabelle tilted her head back, teeth flashing.

'Oh, you are *wicked*,' said Petra.

'I'm sure Waugh would approve,' said Oliver's voice from the doorway. 'He was, of course, an infamous social climber. But you'd know all about that – wouldn't you, Ada?'

There was an unpleasant pause.

'Don't flatter yourself,' I said, applying lip balm with an insouciance I did not feel. 'If I was set on gatecrashing the *haute monde*, I think I could do better than this bunch of clowns.'

More laughter. I could tell the girls were on my side. I wasn't the only one who needed to be careful; it was Oliver's second attempt to publicly embarrass me, and it would do him no good to be thought a bully.

'Very true.' He came further into the room. In his blue striped pyjamas, he looked about twelve. 'Well. I just stopped by to kiss my favourite girls goodnight.'

Mwah, mwah, *mmmm*. It was his standard performance: lechery masquerading as camp. When it was my turn, I got an additional squeeze, which tugged the soft flesh of my waist. 'No hard feelings.'

'Absolutely.' But we'd both sensed the other flinch.

Our first morning in the city began in the Piazza della Signoria. Nate was guiding us through the sculpture gallery in the Loggia dei Lanzi, but I was preoccupied with trying to match our location to the Merchant Ivory film of *A Room with a View*. I'd watched it with Delilah on at least four occasions.

'Stop perving, you lech,' said Oliver.

I started. Until that moment, I hadn't been aware of Lorcan and Petra, nuzzling each other right in the middle of my line of sight. I'd been looking straight past them at the fountain where the knife fight was filmed. But I should have known Oliver wasn't done with me.

'Look at you – all hot and bothered. You're turned on, aren't you?'

He batted those long eyelashes. *Just a bit of friendly banter.* Had everyone else heard? I cast around for some kind of comeback but could think of nothing, and then the moment passed.

We trailed after Nate, who had come to a halt in front of *The Rape of the Sabine Women*. '… carved from a single block of marble in the Mannerist style …'

'In the old days, we just called it *droit du seigneur*,' Oliver said out of the side of his mouth. He meant the remark for JJ, who laughed obligingly but looked confused. A little way apart, Annabelle was surveying the twisting bodies – the gaping mouth and outstretched, pleading hand – with a small frown. I saw Oliver's eyes were fixed on her face. Hypocrite.

So as soon as it was time to move on again, I leaned into his ear. *'Droit du seigneur*'s the only way guys like you ever had a chance with girls like Annabelle.'

'Excuse me?'

'Your crush – everyone's talking about it.' It was just Rocco, as far as I knew, but never mind. I kept my tone light. 'You're delusional.'

Just for a moment, Oliver looked like something you might come upon in a dark wood.

'And you're a cunt.'

Nate turned and stared. He couldn't have heard our exchange, but he knew distraction when he saw it.

'I'm sorry, am I boring you?'

Nate was the only one of our tutors who could act like a fuddy-duddy school teacher and get away with it. His expression, a little bleak at the best of times, looked particularly severe in the shadow of Perseus brandishing the Gorgon's head.

We moved on.

'Time for a *spanking*,' Missy giggled.

'God, I love it when Nate talks dirty,' sighed Kitty.

Annabelle rolled her eyes.

———

I deeply regretted my clash with Oliver. I'd thought that establishing my country-house credentials would have been enough for him, yet we'd somehow moved from casual dislike to confirmed hostility. The Brideshead remark must have touched a nerve, then he'd needled me ... and I'd wanted to draw blood in return. Maybe I'd gone too far, but I was shaken by his response. I'd seen something venomous, fanged. Or had I? I reported an edited version of our exchange to Petra, who told me to forget about it. 'Sounds like macho posturing. I mean, Oliver's adorable, but he's a total shrimp. You know his three brothers are all over six foot? He's probably just overcompensating or something.'

Petra and I would both be studying English at UCL, so we first bonded over our Oxbridge rejections. Strolling in the Boboli Gardens, Petra confided that she'd been wild to get into Cambridge because everyone knew the drama scene was as good as RADA and maybe even better in terms of getting talent-spotted. But, she said, the pressure got to her, and in her interview to read English at Trinity she gave 'basically the worst audition of my life'.

I framed my own failure a little differently. 'It was my father's college – he'd always wanted me to follow in his footsteps. It was just assumed I'd go. I never really had the chance to question it. But when I walked into the interview and looked around, I had this surreal out-of-body experience. Why was I doing this? For Daddy's memory? For my mother's sake? Not for me, that was sure. So I just mumbled a few words and got out of there as soon as was decent.'

Petra looked impressed. 'There's more to you than meets the eye, isn't there? I'm starting to suspect you're something of a secret insurgent.'

I could tell she was pleased with this observation, so I followed it through. 'And *this* is why it pays to beware of actors.'

'How so?'

'You're far too psychologically astute. It must come of inhabiting all those different roles. You can get into anyone's head.'

She smiled. The gardens' fountains and grottos were prettily unkempt, and Petra looked entirely at home here with her floating scarves and tresses. However, her own dishevelment was, I was sure, fashioned with care. No longer the cutie-pie child actress with the curls, she was searching for her USP even more urgently than the rest of us. I understood this uncertainty, and I could make use of it.

I was making progress elsewhere, too. Repairing relations with Rocco had turned out to be easy: back in Venice, I'd asked him to explain Orphic Cubism in the Guggenheim, and listened respectfully to the lecture that followed. I was slightly surprised to discover that Rocco's passion for art was sincere, but once I realised this, I began to like him better. For the rest of the course, I would occasionally ask him what I should think about some piece of art or another. Take someone seriously, and they can't fail to find you endearing.

Everyone liked JJ, and he returned the compliment. 'Oh, Mal's actually quite sweet, I think,' I heard him say placidly, one time when Oliver was being particularly snide. JJ had a girlfriend back home, and he spent a lot of time writing her laboriously soppy postcards, as well as phoning and messaging where at all possible. On our first day in Florence, I caught him moping over his phone with an uncharacteristically forlorn expression. Georgie hadn't returned his goodnight message from the night before – was something wrong? Had she taken offence at his last voicemail? Didn't she like the photos he'd sent?

JJ was sheepish, knowing how this would expose him to mockery – indulgent from the girls, but ruthless from the boys. I made sure to treat his concerns with appropriate gravity. Afterwards, he would take me aside for further consultations. I was called upon to interpret some of the more passive-aggressive messages, as well as rationalise delays in communication and choices of emoji. Luckily for me, Georgie was either flaky or fickle, so there was plenty of material to work with.

Willa took note of my conferences with JJ and came to the wrong conclusion. 'I'm starting to think JJ may have a *teensy* crush,' she drawled one evening, when we were touching up make-up in our shared bathroom.

'He's devoted to his girlfriend.'

She adjusted her cleavage complacently. 'That's what they all say.'

Willa was the kind of girl who grudgingly respects her competitors, while preferring to ignore the rest of her sex. 'I don't know why,' she'd say archly, 'but I've always got on better with boys.' I was hardly a rival, but by supposedly tempting someone to stray, I went up in her estimation. The fact that Rocco and, increasingly, Lorcan also seemed to approve of me was something Willa found baffling. What was my secret if it wasn't sex appeal?

Still, as my friendships with three of the four boys (Oliver was a lost cause) grew more established, Willa's interactions with me became noticeably warmer.

Florence marked the point where I felt able to relax a little. Since Kitty and Missy were amiable and easy to please, the only person I'd failed to win over was Oliver. And Annabelle, I supposed. She remained frustratingly opaque, but I consoled myself with the fact she was the same with everyone.

There was still more work to do. I wanted these friendships to be forged on something stronger than mere liking; I wanted them to become an indelible part of my story. These people could help me become my best self. I'd learn how to have their confidence without the entitlement, their charm without the insincerity. I wasn't beautiful and I wasn't rich, but I sensed I could still have the lustre these gifts bestowed. I could still become someone who was treasured.

In the meantime, I found the machinations involved demeaning. Now and again I felt a twinge of self-disgust. Of course I'd have preferred to let these friendships blossom organically. I was coming from behind, however, and had a lot of catching up to do. This was one of the things that annoyed me about Mallory: she did nothing to help herself. She simply blundered about, unwilling or unable to finagle her manner into something more in keeping with the company.

Lorcan and Annabelle remained the ultimate prize. Wherever they led, others would follow. If I was friends with them – *real* friends – I knew I'd be untouchable. Always. As it turned out, that day with Petra in the Boboli was also the day the key to Lorcan and his family revealed itself.

By the time Petra and I caught up with the others, they were busy setting up for the afternoon's art session. The chosen spot was a grassy terrace overlooking the city; Yolanda distributed oil pastels and encouragement. Lapped by violet hills, Florence lay in a blushing orange haze. The cathedral's dome was a rich terracotta; its bell tower had a mother-of-pearl gleam. Inevitably, our labours reduced the scene to childish rainbow smears.

Missy was the first to lose patience. She had put a figure in the foreground, before changing her mind and trying to turn him into a tree. 'Look at the mess. God. It's like someone's taken a dump on the page.'

'You have a *pentimento*,' said Nate, coming over to inspect. He'd been smoking by the wall, surveying the scene. I flattered myself that he was thinking what an attractive picture we made, with our fresh faces and bright eyes, our drawings rich with the exuberance of Italy and youth.

'What's a penti-whatsit when it's at home?'

'A *pentimento* is an image that had been painted over, but starts to become visible again. It usually happens with time, as paint thins. Then you can see where the artist made his changes.' Missy continued to pull faces, but Nate's was serious. He spoke slowly and carefully. 'The word comes from the Italian *pentirsi*. It means to repent.'

'Can you give us an example?' Annabelle asked, her shining dark head bent over her pad.

He waited a long moment. His eyes were fixed on her with strange intensity; it was as if he was willing her to look up. 'I hardly know where to start.'

'Well, one famous example is Seurat's self-portrait in his picture *Young Woman Powdering Herself,*' said Yolanda, getting out her phone. 'Look.'

We were more than ready to be distracted. The afternoon light was fading; drinks were soon proposed.

The truth was, although we despised the stereotype of the drunken British chav, we spent the majority of our days gently hung-over. Most people had wine at lunch and there was always carafe after carafe at dinner, followed by grappa or other venomous liqueurs. Afterwards, we'd head to bars, and sometimes a dingy club, and the drinking would continue.

I tried to hold back for reasons of economy as much as sobriety, though it seemed to make little difference to the amount of money I was burning through. Restaurant bills were split equally, though rough allowances were made for those who didn't have pudding or wine. To go teetotal in the evening was not an option. It set my teeth on edge when someone (Oliver or Willa, usually) would insist on a 'halfway decent' bottle of something that was always three times as much as I would have been willing to pay. And the boys would inevitably order multiple sides, as well as steak or some other pricy carnivorous platter. They would look at the bloody heap in front of them as proudly as if they had birthed it.

That evening, however, I determined not to fret about the bill. I was feeling buoyant after my conversation with Petra and her willingness to confide in me. At dinner we sat together and she whispered she was worried about Lorcan. 'He *says* he's happy to take things slowly, but what if he's just saying that? I mean, from what Willa says, he used to be a total man-whore. So how do I *know*?'

'You don't,' I said wisely, 'but Lorcan's the sort who's going to be attracted to a woman who knows her own mind.'

She nodded and clutched my knee. 'I knew you'd understand ...'

Recklessly, I ordered swordfish carpaccio and roast pork loin, and *zuccotto* for dessert. Everyone seemed suffused with the same jubilant spirit. Even Annabelle grew flushed and garrulous.

'Aren't we the best Dilettanti you've ever had?' Willa demanded of Ben, as we swaggered back to the hotel. And although her tone was arch, I knew she meant the question sincerely. We wanted to be told that, yes, we were in fact special, magically elevated above every other collection of students who took this tour. Our witticisms, our camaraderie, our insightfulness was sure to be fondly recalled years from now.

'We're all the best,' said Ben, flinging his arms wide. '*Everything's* the best in Italy.'

'But you won't forget how fabulous *we* are,' Kitty insisted, 'because everyone else will be lame in comparison.'

Nate, walking quietly near me, gave one of his rare, private smiles. 'I'll remember.'

'Do you promise?' said Annabelle, unexpectedly joining in the game.

'I will,' he said, his look of intensity returning. 'I do.'

Back in the hotel with my three room-mates, the swoop of the ceiling and tilt of the walls didn't seem like harbingers of the hangover to come, but a merry reflection of my own high spirits. I rolled into bed entirely happy.

Sometime later I awoke, throat parched, my head already beginning to pound. Moonlight spilled from a gap in the shutters. Or was it the grey of dawn? I saw Annabelle slip back through the door, shrugging off her clothes with easy haste. She smiled to herself in the gloom, and it was the same smile as Nate's. Coaxing, secret.

CHAPTER EIGHT

Although I was not yet sure of Nate and Annabelle's secret, I guessed, instinctively, that moment in the pale dawn. Perhaps it was because of how he'd watched her during the art class: that look of almost painful concentration. At the time, I thought Nate had paused when asked for an example of a *pentimento* because he was temporarily stumped. After all, it was Ben, who had the day off, who was the art historian. Nate was a classicist. So, of course, was Annabelle.

Nate's pause had not been one of uncertainty. It had been for emphasis. His talk of repentance was for Annabelle alone. He was trying to make amends for some lovers' tiff.

I hardly know where to start.

The moment afterwards: the air between them electric, thrumming with possibility.

Of course Nate would choose Annabelle, I thought. They were both, in their different ways, the kind of people who kept you looking and listening, all the while holding themselves a little apart. It did not occur to me to think of Annabelle as the victim of a predatory older man. She did not seem the teenage-temptress type either, because that suggested the kind of pointed effort she wouldn't stoop to. Even her underwear – plain monochrome – was without frills.

Perhaps, years later, Annabelle would confide in a friend or lover that when she was very young, she had an affair with a married man, her teacher. 'Oh,' she might say, 'I was so naïve.' Perhaps she would say this fondly, perhaps with regret. But I could not imagine Annabelle revisiting the episode with self-pity. Such an experience would mark her, but it would be a mark of distinction: of lessons learned and worldliness acquired. Annabelle was not like Petra. Petra, I could already see, was one of those people who pin their identity to the *Sturm und Drang* of their relationships.

At that point, I admit, I did not really consider the other woman involved. Since Nate appeared neither carefree nor caddish, his betrayal of his barren wife seemed as much his tragedy as hers.

Of course, mere suspicion was not enough. The next free morning, while some of us napped, others shopped and Annabelle said she was 'going for a walk', I decided to follow her.

But my venture was nearly over before it began thanks to Mallory, who cornered me outside the *pensione*. 'Hey, Ada! Whatcha up to?'

'Uh … I just fancied a wander. I thought you were shopping with Willa and the rest?'

'Yeah, I guess I maybe got the arrangements wrong? I mean, I thought we were supposed to meet here, but … oh well.' She tried to laugh, eyes rolling in a silly-old-me grimace.

So they'd given her the slip. 'Mm. That's too bad.'

Annabelle had stopped at the end of the street to answer a phone call but she could move on at any second. I was trying to look over Mallory's shoulder without being too obvious about it.

'Want some company?'

Her tone was so hopeful I almost felt guilty. 'Actually, I'm sorry, but I need a bit of alone time. I'm … I'm trying to get some thoughts together for a story.'

It wasn't a total lie. I was trying to take my literary aspirations more seriously, though I found myself a frustratingly unreliable narrator.

'Oh, wow. Sure. That's so interesting. And inspiring? You know, I'd really love to–'

'*Mal.*' Her puppyish enthusiasm would ruin everything – Annabelle had moved around the corner and out of sight. 'Honestly, I know you Americans are an excitable bunch, but maybe you could try *not* to embody *all* the clichés?'

She blinked at me. 'I – what do you mean?'

'Look, it's a cultural thing. A cultural difference. Brits tend to dial things down. We're all stiff-upper-lipped and repressed, remember? So you're not doing yourself any favours by being so, well, *full on* all the time.'

She blinked some more. Oh, shit – had I made her cry? But no. 'Thank you, Ada,' she said, with a sincerity that made me wince. 'It's so sweet of you to look out for me. And I get what you're saying, I truly do. But all that stiff-upper-lip stuff … it's just not in my nature.' She actually smiled. 'OK. Ben says there's a gelato stand near here that makes a trifle flavour. *Zuppa Inglese* – English soup! Cool, huh?'

I watched her go, baffled. I'd spoken out of frustration, and meanness, but I'd also given her good advice. Mallory, I decided, was her own worst enemy.

I was sure Annabelle was long gone, but to my surprise I caught up with her without much difficulty. She was walking fairly confidently, only pausing to check her surroundings a couple of times. If she turned back and saw me, I calculated I could quite easily exclaim about the coincidence without arousing suspicion. Florence is a small city, after all.

The meeting point was, of necessity, I suppose, none of the obvious beauty spots. Nate was waiting for her in a small café in a nondescript square. They embraced easily, freely. Just another pair of lovers. He touched her hair. She, laughing, tugged at his lapel.

Are you seeing anyone, Bels?

In a manner of speaking.

How effortlessly adult she was. How much younger Nate looked with her in his arms. Boyish and tender.

There had been a furtive excitement in trailing Annabelle through the streets. I'd thought I'd tasted a little of their affair's illicit thrill. Now, as I watched them settle down to their coffee and kisses, I felt like a small and grubby child. At that instant, I was enraged by both of them.

I was ashamed of these occasional bursts of bitterness. I wanted Italy to be a love story, even if the romance wasn't specifically mine. It's strange to think that, even now, after everything, I still find it hard to acknowledge the hate.

———

I spent my time in Italy in a state of hyper-vigilance. I was never so absorbed by its treasures that I stopped being alert to the jostles of thought and feeling, expectation and intent, in the people around me. In this respect, perhaps, I was bound to discover the affair. From the moment I saw Annabelle smiling to herself in the dark, her secret seemed so obvious as to be inevitable. It surprised me that everyone else was oblivious.

Or were they? I began to think that Lorcan did, in fact, know about what his half-sister was up to. There had been a couple of occasions when I'd caught him eyeing Nate and Annabelle in a curiously cold, assessing sort of way. And although he was unfailingly pleasant towards Annabelle, it was without the easy playfulness he extended to us other girls. I'd thought this was because they were still navigating their sibling relationship, but now I wondered if it was because he knew what she was doing and disapproved. Nate was his cousin, after all. Presumably Lorcan had been the one to introduce them.

I resolved to broach the subject with him. The risk was huge, but so was the potential pay-off. It could elevate our relationship to a whole new level.

My chance came on another day trip, this time to Pisa. The focus of our visit was the late medieval frescos of the Campo Santo, specifically *The Triumph of Death*. Allegory in art was one of Ben's pet enthusiasms, and after seeing the sights he asked us to reimagine Petrarch's poem *I Trionfi* ('The Triumphs') as a game of Top Trumps. Given extracts from the poem, we were put in pairs to discuss how the various powers – Chastity, Eternity, Love, Time, Fame, Death – prevailed over each other.

It was not a particularly inspiring exercise, but even the most cynical among us found it hard to disappoint Ben. My gratification with the assignment came from the fact I'd been paired with Lorcan. As the two of us settled down on the slightly damp lawn outside the Duomo, I felt a surge of nervous energy. The allegory was a love poem, after all. Our discussion might go in all sorts of interesting directions.

I plunged in. 'OK, so Chastity triumphs over Love, because the poet's beloved Laura won't sleep with him. Death destroys Laura before she can change her mind. Petrarch makes them both immortal through his poetry. Not immortal enough, however, as over Time his Fame gets forgotten. Then Eternity kicks everything into the long grass. Does that work?'

But I had taken the subject too seriously: Lorcan was unimpressed. 'How about we mix it up a little,' he drawled. 'Because Fame trumps Love, don't you think? People will sell their souls, let alone their sweethearts, for a shot at celebrity. Time trumps Fame and Eternity trumps Time.

'*However*, Death trumps Eternity, because Eternity is essentially God and, thanks to Nietzsche, we all know God is dead.

'And, finally, Chastity trumps Death. Because if people stop screwing, they stop procreating. No more babies, no more people, no more victims for Death. Death literally wastes away. So Chastity wins. The end.'

I wondered if this was an oblique comment on his relations with Petra. Still, I seized my chance. 'If so, I don't think your immediate family got the memo.'

Lorcan's head whipped round. His face was suddenly all angles

80

and shadows. 'What do you mean by that?'

The light in his eyes was ice-pale. It was an effort to keep my tone neutral. 'I mean your cousin and your sister. I nearly stumbled into them last week on our free afternoon. They were very obviously on a date.'

'Jesus fucking Christ. Fucking *idiots* ... Have you said anything to anyone else?'

'No. Of course not. I would never have brought it up if I wasn't fairly certain you already knew.'

'How beady-eyed of you.' The fury had abruptly passed; his tone had a whisper of flirtation in it. 'I can see you need watching, Howell. Petra tells me you're a bit of a dark horse.'

I decided I quite liked this. 'Does Petra know?'

It was gratifying to see him shake his head. This was to be our secret.

'*I'm* not even supposed to know. Ani and I went for drinks a while back and ... well, Annabelle had a few too many, and out it slipped. She got a bit emotional – not her usual style. It was rather awkward all round.'

'How did she and Nate meet?'

'Pa organised it, ironically. A big thing about rehab is making it up to people you've wronged. Mending fences and all that. So once he ditched the booze, he made a point of reaching out to Annabelle. He knew Nate was a classicist, so he asked me to see if Nate would help prep Annabelle for her Oxford interview.' Distractedly, he began ripping up clumps of grass. 'I mean, I know things have been rough with Nate and Clem for a while. She wants a baby and it's not happening so ...'

I waited, trying to make my presence as unobtrusive as possible, as Lorcan continued to tear at the lawn.

'OK, so you know Annabelle and I have different mothers. Our old man's on wifelet number three.'

I remembered: the common-as-muck cliché his father had met in rehab.

'The thing about Pa is that he's both filthy rich and stingy as hell. He left Mummy with practically nothing, and Annabelle's mother did even worse – she ended up taking him to court for child maintenance, and he *still* managed to screw her over.'

I was sceptical about what 'practically nothing' really entailed. There was the scenic country vicarage, the elite public school, the gap-year series of destination holidays … Annabelle, it was true, was noticeably careful with her funds. Still, she'd been privately educated at a London day school. You couldn't get her kind of polish on the cheap.

'How does your dad make his money?'

'He's a bin-man.'

'Huh?'

'Governments pay him to dispose of toxic waste. Though, between you and me, I'm pretty sure all he does is ship the stuff off to some third-world shithole and dump it in the jungle. Pa likes to say he's saving the planet, of course. That's another game of his: he's always threatening to leave his loot to some whacko environmental cause. Even wifelet number three looks a bit peaky whenever the subject of Greenpeace's bequest comes up.'

'What are you saying? If your dad found out about Annabelle and Nate, he'd, er, cut her off?'

'Ha. No. I mean, he's turned into a bit of a pious prick but he's not a *total* hypocrite. Plus, now the two of them are reunited, he thinks the light shines out of Annabelle's arse. No, it's more that he'll find some way of blaming me. While up till now, Annabelle's been a certified goody-two-shoes, Pa's always been a bit suspicious of yours truly. Reckons I'm dissolute.'

Now I laughed, in spite of myself. 'How very nineteenth century of you. Gin and harlots, I presume?'

'Let's just say I had a rowdy couple of years at school. Acting out, pissed off at the world. Your average teenage bullshit.' Lorcan spoke as if his teenage years were far behind him. 'Nowadays I'm on the side of the angels. As you can see.' He looked at me from under his lashes. 'But there you go. Turns out there's nothing as sanctimonious as a reformed hell-raiser.'

'Wow. I'm sorry. He sounds like a nightmare.'

'Oh, he is, he is. And the worst of it is, he's utterly charming with it.' All of a sudden, Lorcan's face slumped. 'I might even miss the old monster once he's gone.'

'Gone?'

'Liver cancer. The doctors reckon he's got about a year, two if he's lucky. That's the other reason he's suddenly become such a fine upstanding paterfamilias.' His mouth crooked. 'The triumph of death indeed.'

Lorcan and I were late rejoining the rest of our party. 'That looked rather deep and meaningful,' Petra remarked, eyebrow raised. It was not in my interests to add to her insecurity. So I pulled a face and said that Lorcan had been giving me advice on how to deal with awkward step-parents. Brian, I feared, was swiftly becoming a fixture of the Brockley terrace.

In truth, I had to hide my jubilation. Lorcan had confided in me. This put me ahead of Petra, at least for the moment, since Lorcan would no doubt want to shield her from his familial can of worms. Personally, I found his tale of adultery, delinquency and tainted wealth rather impressive.

In the central scene of *The Triumph of Death*, a group of beggars call upon Death to relieve their suffering. They stand to the side of a pile of corpses; above them, angels and demons fight for the departed souls. To the left, a band of noble young huntsmen recoil at the sight of three rotting cadavers. To the right, more courtiers make merry in a pleasure garden, oblivious to the figure of Death advancing on them with its scythe.

'*Et in Arcadia ego*,' said Annabelle.

Ben expanded on the theme. Here we see how Death is the ultimate leveller, he told us, pointing to where the bodies of peasants, merchants and holy men lay jumbled together. The fresco, he said, was devised as a rebuke to the sinful decadence of the aristocracy.

Yet to me, this rebuke was also an acknowledgement of their attraction. Religion has always claimed to champion the underdog; it is only in recent times that we expect this of art, too. While this position may be virtuous, it's not necessarily natural. For although the central scene of *The Triumph of Death* is ostensibly the heap of corpses and beggars, the true drama of the fresco lies with the gorgeous young nobles to either side.

Isn't there more colour, more tragedy, when Death carries off a prince or princess in their pomp, rather than some drab peasant in a muddy field?

CHAPTER NINE

Kitty belonged to a fashionable evangelical church in Chelsea. Now and again she would surprise us with a burst of religious feeling, and the expedition to Pisa was one of these occasions.

'The earth in the cemetery comes from Golgotha,' she told us importantly, coming over from where she'd been in conference with Ben. *'Where Jesus was crucified*. No wonder there's something about the atmosphere here. It's strangely sombre, don't you think?'

We surveyed the historic buildings of the cathedral square, as white and lacy as wedding cakes. Tourists struck comic poses for Leaning Tower photo-ops. The sun shone. 'But it's so pretty,' said Mallory. 'Too pretty for spookiness.'

Kitty frowned. 'Maybe you're just not very sensitive to it because of your background.'

'How do you mean?'

'Because you're American.'

'Oh,' said Mallory. 'For a moment, I thought you were going to say it's cos I'm Jewish.'

'God, no. Not at all. I – well, I only meant the history of America is relatively, you know, *short*. Whereas if you grow up in a place with lots of heritage, it's maybe easier to connect with other ancient cultures.'

Mallory squinted at the Duomo. 'Mm … it's kinda interesting how Renaissance art takes the Jew out of Jesus.'

There was a slightly uncomfortable pause.

'OK,' said Rocco, 'but great art transcends its subject matter, yeah? Even if there's a religious theme, you don't have to be a believer of any kind to connect with it. It's about the *fundamentals* of human *experience*.'

'Not all experiences are universal, though, are they?' Mallory said mildly. 'Some are specific.'

We felt abashed, and then resentful. Because Mallory was not religiously observant, and ate spaghetti al vongole and salami with the same relish as the rest of us, this sudden reminder of her minority status seemed almost unfair. It was as if she was asking for special consideration. I suppose if she herself had been special in any way – distinctive, intriguing – we might even have given it.

Inevitably, Mallory had a crush on Lorcan. Her admiration was clumsy as well as self-effacing; I admired his patience with her. 'Thanks, luvvie,' he'd say, when she'd shyly compliment him on his Italian or buy him and Petra their morning coffees. 'You're a doll.'

His and Petra's relationship was a volatile one. Petra had determined not to sleep with him for the duration of the course, partly for logistical reasons and partly because she claimed to want to take things slowly. 'I'm usually a caution-to-the-winds-type person. Follow the heart and to hell with the consequences.

But here in Italy ... it's all gone a bit *baroque*. Like everything's already dialled up to eleven, you know?'

I thought this was a smart move. For all Petra's talk of ambition, she was the kind of girl who, deep down, would much rather be an artist's muse than an actual artist. Lorcan was no artist, but Petra's efforts to be original and desirable and mercurial were not lost on him.

For my part, a certain low-level sexual frustration was probably no bad thing, in that it kept me sharp. I worked hard not to let my attraction to Lorcan grow beyond a faint background hum. This is not to say that if, at some wild moment, Lorcan had made a move on me I wouldn't have reciprocated. He was one of those people whose charisma has an unsettlingly erotic charge. One was always aware of it, like a thread of warm silk moving across the skin.

Since our day in Pisa, we had become co-conspirators. From time to time we would catch each other's eye, in wry acknowledgement of what we knew and shared. I watched him watching Annabelle and Nate, and felt it was only a matter of time before he'd need me.

But what of Annabelle? She was beyond the reach of Lorcan, of me, of everyone. The rest of us were merely the background to her *grand amour*. Spear carriers and static. No wonder she seemed so removed.

Yet even if she didn't know it, I understood her better than almost anyone else there. I wished there was some way to communicate this. She should have been easier to befriend than Lorcan simply because she was female. With another girl, sex was something to bond over, rather than a possibility – however abstract – that would only ever get in the way.

I made my approach during the trip to Orvieto. We'd spent an hour exploring the narrow lanes and stone chambers of the Etruscan burial ground, which I'd hoped would set an appropriately ascetic scene for mutual soul-baring. But whenever I came close to getting Annabelle on her own, one of the boys would spring out from whichever damp tomb they'd been hiding in and explode the quiet with horror-movie shrieks and groans. I had better luck on the minibus. There, I manoeuvred myself into the seat next to Annabelle at the back, while JJ led a group sing-along from the front. The general hubbub gave us relative privacy.

Annabelle spent the first ten minutes of the journey looking out of the window and fidgeting with her scarf. It was new, which had caught my attention because she did so little in the way of shopping. The design was derived from Persian tiles and was an intricate pattern of turquoise, purple and indigo. Back in Florence, I had seen Nate look at just such a scarf as we'd perused some shops near the Scuola del Cuoio. The tile print was an apt tribute to Annabelle's Iranian heritage, and the jewel-bright colours were striking against her hair and eyes. But Annabelle didn't go in for bold patterns and colours. Really, it was more Petra's style. Nate should have known better.

Time to make my move. I looked down at my phone and audibly caught my breath. Then I dug a nail into my thigh until tears sprang in my eyes. I was already flushed with daring; when

I looked up, as if blindly, I knew my face was suitably stricken.

'Ada, are you OK?'

'Oh. Yeah. I'm fine. I –' Shaky breath, brave smile. 'It's some random message from my ex. It caught me off guard.'

'This is the man from the bar you worked at?'

I nodded. After using Garreg Las to establish my olde worlde credentials, I was more relaxed about sharing the (comparatively) hardscrabble particulars of life in Brockley. Rich people like a plucky underdog, as long as it comes with a pedigree.

'Yeah. It got messy. He was a few years older than me, and really bright, but had crashed out of university. Drank too much, hated his family ... your basic rebel without a cause.' I rolled my eyes at my naiveté.

Annabelle nodded.

'Anyway. He was into poetry and so on, took a big interest in my writing. I fell hard. Then – whew – I can't believe I'm telling you this – but his drinking got worse. So did his temper. And then one time he hit me.'

'God, really? I'm sorry. I hope that's when it ended.'

She didn't have Lorcan's natural warmth, but her full attention was still a luminous thing.

'Pretty much.' I grimaced. 'He hated himself afterwards. I mean, I don't think he's *evil*. Now he says he's cleaned up his act ... who knows. I'm glad to be out of it. Even when things were good, our relationship was never exactly healthy.'

'Don't be too hard on yourself. Isn't wanting things that are bad for us what makes us human?'

I waited. But she didn't elaborate.

'I'm sorry to dump this on you, out of nowhere. It's not like we know each other that well.'

'Honestly, it's fine.'

'Perhaps it's easier sharing this stuff with people who don't have a history with you. There aren't any preconceptions to get in the way.' Again, Annabelle didn't respond. 'You won't mention this to the others, will you? It's something I'm still processing.'

'Of course. I understand.'

Final overture: 'Are there any exes you'd like exorcised?'

She shook her head, smiling. 'Maybe they need to exorcise me.'

I was annoyed. I hadn't expected her to come right out and admit the affair with Nate, but I'd anticipated some kind of hint, or at least an intimation of fellow feeling. I'd shared something deeply personal – something dark and complicated, grown-up – and got nothing in return. It didn't matter that my story was a lie. I felt cheated all the same.

Our first day in Rome was spent in homage to the Romantic poets. We visited the Keats–Shelley museum by the Spanish Steps in the morning and the Protestant cemetery in the afternoon. Keats's grave was in a meadow in the shadow of an ancient pyramid. It was a silvery grey afternoon; cypress trees whispered overhead, and the long tangled grasses were haunted by cats.

At Ben's urging, we girls picked violets to press between the pages of our guidebooks. Then everyone took it in turns to read aloud the poetry of the Romantics. We hadn't yet grasped what a luxury it is to feel tragedy without being marked by it. But the Italy we were exploring wore its heart on its sleeve, and the longer we spent there, the easier it became to put our defensive adolescent irony aside. (Only Mallory spoiled the mood, hopelessly mangling 'Music, When Soft Voices Die'. Her rendition of 'odours, when sweet violets sicken' had Kitty and Missy in fits.)

When it was Nate's turn to read, he chose Byron:

'She walks in beauty, like the night
Of cloudless climes and starry skies;
And all that's best of dark and bright
Meet in her aspect and her eyes ...'

His delivery was dry and almost colourless. He scrupulously did not look at Annabelle. But it didn't matter. I could almost taste the heat coming off both of them. It was extraordinary nobody else noticed. I looked over to where Lorcan lolled against a gravestone, and he mimed sticking his fingers down his throat.

Rome is a sentimental city. Buskers played *Somewhere over the Rainbow* on every other corner; rose sellers stalked the streets. Couples were everywhere: kissing on the Spanish Steps, tossing coins in the Trevi, posing for the cartoonists in Piazza Navona. Even the Colosseum – that monument to human cruelty – looked almost ethereal lit up at night, with lovers embracing in its shadows.

We were discussing the incongruity of this at a neighbouring bar when Yolanda asked Nate if she was right in thinking that he and Clemency had honeymooned in Rome. 'You must be looking forward to her visit next week,' she said casually.

Last year, we knew, Ben's partner, Ralph, had come out for a weekend. So Clemency's visit was not in itself particularly surprising. Dilettanti Discoveries liked to present itself as a 'family', in that its organisers drew on a network of colleagues who were also friends and often relations. It wasn't unusual for our tutors' local friends to join us for coffee or a walking tour. While we were in Siena, the course founder, Rex Whitelaw, a dapper old man with a neat white beard and a twinkle in his eye, had flown out to take us to lunch, as was his custom.

Still, this particular visitor was more eagerly anticipated than most. 'Of course, she's bound to be stunning,' Missy lamented at the next morning's coffee break. Her devotion to Nate was a running joke that no one took seriously, least of all herself. 'And she's an architect, so she'll be super-brainy too.'

Annabelle was sipping a macchiato in her usual composed fashion. However, I thought there was a new tautness to her face. As Clemency's visit grew nearer, she was first a little distant with us and then, as if to compensate, became uncharacteristically gregarious. Nate, however, looked ill. He said he was fighting off a cold.

'The only thing he's sick with are nerves,' Lorcan said in an aside to me. 'Clem must have sprung this on him at the absolute last moment. I don't think it's an actual *ambush*. But it might as well be.'

Clemency would be the guest of Annabelle and Lorcan's father and stepmother. With the kind of spontaneity available to the rich and leisured, they had decided to rent a villa in Rome for a week. I was surprised that Clemency had been included, since she and Nate were only connected to Mr Holt through Lorcan, but she was apparently close friends with Tess, the infamous trophy wifelet. 'Tess has been trying to ingratiate herself with my extended family for ages,' Lorcan brooded. 'Of course, she has no idea what she's let herself in for. Really, it's almost comic.'

The day of Clemency's arrival was the day of the pasta-making class. It was run by an Anglo-Italian couple in a medieval farmhouse in the Sabine hills. For lunch, we ate the fruit of our labours out on a paved loggia, overlooking vineyards and olive groves. Spring was well on the way and the saturated freshness of the blues and greens before us was almost painful in its intensity. We had one more week in Rome, and then it would all be over. I hoped I wasn't the only one whose heart ached at the thought.

Between courses, I went to fetch more bottled water from the kitchen. In the hall, I came upon a woman with a suitcase. 'I'm sorry,' she said. 'I did try the bell.'

It was not surprising we hadn't heard her; in addition to our mealtime hubbub, jazz was playing on a stereo.

'I'm Clemency ... Nate's wife?'

She looked a little uncertain and I realised I had been staring. 'Great,' I said. 'Lovely. Of course. Come on through. Nate's this way.'

His wife was a willowy strawberry-blonde, dressed in skinny jeans and a white peasant blouse. She had a fine-boned China-doll prettiness, but, close to, I saw this came with the kind of pale English skin that doesn't age well. Although she was only thirty-six, there was already a web of fine lines around her eyes. In her voluminous blouse – reminiscent of a child's pinafore – she simultaneously looked both older and younger than her real age.

'I thought I'd surprise him so I came straight from the airport, then the cab took a wrong turn in that village down the hill. My Italian's a bit rusty, so it's just as well asking for the school of pasta wasn't too taxing.' She spoke quickly and breathily, blinking hard. It was impossible not to feel the drama of the moment as I showed her through to the loggia.

Nate got up with clumsy haste, so that his chair scraped against the floor. 'Clem.' His voice caught a little. 'What a treat.'

They efficiently embraced. Annabelle was smiling pleasantly along with the rest of us. I remembered my own arrival, and how it felt to be silently assessed over the remains of somebody else's meal. Clemency was as quick as Nate was, but without his dryness. Almost immediately, we could see how Nate's somewhat austere manner was softened by the playfulness of hers. All the same, she did not seem wholly at ease. Her laugh was too giddy, her eyes a little too wide. She would lapse into abrupt silences and pick, nervously, at the dry skin on her lower lip.

Perhaps we were too eager to look for signs of weakness. Thanks to Willa's indiscretion, the principle thing we knew about Clemency was her infertility. Some of us, of course, knew of another injury. She was among strangers who knew more about her secret wounds than she did. It was disconcerting to have this kind of advantage over a grown woman.

At the station, waiting for the train back to the city, I was standing close to husband and wife. They were discussing whether she would join him for dinner.

'No, no,' Clemency was saying, 'I think it's better if I eat with Tess tonight. She's being very kind. You stay, hang out with the kids.'

Nate reflexively winced. To think of Annabelle as one of 'the kids' must have stung. Clemency saw his face change, and at that moment hers flickered too. I realised there was another reason to regret her choice of words: they unwittingly evoked the children the two of them should have had.

Further along the platform, I watched Annabelle smooth down her hair. She was checking her reflection in the window of the waiting room. Now that there was no escaping her status as the scarlet woman, surely cracks would begin to show on her veneer. I wondered what might come through them: some creeping growth, sinuous and over-ripe.

CHAPTER TEN

On the train back to Rome, Petra admitted to feeling some anxiety about Lorcan and Annabelle's family visit. Was she going to be invited to meet their father? If so, how was she to be introduced?

'Obviously, I'm not going to go into the details, but there is a lot of family dysfunction behind the scenes,' she told me darkly. 'A *lot* of tension. Lorcan likes to stay sunny-side-up, but he's actually quite conflicted about it.'

I know, I longed to say, but held my tongue.

Petra tossed back her curls. 'At least one thing's settled. I'm definitely going to sleep with him now.'

Sex was suddenly, starkly, everywhere. That night, in a dingy club in the Trastevere, our group bumped into a gaggle of Australians on a study-abroad semester. The tallest and rangiest of the guys claimed Willa. Oliver and Rocco were soon doing the public school bump 'n' grind on the dance floor, two girls apiece. Petra and Lorcan had disappeared, presumably to seal the deal. Annabelle was also nowhere to be seen. I downed a series of neon-orange cocktails and at the end of the night found myself sweatily entangled with one of the bartenders. He was stocky with a mono-brow; both our mouths were slimed with sugar from the drinks. My head sparked and pulsed as his hands roamed damply around my body.

I was horribly hung-over for the next morning's tour of the Galleria Borghese. I was embarrassed, too, by kissing the bartender. He had not been particularly attractive – did everyone think I was desperate? The boys exchanged lascivious notes on their own conquests. Oliver had been given – or so he claimed – a blow-job behind the bins in the smoking area. Lorcan and Petra wandered the halls hand-in-hand, in a swoony post-sex bubble.

And although I was disgusted with myself, I still felt a residual twinge whenever I remembered the man's hands on my back. That yank of heat, deep within the belly …

'Do you see how the cleft in the golden peach is echoed in the lad's chin?' Ben enjoined us, in front of *Boy with a Basket of Fruit*. 'And then again in his bare right shoulder? Good enough to eat!'

We tittered, uncertain as to how rude he had meant to be. Caravaggio's boys, with their sooty eyes and sulky mouths, seemed of a piece with the wanton mood of the morning. In front of the *Venus Victrix*, Oliver made an obscene grabbing gesture. The statue's breasts were small and lusciously plump. More bare breasts gleamed from the walls – Danae, molested by cherubs; Leda, by a swan. Susanna and Diana, surprised at their bathing. 'Mind-bending, isn't it,' said Ben, of the *Rape of Proserpina*, 'how Bernini is able to turn cold marble into something so sensual.'

I stared at the swell of Proserpina's flesh and how Pluto's grip dimpled her upper thigh. Skin turned to bark in *Apollo and*

Daphne, as the nymph's mouth gaped in stony horror at the god's touch. I felt a surge of nausea.

Clemency saw me grimace. 'You know,' she murmured, 'I sometimes think Plato had a point with his distrust of art. It beautifies unbearable things.'

I thought I detected a tremor in her voice. I didn't feel able to confess I was in the grip of a hangover, rather than suffering from some finer feeling. I questioned, not for the first time, why Clemency was accompanying us around the gallery when Nate had the morning free. I looked again at her brittle wrists and the creases around her eyes. This seemed to me a critical moment. I was beginning to understand how, for all its false consolations, art shows us how we learn from pain. I wanted to express this. I wanted to articulate something profound about love and suffering. I wanted to say *I'm sorry*.

Yet the words I was looking for kept retreating from me. My head throbbed. 'It's all quite male gaze-y, isn't it?' I said lamely.

Someone tugged at my hair – it was Lorcan, passing by. 'We're nothing without our lechery, you know. As the poet said, the female of the species is more deadly than the male. So how else are we going to subjugate you?'

Lit by a slant of sun, his hair was gilded and eyes silver, his skin bronze. He moved out of the light and the effect was gone. Even so, the afterglow lingered.

Clemency smiled a little in his direction. 'Boys like Lorcan terrified me at your age.'

Was she suggesting that I was intimidated by him? I didn't believe her, anyway: at eighteen or nineteen, Clemency's doll-like prettiness must have been at its peak. But her next words softened me.

'You're all rather terrifying, actually. I feel you must be a different breed to the muddled sort of teenager I was.'

'How did you and Nate meet?'

I already knew it had been at Oxford. But I was curious as to how she'd tell the story.

'At university. Nate introduced me to art, you know. For our first date, he took me to a Chagall exhibition. And then he bought me a print of *The Birthday* for mine. Chagall painted it as a tribute to his wife. He said, "I had only to open my window, and blue air, love and flowers entered with her."'

'That's beautiful.'

'It is ... Have you come across the word *pentimento* yet?'

I was interested by this apparent non sequitur, so I shook my head.

'Something else I learned from Nate. The word comes from the Italian for "repent". When paint ages, the artist's first draft is sometimes revealed under it: their *pentimento*. I've always liked the idea. How, as time goes on, the finished surface thins and you can see through the layers – back to abandoned ideas. The lost or mistaken. Because they're always with us, aren't they? All our regrets. All our hidden things.'

She was looking towards Lorcan again, and I saw Annabelle had joined him and Petra. They were laughing together. Clemency put up her hand to her cracked lip, peeling away another fleck of grey skin. A bead of blood trembled underneath.

———

I was watching Clemency; I was watching Annabelle; I was watching Nate.

Clemency's arrival had prompted Annabelle to make subtle efforts to reengage with us. She was warmer, more expansive and involved. 'I've realised Annabelle's maybe quite shy?' Mallory reflected. 'Like, she's so refined I thought she might be a bit stand-offish. But she's a real sweetie once you get to know her. I feel like she's just taken a while to relax?'

Nate, by contrast, was visibly on edge. He was the lead tutor for much of our activities in Rome, thanks to its abundance of classical antiquities, but the hectic energy he brought to his tutorials seemed forced and made everyone faintly uneasy.

'He's useless,' said Lorcan disgustedly. '*Obviously* the writing's on the wall. It's only a matter of time before Clem susses him out or – more likely – Annabelle dumps him.'

It was true that, now Clemency had arrived on the scene, Nate seemed considerably less impressive. And then there was Oxford. No doubt Annabelle would be much in demand among the floppy-haired young demigods who thronged the quads.

Almost without realising it, my own loyalties had shifted. If someone like Clemency stood no chance against a girl like Annabelle, then nobody did. I still admired Annabelle, fervently. But I liked her less.

'Has Annabelle asked for your advice?' I asked Lorcan.

'No chance. I know she massively regrets telling me about Nate. She's been cold-shouldering me ever since. And to be honest, I'd rather I didn't know.'

'Do you think Clemency suspects?'

'Hard to say.'

I thought she did. She knew someone had betrayed her confidence, at least. Back in the Borghese gallery, Ben had mentioned something about Caravaggio depicting David's pity for Goliath. 'Screw pity,' Clemency had said abruptly. 'Pity without compassion or real understanding ... it's poisonous. I'd rather have indifference. Or even hate.' And the group of teenagers around her had looked away, embarrassed.

'It must be awful for her.'

'Mm. Poor old Clem,' Lorcan said vaguely. 'She's always been on the highly strung side; I think there was a breakdown at uni. That's where she and Nate met, you know. I don't believe in taking relationships seriously until your thirties at least. People outgrow each other so fast.'

Alas for Petra. I'd fretted that her and Lorcan's new closeness would mean he had no more room, let alone need, for me. Instead, the privilege of my position was confirmed by his next words.

'Thanks for this, doll. You've got the patience of a saint. No – I mean it. Here you are in the Eternal City, in hot pursuit of *la dolce vita*, and I'm boring you stiff with my sordid family dramas.'

'It's not sordid. It's sad. Complicated and sad.'

He shook his head, smiling. 'Oh, we're all monsters really. You'll see.'

'How do you mean?'

'Pa's in town tomorrow. He's insisting on taking everyone out for lunch. Honestly, it'll be like one of those miserable art-house movies. You know – where a bunch of dysfunctional twats sit around a table taking potshots at each other with the vol-au-vents. Or antipasti, in this instance.'

I was thrilled by the idea.

Our latest conversation had taken place while walking back from St Peter's. I felt quite able to disregard Lorcan's remark about what I should be prioritising in Rome. So what if my most meaningful memories of Italy turned out to be conversations – moments of connection – just like this? Art is no substitute for experience, I told myself. No matter that I was not a direct participant in the dramatic entanglements Lorcan put before me; I trusted that, with luck and patience, my time would come.

Petra was to be introduced as Lorcan's girlfriend at lunch, and her new-found sense of security showed itself as an increasing sleekness. She'd evidently decided I posed no possible competition, let alone threat. This was something I tried not to be offended by.

The Holt lunch was to take place on our last day in Rome. None of us was immune to the pull Lorcan and Annabelle's family exerted, yet we were distracted from the start, our sense of anticipation drawn elsewhere. Oliver had lately reasserted himself with an invitation of his own. His family connections included a long-standing friendship with one of the rare survivors of the Venetian aristocracy. This family, the Monegarios, had recently inherited a palazzo on the Fondamente Nove. They already had their own far grander establishment on the Grand Canal, and so intended to convert the place into apartments for the wealthy foreigners who snapped up most of Venice's real estate. In the meantime, the palazzo lay empty. The younger Monegarios were going to host a party in it that weekend. And here was Oliver's ace in the hole: we were all invited.

The course was due to end with return flights from Rome on Saturday morning. Oliver proposed we change our travel arrangements to fly home on Sunday from Venice instead. We would catch the train to the city early on Saturday and camp out in the palazzo overnight. 'Let's bow out in style,' he said. 'Our own Venetian carnival.'

Oliver, with Willa as his back-up, was relentlessly dismissive of the difficulties of changing homecoming plans. It would only be worth doing if everyone did it. One for all, all for one, et cetera. My qualms about the costs involved seemed trivial and mean-spirited – especially as Mallory was buying a new ticket to New York without so much as batting an eye.

'Oh, come *on*, Ada. Don't pretend there's some wildly important assignation you're in a rush to get back for.' Since Florence, Oliver and I had been treading carefully around each other, and I didn't want to antagonise him again. Besides, I had already gone so far over my budget, any further economies seemed false ones.

Though we didn't like to admit it, all of us were feeling a little jaded by now. Weeks of minimal sleep, heavy meals and even heavier boozing had taken its toll. Our skin was sallow and prone to break-outs. Our clothes, inexpertly hand-washed or else pummelled in laundrettes, were over-familiar and tired looking. Our nerves were beginning to fray. This unexpected extension of our Grand Tour was a chance to put any small frustrations and disappointments aside and be our most impressive selves again.

CHAPTER ELEVEN

Annabelle and Lorcan's father had rented a villa close to the Borghese. The lunch was catered and served by a neighbouring restaurant. I wondered if Mr Holt's preference to entertain us at home was because of his illness, about which I felt a morbid curiosity. I knew from Lorcan that he was a former alcoholic, he was wealthy, and also monstrous. That he was dying only made him more formidable. We had spent the morning in the catacomb of Sant'Agnese; I fancied the chill of the burial chambers would follow after us, like an invisible mist.

The villa was not the baroque palace I'd imagined, but plain and contemporary in style. The trophy wifelet was similarly unexpected. Tess was in her late thirties, with close-cropped dark hair and a nose stud. She had a tired smile and only a trace of Geordie in her accent. Nor did she and Mr Holt seem such an unlikely couple. At the age of sixty, Leo Holt was still handsome, his thick head of hair only just beginning to grey. He was gaunt, but this and other signs of ill-health – the sallow skin and ringed eyes – only enhanced his resemblance to an ageing rocker. Both he and his wife were dressed in skinny black.

He had met Willa before and greeted her warmly, which I could see irked Petra. I hoped that next time we encountered each other I would receive the same friend-of-the-family welcome. 'There's nothing so delightful as girls in pearls,' he said by way of hello. His breath had the sour undernote of sickness; I couldn't tell if he was mocking me or if I was supposed to be in on the joke.

There was an attempt at a seating plan, but this meant that Annabelle would be next to Clemency, so she contrived to be elsewhere, and in the resultant muddle Mallory ended up taking her place next to Mr Holt. This struck me as unfortunate, for I felt it important that our group was shown to its best advantage. I found myself between Yolanda and Lorcan, and facing Kitty.

Clemency was opposite Yolanda; they immediately leaned towards each other and resumed the discussion of Arts Council politics they had begun on the walk over. Clemency's fragility inspired a special kind of carefulness in those around her, and Yolanda was no exception. Still, I was surprised by their camaraderie. There was always something effortful about Yolanda, who tried too visibly for us to wholly warm to her. We were polite, rather than enthused, during the debates she encouraged on the whiteness and maleness of our studies.

With Yolanda tending to Clemency, and Lorcan engaged with Petra on his other side, I felt marooned. Kitty and I never had much to say to each other. Even Mallory was chatting happily away. Under the glow of Mr Holt's apparently undivided attention, she was almost vivacious.

'Oh, Pa loves Americans,' said Lorcan as an aside, when he saw me looking. 'It's part of his contrarian man-of-the-people pose.' He was distracted, with a hectic flush; neither he nor Annabelle appeared at ease. I was on edge myself. Mr Holt, perhaps because of his condition, felt the cold and as a result the heating was turned uncomfortably high. The restaurant that was catering our lunch specialised in *quinto quarto*, otherwise known as offal. Due to a misunderstanding with the waiter, I'd got a plate of tripe instead of the fish that was also on offer.

After the first course had been cleared away, Mr Holt got to his feet. He wasn't the sort of man who had to clear his throat or tap cutlery against glass for a table to fall silent. 'Here it comes,' Lorcan muttered under his breath.

'I didn't grow up with the refinements my children enjoy,' was how Mr Holt began. 'This isn't to say it was a life of hair shirts and gruel sandwiches. Not at all. But I was nonetheless raised to believe that to study the arts was a luxury the likes of me couldn't afford. Culture, my friends, is a word that for centuries has sat atop a gleaming plinth and looked down its nose at the masses.

'My children inform me that this has changed. And looking at the bright young faces around me today –' mischievous smile '– I'm sure you wouldn't dream of looking down your noses at anyone.

'Still, it's only lately I've learned your secret. Culture is the best educational tool we have – better even than science or philosophy. Why? Because a person doesn't have to be especially clever or industrious to engage with it. And I mean that as the greatest compliment! Truly.

'Like falling in love, connecting with art's the easiest thing in the world. And also the hardest. Love and art – both a gift and a challenge. They disrupt as well as renew. Because that's what Renaissance means, doesn't it? Rebirth.' He turned to his wife and raised his water glass. 'To new beginnings. To art and love.'

'Art and love,' we chorused.

I was disappointed with this speech. There had been no fireworks; it seemed to me both snide and sentimental. Still, I joined in the smiles and the applause. Mallory was even wiping away a tear.

'You can see where Lorcan gets his charm from,' said Kitty, once we had settled again.

It was at that point I realised Clemency had left the room. She had grown very quiet over the course of lunch, pulling at her lip and picking at her nails, her expression glazed. Nate was down the other end of the table, in between Oliver and the third Mrs Holt. I had noticed him attempt to catch Annabelle's eye on several occasions, but she was studiously avoiding him. He, along with everyone else, was shouting slightly to be heard. The high ceiling and hardwood floor of the dining room threw the noise of the party above and around in an increasingly clamorous din.

I felt hot and sick. I'd had one experimental mouthful of tripe and, though it was merely chewy, tasting of nothing very much but the tomato sauce it was cooked in, I fancied it was somehow festering in my stomach, infecting me with the odour of farmyard and decay. The more wine I drank, the more pronounced the tang seemed to be. My throat was sore. By the time I was spooning up a somewhat gluey *zabaglione* I was in need of escape. When I found the downstairs bathroom occupied, I climbed the stairs to look for another.

The house was all hard angles and high-gloss surfaces. After spending so much time among the antique, the effect was disorientating. The first two doors I tried led to Mr and Mrs Holt's bedroom and then a small office. The final door opened to a guest bedroom, as impersonal as a hotel's. The door within led, I guessed, to an en suite. I was halfway across the room before I saw the spot of blood on the white carpet.

I stopped, transfixed. My first thought, absurdly, was of Mr Holt. Then I heard a low groan from behind the bathroom door.

'Um. Hello?'

A stifled gasp. And then Clemency's voice, in a whisper so frail it made me wince: 'Just a moment, please.'

'Are you all right?' I asked, witlessly.

'Yes. I … I will be.'

Another low, guttural noise. The hiss of breath through clenched teeth. I dithered, then pushed the door in a little. I saw a smear of blood across pale bathroom tiles. I let the door close. My throat was thick with the taste of farmyard again; of innards, death.

'Can I get – should I get you a doctor?'

'No need.'

Her voice was a thread firmer.

I waited. Minutes passed. The toilet flushed, water ran. Two or three long minutes after that Clemency came out, wearing a white bathrobe. She looked calm and very clean. But my head was swarming with scenes from horror movies and Gothic folk tales. Behind the pristine door, I imagined bloody handprints, clots and spatters; pulsating lumps of gore.

'It's all right,' she said distantly. 'Hardly anything to lose this time. I was only six weeks gone.' A small tense smile. 'That was my tenth. You'd think I'd be used to it by now.'

My own insides cramped. 'I'm so sorry. I'm sorry. It's … awful. Terrible. A terrible thing.'

Clemency wasn't listening. 'The womb is supposed to be where life begins. Mine, it seems, is a graveyard.' She gazed past me, out of the window onto the Roman rooftops. 'Coming to Italy was a mistake. I thought being a tourist would be a distraction. But actually it's the worst place to be. All those fucking Madonna-and-Childs.'

She said the last quite matter-of-factly. Her bathrobe was man-sized; wrapped in its swathes, she looked like a child herself. Yet she seemed, in a strange way, more collected than I had seen her before.

'I suppose you'd better fetch Nate.'

I was in two minds all the way down the stairs.

I went to Nate and put one hand on his shoulder. I felt a tingle of importance, despite myself, as I bent to murmur in his ear. 'I'm afraid Clemency's been taken ill. She's waiting for you upstairs.'

At once, Nate's eyes darted to Annabelle. She was laughing at something with Rocco. Casually draped around her neck was the Persian-tile scarf.

Enough was enough.

'By the way,' I said, 'is this yours?'

I passed him the postcard I'd gone to considerable pains to track down. It had taken time and trouble, but eventually I'd found a set of notecards in a little poster and print shop near the Vatican. Among the half-dozen pictures repackaged as 'Art 4 Lovers' was *The Birthday*, by Marc Chagall.

A couple embrace, the man bending over backwards to kiss the woman, soaring up like a kite in their simple living room. It is an image of transcendent joy. *Blue air, flowers, love.*

Nate fingered the card, clumsily. 'Ah ... Uh ... How –? Where –?'

'It was lying in the hall, near your bag.' Nate stammered something else. He jammed the card into his pocket. In the doorway, he stumbled, and the noise made Annabelle turn and stare.

I have to be honest: I wanted Annabelle to bleed, just a little, when Clemency had bled so much. I wanted her to be vulnerable so I could be strong. For I would know how to comfort her if she asked. *He's not worthy of you*, which was true. *You have nothing to be ashamed of*, which wasn't.

Our final dinner in Rome was a subdued affair. Only Mallory was on good form. The attentions of Mr Holt had invigorated her.

'I loved your speech,' she said, when they said goodbye. 'I'll remember it always.'

'Then remember this too,' I heard him say, clasping her hand in both of his. 'Armour may look tough, but all it does is mask the anxiety inside. It's not someone else's responsibility to break down your armour. *It's your responsibility to let them in.*'

I suspected Mr Holt was amusing himself by parodying the kind of motivational hokum he must have encountered at rehab.

I still wasn't sure how heartfelt his speech had been. But Mallory turned pink with pleasure.

The rest of us were tired and sullen. Petra had quarrelled with Lorcan over some perceived slight at the lunch party, and both were sulking. After coming by the restaurant to make a hurried farewell, Nate had returned to Clemency, prompting somewhat bad-tempered speculation as to why he had bailed on the last official night of the course. Annabelle looked wan and left early. JJ and Rocco, who had taken their competitive offal-eating to unwise extremes, were distinctly bilious. My sore throat had worsened into the beginnings of a cold. Most of us stuck to soft drinks.

Ben and Yolanda gamely tried to infuse the evening with festive spirit, but our final farewells were made with the brittle extravagance of children who have stayed up too long past their bedtime. Tomorrow, we consoled ourselves, we would start again. Tomorrow we would fall back in love, with art and beauty and each other.

CHAPTER TWELVE

Most people slept for the duration of the four-hour train ride to Venice. I thought this meant Lorcan and I could talk, for I was eager to discuss the lunch and its aftermath. Whatever Petra's quarrel with him, it had not been resolved. He had left the bar early, without her, to stay over at his father's, and she gave him a distinctly frosty welcome when he skidded into the train station with seconds to spare. Petra's whims had become a running joke between the two of us, a source of affectionate exasperation we could communicate by the merest twitch of lip or eyebrow. (Petra required her complaints about Lorcan to be taken considerably more seriously, of course. It was a delicate balancing act.)

Today there was nothing light-hearted about Lorcan's annoyance. 'OK, maybe it would make life easier if I could tell Petra what's been going on, but now she'll just be spitting nails I didn't fill her in from the start. It'll mean yet more drama and histrionics, which is the last thing any of us need. Christ – the fallout from Annabelle's fuckwittery has no end.'

He gave his sleeping sister a baleful look.

I didn't know if Lorcan knew about the miscarriage, and I wasn't quite sure how to ask him. I had been privy to a loss that was both savage and intimate. By bearing witness – to *real* blood, *real* pain, not their exquisite canvas counterparts – I felt I had acquired a new, adult worldliness. But Lorcan was brooding and preoccupied. When I asked him if he knew how Clemency was, he merely shrugged.

Mallory was watching us with open curiosity. She had been attempting to sidle up to me all morning. When Lorcan wandered off to look for the buffet car, she came over to take his place. 'That speech Mr Holt gave, about art and love, and how challenging they are, it really resonated, you know?'

I made a non-committal grunt.

She was fidgeting, frowning. 'It makes you think. It really does. It's–'

'Mm. You're right, Mal. It was a good speech.' I yawned, then closed my eyes, feigning sleep. After Florence, I was sure to keep my interactions with Mallory pleasant. If I needed to give her the brush-off, I did so politely. That was enough, wasn't it?

Today I had the excuse that I was definitely getting ill. My head felt heavy and it hurt to swallow. I wondered if I'd pressed Lorcan too hard, and if he was now irritated with me as well as with Petra. Sometimes I worried I hadn't done enough to cement my friendship with the two of them. One more day and night and then we'd be scattered; any interest I held, the usefulness I offered, would be gone.

Panic flared. What if I had wasted this opportunity after all? Attempting to make myself indispensable had hollowed me out. I thought of all the sightseeing trips that had passed in a blur, of meals where I'd barely savoured the food. Art, culture, history, philosophy … I had meant to wallow in them, to luxuriate in the life of the mind, as well as the more sensual pleasures of a *vita bella*. But what would I be left with when everyone parted ways? The end of my overdraft. An extra half-stone in pasta weight. A bundle of dog-eared postcards. A thousand photographs of people I hardly knew.

Perhaps, I fretted, I should have tried harder with Annabelle. Or handled things differently, at least. She was visibly fragile this morning. The fragility of the dumper or the dumped? It seemed to me that Annabelle had as much reason for ending things as Nate. He'd gone back to London at one point in our Venetian stay; it had been a twenty-four-hour trip, allegedly for a conference. Clemency being six weeks pregnant cast this in a rather different light. Annabelle's eyes were red-rimmed and she was hunched in on herself. No scarf. But when she saw me looking she held my stare, almost aggressively, until I was forced to turn away.

Venice was sparkling after a week of rain. A bank of clouds hung over the Rialto like a pile of densely whipped cream – Tiepolo clouds, in confectionery shades, on which you'd expect to see an aerial carnival of boozy nymphs or bosomy angels, all gauzy drapes and rose-flushed limbs. The sky behind them was eggshell blue.

The sight raised our spirits. Annabelle and Lorcan exchanged laconic fist-bumps. Even Petra managed a smile.

We were met on the Fondamente Nove by Lorenzo, the younger Monegario son. Oliver had impressed upon us that the Monegarios were not only a famously aristocratic clan, with a number of Doges to their name, but high-flyers in the modern sense. Their more recent fortune was built on shipping; they were big patrons of the arts and had property in London and New York. Lorenzo himself was in his first year studying engineering in Milan and looked like an Italian version of JJ, merry brown eyes squinting at us through a flop of overgrown hair.

Kisses and 'ciao's were enthusiastically exchanged with one and all; Oliver was greeted like a long-lost brother. He and Willa, who had formed an alliance as the chief party-people of our group, underwent a miraculous transformation. The creases seemed to fall out of their clothes; their backs straightened; their eyes found a fresh sparkle.

The rest of us chimed in with indistinct noises of enthusiasm and gratitude.

Lorenzo gave a gracious wave. 'Please. It's nothing. Lower your expectations, OK, because the palazzo is nothing like your National Trust. No. It's a crazy old place. But then, my cousin was a crazy old man. You will see.'

Like many grand Venetian houses, the sixteenth-century building didn't look anything special from the rear. The walls were plain, the windows few. To enter it, we turned off the Fondamente into a cramped calle and through a door that opened onto the back stairs.

Our host led the way up to the *piano nobile*. Here, we found ourselves in a *salone* with a wide marble floor and elaborate stucco ornamentation. The principle furnishings were a number of chaise longues upholstered in faded brocade, a grand piano and a vast Murano chandelier, dripping with plumes and curlicues of coloured glass. Glazed doors opened onto a balcony overlooking the canal.

'This,' said Rocco, very solemnly, 'is *seriously* cool.'

Lorenzo laughed. 'Ah, but do not look too close. It's junk and fakes. Or mostly. A couple of mirrors are good, and the tapestries. And one or two chairs … The old man, he used to work in the theatres, you know? He had little money so he used tricks instead.' He strode towards the glazed doors. 'The view is not bad. That is something you cannot counterfeit!'

We took turns to crowd onto the balcony, which overlooked a canal and an attractive but unremarkable parade of houses. To our left, however, was the lagoon and the cemetery island of San Michele, encircled by low red-brick walls and crowned with cypress trees. The pale imprint of the Dolomites was just visible to the north, floating on the skyline like the ghost of snow.

The dining room was to the left of the balcony end of the *salone*. There was a table for twelve and tattered crimson wallpaper. A sitting room was to the other side, bedazzled with eighteenth-century mirrors. But we soon saw what Lorenzo had meant by 'tricks'. What appeared to be painted beams had been decorated by peeling transfers. The velvet hangings were polyester; the turbaned moors on pedestals had been carved out of polystyrene. While the bedroom furniture resembled funeral monuments, the kitchen was small and cramped, with grubby Formica units.

'Is this fake too?' Missy enquired about the slightly too colourful fresco that lined an upstairs reception hall.

'*Certo*. It was done by one of the old man's theatre friends. A set painter. But this one, it is not so bad, I think.'

The fresco was of a Renaissance festival and a procession of costumed figures. They stood on chariots, like carnival floats. A naked woman, drawn by swans. An angel with a golden trumpet. A skeleton with a scythe.

'They're the Triumphs, aren't they?' I said.

'So you know your Petrarca! *I Trionfi*. Very good. But these are supposed to picture the *tarocchi*.'

'Tar-whatty?' said JJ.

'Ancient playing cards. What is the English word?' Lorenzo clicked his fingers. 'Ah! Tarot. You know?'

Kitty pursed her lips, presumably offended by tarot's occult associations. The rest of us peered closer. There was Justice, with her sword and scales. A grinning Devil. A motley Fool. But we were soon distracted by the discovery, in the same hall, of a trunk full of carnival masks. Although they were the kind you could find in any souvenir shop, their surroundings gave them a gimcrack glamour.

The tour ended with the formal entrance to the palazzo. Originally, our guide explained, visitors arrived by boat at the water gate and went from there into the courtyard, where there was a flight of steps up to the *piano nobile*. In more recent times, a partition had been put up at the west end of the *salone* to create a poky lobby. We stepped outside to find the stately entrance that had been missing at street level.

This door had pilasters to each side and a grotesque mask on the keystone. Ivy clung to the stairs' rusting balustrade and the walls' crumbling plaster and worm-eaten bricks. A colonnaded walkway ran around two sides of the courtyard; in the centre, an overgrown fig-tree spouted from the well.

Cautiously, we made our way down. There was a door to the

calle as well as the water gate, though the street exit was blocked by sacks of rubbish. The surrounding windows were shuttered and grilled. It was dank and rather desolate, yet a gloomy grandeur prevailed.

Oliver rolled his eyes as people started taking photographs. 'Can you try and act a bit less like a Japanese tour party?' he muttered.

Our host heard him. 'Photograph as you wish! Please. Once the renovations are done, all this will be unrecognisable.'

'But it's so romantic as it is,' Mallory said, taking a selfie at the foot of the stairs. 'It's like we're in Sleeping Beauty's castle.'

Lorenzo laughed. 'Rich foreigners want romance, yes, but only the five-star kind.'

I felt a pang. The building's ramshackle magic was surely preferable to the bland opulence required by the international elite. I thought of Garreg Las, despoiled by feature wallpaper and gold taps.

'Never mind the makeover, OK?' Lorenzo clapped his hands together. 'The builders and the architects and the estate agents are for another day. For now, this is our palace, to do as we like.'

Lorenzo left us with keys and directions to the local supermarket. He would rejoin us in the evening. It would be a small gathering, he told us, of the younger family members and a few of their friends who were in town for the Easter break. In the meantime, we had the place to ourselves. We spread out through the upper floors, slinging our bags onto sagging mattresses, before going out for supplies.

The afternoon light was already fading when we returned. Only three of the twelve electric candles on the chandelier worked and so we supplemented them with tea lights in jars. JJ pushed back the battered lid of the piano to reveal a set of ivory keys as yellow as old teeth. When he sat on the stool and flexed his fingers I braced myself for 'Chopsticks' or maybe 'The Entertainer', but to everyone's surprise, he launched into the *Moonlight Sonata*. 'It sounds like bad jazz,' Kitty remarked, and it was true the piano was so out of tune the melody was almost unrecognisable. Yet in such a setting, the discordant notes had a plangent grace of their own. As we gathered around the piano, glasses of prosecco in hand, sentimentality descended like a warm mist. I looked over to try and catch Lorcan's eye. Instead, I realised that Mallory's were fixed on me.

She ran me to ground later while I was engaged in draping fairy lights around the sitting-room mirrors.

'Have you got a minute?'

'Well, your timing's not *ideal*.' I was balanced on a coffee table, trying to loop a string of lights over a curly bit of frame.

'I know, but it's kinda important.'

I realised that if I didn't give in now I'd be pestered by her for the rest of the evening. 'OK, fine. What's the problem?'

'I need your advice, I guess. I want to know what you'd do if you saw two people sneaking around, doing something that would cause a lot of hurt. A lot of *damage* ...'

Shit.

'Spit it out, Mal.'

She scrunched up her face. 'So I saw … that is … I think I saw Annabelle. With Nate. Our tutor? As in, they were together. They were *kissing*.'

'Are you sure?' I asked, playing for time.

'Remember Annabelle went home early last night because she didn't feel too good? Well, when we got back to the hotel there was a note in our room saying she'd gone to the late-night pharmacy. But as it turned out, I'd left my phone behind in the bar. So Ben called the bar from the hotel and got me a cab to go collect it. That's when I saw them.'

'In the bar?'

'No, in the street. I was looking out the window of the cab. I mean, it was nearly midnight and dark and all, but I definitely recognised them. It was, like, super intense. And when she got back, it looked like she'd been crying?'

I frowned. 'Whatever you think you saw, it's none of your business.'

'I know. I'm totally conflicted about it. It's just – Mr Holt's speech – it made a big impression on me. And whenever I think about Clemency … She's already had a lot of pain in her life? And she's such a beautiful, delicate person …'

'So why are you telling me this? You want my permission to tell Clemency her husband's a cheat?'

'No,' she said uncertainly. 'At least … I don't want to get anyone in trouble. But I thought you could maybe tell Lorcan and he could maybe talk to his sister. He could, like, warn her or something.'

'Why not talk to Lorcan yourself?'

Mallory blushed. Of course: she had a crush on him. I saw that she had made a special effort for this evening: her frizzy black hair had been straightened smooth; she was wearing high heels and a low-cut top.

Most likely, she didn't even want my advice. All she wanted was a little consequence, the pomp and circumstance of a secret she was the first to impart. Mallory, however, wasn't crafty or courageous enough to turn the situation to tangible advantage. 'You guys seem good friends,' she said. 'And right now he and Petra are pissed at each other. So I thought it might be better coming from you.'

This warmed me, despite myself. 'Honestly, Mal, I think you'd better stay out of it. The situation's more complicated than you realise.'

Her eyes widened. 'Does this mean you already knew? Does Lorcan?'

'Never mind all that–'

'But don't you think Clemency deserves better?' She was still frowning, still twisting her hands. 'And Annabelle too. Nate's her *teacher*.'

Her distress was starting to annoy me. There was no need to be so pious about it. 'Then have a quiet word with Annabelle,' I said. 'Don't make it obvious that you know. Just tell her that you can see she's upset about something and that you'll always be there for her, as a friend, ready to listen and support. It'll mean a lot.'

It was unkind of me, I'll admit. But it was intended to be Annabelle's punishment, not Mallory's. I could picture Annabelle's rictus smile as Mallory babbled on, oblivious.

'Are you sure?'

I nodded. Anything to be left in peace.

I was saved from further interrogation by the arrival of Lorenzo and company. For the first hour, natives and visitors kept to their own groups, though once the alcohol had begun to take effect, I joined the others in some tentative intermingling. The Monegario posse spoke English with a transatlantic drawl; boys and girls alike were uniformly sleek as well as tanned. In normal circumstances, I might have found them terrifying, but I was a Dilettante now. For here we were, rubbing shoulders with 'the elite of continental society' in an ancient palazzo – Grand Tourists in every sense.

Someone had moved the box of carnival masks downstairs. There were cloaks and jackets too, and people were soon trying them on, striking poses that were only partly ironic. I could imagine the Instagram hashtags already. Dilettanti Discoveries disapproved of social media; Ben was always threatening to confiscate our phones if he found our use of them distracting. We were supposed to chronicle our experiences by writing journals and collecting postcards and ticket stubs.

Tonight it felt as if our memories were already crystallising, almost before our eyes. Everyone was loveable, everyone attractive. Mallory appeared to have recovered from her crisis of conscience and, draped in a red carnival cloak, was taking selfies with Kitty and Missy. Annabelle was in fits of laughter with Petra. 'You're stand-up gents,' I heard Rocco slur to JJ and Oliver. Lorcan had slung his arm round my shoulder; Willa was topping up my drink. We were already planning our first reunion. 'And then there will be all the twenty-first-birthday dos,' said Missy.

'Graduations,' chimed in Kitty.

'Weddings!' somebody shouted.

'Funerals!' shouted somebody else and, laughing, we bumped fists and clinked glasses.

How I longed to be essential to these people. Already, I couldn't imagine myself being without them.

CHAPTER THIRTEEN

Someone was insistently pressing on the buzzer. The music wasn't overwhelmingly loud, but the giddy spirit of our group had begun to spread to the wider party; most people were too distracted to notice. 'I'll go,' I shouted to Lorenzo, who was putting the moves on Willa by the mantelpiece. Since the intercom was broken, opening the door meant going down the backstairs to street level.

But when I made my way down the stairs I found I wasn't the only one to answer the bell: Lorcan was just ahead of me. I wondered if I should turn back – after the train journey, I didn't want him to think I was trailing him, buzzing insistently at his ear. I mustn't be a Mallory. Still, something impelled me to keep going.

I rounded the final corner of the stairs to see that Lorcan had opened the door to Clemency.

'Where is she?' A ragged nimbus of pale hair stuck up around her head. Her face was all bones and hollows, her dry lips flecked with blood.

'Shit. Clem–'

'Don't you dare "Clem" me. Presumably you've known about the little slut from the start.' She tried to push past him. 'Let me through.' Her voice cracked. 'For fuck's sake –'

'Hey, hey, hey,' Lorcan said, gently this time, and put his hands on her shoulders. 'Don't do this. Not like this, not now.'

'I'm still bleeding, by the way. From Nate's baby. Do you have any idea how that feels? Do you? Does *she*?'

'Oh, Clem …'

'You!' Clemency had spotted me on the stairs. Her eyes widened. 'What are you doing here?'

'I'm sorry. I – I only came to answer the bell.'

Lorcan shot me a confused look, then turned back to Clemency. 'Listen. This is total crap. I get it. I'm horribly sorry about it all, and I'm on your side. But you're not going to feel any better by having it out with Annabelle. Not like this, not here.'

He spoke to her as if she was a contemporary, or younger. I expected her to bristle; instead, she shivered, and bit her scaly lips. 'Your sister has to know what she's done,' she said, but without the same fire as before.

'I know,' Lorcan said in the same firm but soothing tones. 'I understand. So why don't you and I go for a coffee? Talk things over?'

'I can't think. I – I haven't slept. It feels like I'm burning up, inside and out. Everything's gone crooked. Crooked and bloody.' She scrubbed her face. 'Goddammit. Goddammit to *hell*.'

'Shh. It's OK. Take a breath.'

'I just want her to know what she's *done*. To us. To me.'

'Come on.' Lorcan took Clemency's hand, like a child's, and, like a child, she gazed up at him with teary eyes and a mutinous mouth, suspicious and trusting all at once.

He remembered to call back to me as they left. 'Petra –? Could you –?'

I flapped my hand. 'Don't worry about it.'

I headed back to the party. I found Petra in the sitting room, where my fairy-light arrangement around the mirrors had created a twinkling grotto. 'Lorcan's had to take a call from his dad,' I told her. 'Some family thing. He said he'll be back soon.'

'Hmm.' She looked at me narrowly. 'He's been behaving really strangely. Ever since that godawful lunch. And you know what? I'm starting to lose patience.'

'I'm sure he's sorry. On the train, he was telling me how great you are.' A useful embellishment. 'He's just in one of his moods. You know what he's like.'

'Better than you, certainly,' Petra said with unaccustomed sharpness. She downed her glass and turned back to one of the Monegario youths lounging on the sofa beside her. This one had the sultry looks of a Caravaggio. 'Yuh, so I'm an actress?'

Screw her, I thought, and marched back to the *salone*. Perhaps it was the cold-cure capsules I'd taken, on top of the cheap prosecco, but I was beginning to feel distinctly jittery.

Lorcan returned after forty minutes. By listening out for the buzzer and staying close to the door, I was the one to let him in. He didn't look as relieved to see me as I hoped.

'So ...?' I prompted.

'So I bought her a drink and she calmed down a bit.'

'Booze? Was that wise?' I suspected Clemency had already been drinking.

'I don't know about wise, but it was definitely expedient. She'll be OK, I think. I phoned the people I stayed with my first night in Venice. They're old family friends; they're going to look after her.'

'How did she find out?'

'Oh, Nate had a fit of integrity and fessed up.' Lorcan rumpled his hair impatiently. 'But it's not just that. It turns out my stepmother's With Child. Dad told me and Annabelle last night. Apparently Clem found out this morning.'

'Shit.'

'Yeah. Tess is pushing forty, and my dad's ancient and cancer-ridden. But, hey presto, a brand-new Bambino Holt is on the way.'

I thought back to Mr Holt's speech. So that was what all his talk of rebirth and fresh starts was about. 'God. I ... I don't know what to say.'

'Who does? It was a bit of a kick in the teeth for Clem, obviously.' He moved past me and up the stairs. 'Christ, I need a drink.'

Lying in wait at the entrance to the *salone* was Petra. Her expression was venomous. 'Would you *kindly* care to inform me what the *fuck* is going on?'

Surely, with everything that was going on with his family, Lorcan was out of patience with Petra's insecurities. Perhaps this was the moment their Italian romance came to an end. I braced myself for a very public showdown.

Instead, Lorcan gave her his most irresistible smile. 'I'm an utter arsehole and I don't deserve you in any way, shape or form. Does that cover it?'

Petra snorted.

He leant in, brushing his lips against her neck. 'Name my punishment.' His mouth moved to her ear, his hands to her waist.

As he whispered, her face flushed and softened, and she gave a squirm that was part protest, part surrender. *'You ...'*

When I moved away, I heard his low chuckle, as his hands moved to tangle in her hair.

Heading to the drinks table I blundered into Annabelle, of all people.

'Watch it,' she said lightly. She tilted her head towards her brother and Petra. 'What's the latest drama?'

I felt a stab of unexpected savagery. 'It's your drama, actually.'

She raised her exquisitely tapered brows. 'Excuse me?'

'Clemency knows. About you and Nate. She was at the door half an hour ago, demanding to have it out with you.'

It was gratifying to see her mouth gape.

'Don't worry, Lorcan took care of it.' I turned insouciantly away.

It was even more gratifying to feel her hand on my arm, tugging me back.

'How did she find out?'

'Nate told her.'

'He swore he wouldn't. He *swore*. We were over, we *ended* it.'

He ended it, most likely. But only after my postcard had nudged Nate into his so-called fit of integrity. I felt another tingle of importance. 'I'm sure Clem would have discovered it anyway. You weren't exactly discreet. I mean, I spotted the two of you up to no good in Florence.' It was hard to keep the satisfaction from my voice. 'Even Mallory worked it out. She saw you and Nate kissing in the street last night. Your big farewell, was it?'

'Me and Nate? Last night? *How?*'

Distress gave her a fierce and frosty glitter.

'Mal had to go back to the bar for her phone. She'd have seen you en route, I suppose.' I wanted to show Annabelle I was bored, not impressed, by her intrigues. 'I told her to stay out of it, but I suspect she's going to offer you some words of folksy wisdom, all the same.'

Annabelle shook her head blindly. 'I – we –' Her breath caught. Then she straightened and smoothed herself, and her sheen returned. The transformation was no less impressive for being visibly effortful. 'I'm very sorry about how things turned out. More sorry than you could possibly know. But this is between Clemency and Nate.'

'Is it? Clemency's still on the warpath, you know. I wouldn't rest easy yet.'

Annabelle shrugged and picked up a golden cat mask from the box of carnival accessories. 'Well. She'll have to find me first.'

I watched her go admiringly, in spite of myself. Once the initial shock of discovery was over, she had been neither embarrassed nor – to my mind – particularly remorseful. And, of course, Annabelle would always be able to evoke compassion for her part in the drama. She was a teenager, a student. None of this would tarnish her. It was Nate and Clemency who were soiled.

The drinks table was beneath a painting in the style of Titian. The artist had laboriously painted a series of fine black lines over the picture to mimic the appearance of *craquelure* – the network of tiny cracks that appear in old paintings as the pigment shrinks. They made me think of Clemency. I felt sorry for her but there was something repellent, too, about her pain, as visibly ugly as a weeping wound. I wished, for her own sake, that she had been a little more dignified.

The party in the *salone* had swelled in number. A lot of the new arrivals looked to be in their late twenties or older. Glancing around the room, I couldn't see any one I recognised.

The bell was buzzing again. Moments later, another cheerful throng of partygoers spilled into the room. Tagging along at the edge of the group was Clemency.

She looked both wilder and more insubstantial than she had before, as if she were more a portent than a person. I was surprised the other guests didn't look askance at her flaking mouth and bloodshot gaze. She shivered and swayed, flimsy as a paper doll. Then she saw me. Her cheeks flamed red, then white.

'You! Again! Why is it *always* you?'

'I –' I looked around for Lorcan, or anyone else I knew. I was adrift in a sea of tipsy strangers.

Clemency snatched a paper cup and a bottle of grappa from a side-table and poured herself a generous slug. She saw me looking and gave a jagged laugh. 'You shouldn't drink while you're trying for a baby, and you can't drink when you're pregnant … so this here is what you might call a window of opportunity. *Salute!*' And she downed it in one.

'Shall I look for, er, Lorcan?'

'What's he got to do with anything? It's the sister I want.' She poured more grappa with an unsteady hand. 'So c'mon. Where is she?'

'I don't know. Honestly.' And I was about to make my escape when my eye was caught by the knock-off Titian again. It was of a half-naked woman embracing a bull; Europa and Jupiter, I presumed. From here, the fake *craquelure* wasn't visible. The pink and lumpen nymph was a poor imitation of a Titian nude and bore absolutely no resemblance to Annabelle. But as amateur as the painter was, he had still managed to capture a certain complacent sensuality. I felt a flash of malice.

'I don't know,' I said again. 'But last I saw, she was wearing a gold cat mask.'

Turning away, I made sure to lose myself in the crowd. I regretted my words almost as soon as I'd said them. I envisaged Clemency ripping off the mask, tearing at Annabelle's hair and screaming obscenities, as an audience of dumbstruck Italian aristos recorded the debacle on their phones. Maybe Annabelle deserved some of this, but Lorcan didn't. His family secret – *our* secret – wouldn't be just common gossip, but an indelibly sordid tableau. The final scene of our Grand Tour, the most abiding memory of our sentimental journey…

I didn't want to be around to witness it. Or maybe I did – maybe it would have the irresistible pull of a car crash. At the same time, it bothered me that I didn't know where everyone had disappeared to. Clemency, too, had vanished. She and her quarry could be anywhere in the palazzo's warren of rooms. I checked my phone but there were no messages. In the dining room, a couple of playboy types in blazers and open-necked shirts were doing lines of coke off the table. For a moment, I couldn't think what I was doing there.

I was beginning to feel light-headed so I went to the mouldy little bathroom that overlooked the lagoon and splashed my face in the basin. The Tiepolo clouds had darkened over the course of the day, and the night was overcast. San Michele was only just visible in the lights on the log pylons that marked the way for boats. I fixed my gaze on the gold smears reflected in the water and tried to recapture the magic of the evening.

I came out of the bathroom to find Oliver waiting outside. I remembered all of us gathered together earlier in the evening, toasting our vow to always stay friends.

'I'm sorry if I ever rubbed you up the wrong way,' I said impulsively.

'No doubt.' He looked at me sidelong. 'A-plus for effort, I'll give you that.'

Effort. That was the sticking point.

For despite my quiet popularity within the group, for all my vintage pearls and brandy-butter vowels and country-house childhood, in Oliver's eyes I was still never going to be one of them. By 'them' I mean the kind of person Oliver judged an acceptable associate for himself or his friends. Perhaps it was simply the fact I lacked their air of unquestioning entitlement. Right from the start, Oliver had sensed how much I was attracted as well as infuriated by this quality. It was as if he alone could smell the strain on me, like old sweat.

He tapped the mask he'd pushed back on the top of his head. It was of a pink-cheeked cherub; the face below was every bit as pretty, and entirely malevolent. 'I think you'll find we've all been playing dress-up to some extent. Just don't kid yourself the carnival's going to carry on back home.'

I went cold all over. Oliver had given voice to my lurking fear that any feelings of success, or happiness, were an illusion that would vanish into the thin English air.

'Don't pout,' he said, pinching my cheek. To a bystander, it might almost have looked affectionate. 'You've had a good run.'

Music throbbed and moaned. It was only 1 a.m., yet the night already seemed to have lasted forever. I made my way to the lobby at the end of the *salone*, looking for refuge or at least a friendly face. (Where *was* everyone? Had I already been forgotten? Was Oliver right, and I was expendable, after all?) It wasn't much of an entrance hall, cluttered with broken chairs and dead pot-plants. The only light came from the landing at the top of the stairs to my left. That was why I didn't see her at first: a small, pale figure hunched on the floor, arms wrapped around her legs, rocking soundlessly.

'Clemency?'

The rocking increased in speed. 'I didn't know it was her.' Tears slid, silently and unstoppably, down her face. 'Not at first–'

'Clemency? What's wrong?'

She gripped my wrist with surprising force, staring up at me with bloodshot eyes. 'I was glad,' she said fiercely. 'You hear me? I was *glad*.'

My skin prickled all over.

I pushed open the heavy doors out to the courtyard. It was very dark. The stone staircase was steeper than I remembered, and more slippery. The enclosing walls seemed higher, too, the square of night sky at the top impossibly distant.

The body lay in an extravagant heap at the foot of the steps. The picture it made was almost too theatrical to be real. The swirl of red cloak, the spill of dark hair, the pale reach of an out-flung hand. The gold mask glinting from the ground. The ancient walls rearing up around. Everything was perfectly still, perfectly composed. Even in death, Annabelle was an art form.

I suppose I must have been in shock. I closed my eyes. When I opened them again, the picture had changed. The dreaminess was gone. It was replaced by something lurid and ugly, a convulsing force that bulged dangerously against the fabric of the ordinary world. This time, I saw how the girl's head lolled at an obscene angle. This time, I saw the creeping puddle of blood beneath her hair. A man crouched next to her, head in hands.

'Is –? Is she –?'

'It's Mallory,' said Lorcan, his voice thickly clotted. 'And I think she's dead.'

CHAPTER FOURTEEN

Behind me, Clemency gave a strangled cry. She had staggered to her feet, but now she collapsed again and set up a thin, keening wail.

I went down the stairs, clutching the railing tight. Outside, the thump and babble of the party was dimmed but not extinguished. The blood roared in my ears.

I couldn't look at Mallory's face. Instead, I fixated on her feet. One of her high heels had fallen off. She'd been wearing tatty pop-socks: there was something unbearably sad about the sight of one naked toe, poking out of the hole. Near the shoe was her phone. Of course, I thought numbly. She had probably been posing for photos when she fell.

'Did you see it? Did you – see her fall?'

'I was in the lobby with Clem. Then I heard a scream.' Lorcan ran a trembling hand through his hair. 'Shit, shit, *shit*.'

I looked over to where the cat mask lay by one of the pillars of the colonnade. It must have come off before the main impact of Mallory's fall, since the only injury it had sustained was a crack to one plaster ear. It was a cheap knick-knack, made in China most likely, but the spill of moonlight on its curves gave it a sphinx-like majesty.

Clemency was hauling herself down the steps, inch by painful inch, still making her terrible keening cry. When she got to the bottom, she crouched on all fours by the body, staring into Mallory's blind eyes. 'Oh God.' Then she sat back and put her face in her hands, rocking back and forth. 'She's somebody's baby. Somebody's baby. She's somebody's baby girl.'

Lorcan looked from Clemency to me and back again. 'What do we do?' He wore a loose, stunned expression. His helplessness steadied me. I ran a finger along the ripple of my pearls. *Stay calm.*

'Ambulance. Police. What's Italian for 999?'

But the phone I picked up was Mallory's. I didn't feel that I was doing anything wrong. I suppose I was looking for answers to questions I wasn't quite ready to ask. Questions that frightened and also excited me ... Although the screen was shattered, the phone was still functioning. I knew Mallory's pin: it was typically basic, and I'd seen her tap it in often enough. *2143*. It was the work of seconds to bring up the last photos she took: two selfies of herself standing at the top of the steps, in carnival costume.

Lorcan frowned. 'That thing can't still be working. And shouldn't we – I dunno – not touch stuff?'

'Yeah. You're right. Sorry.' I put Mallory's phone back on the ground and got out my own. 'Wait – I should get Lorenzo. He can help.' I'd remembered the lines of coke in the dining room; our host would appreciate some warning before the authorities arrived. Then I looked at Clemency, who had crawled towards the wall and, with quiet violence, begun to vomit. 'Is she going to be OK?'

Lorcan squatted beside her and put his arm around her thin shoulders. 'Listen to me, Clem. It was an accident, all right? A tragic accident. Mallory came out for some air. Then she slipped and fell. Do you understand? The police and the ambulances will soon be here, and they'll take care of everything. Just … try and be calm, will you?'

She shivered. 'An accident. Yes. We've all fallen.' She began to rock back and forth again.

I found Lorenzo quickly. I had never seen anyone sober up so fast. Annabelle met us in the lobby; Lorcan had phoned to give her the news. Her skin was almost translucent, her eyes vast and dark. When we got down and surveyed the body, she started to shake. 'Oh, Ada,' she said, and there was a sob in her voice. 'I was such a bitch to her. She came up to me in the kitchen, rabbiting on, and …'

'I know. I –' I felt my own voice catch. 'I'm sorry too.'

Lorcan reached for Annabelle's hand and laced his fingers with hers. 'We're all sorry,' he said quietly. They looked at each other and I saw, for the first time, a family resemblance in the rueful twist of their smiles.

Lorenzo, meanwhile, was pacing back and forth, in the midst of various agitated phone calls. 'I have telephoned the authorities. My father also. We should make sure nobody else comes out here.' He squinted at Clemency and the puddle of vomit by her side. 'Senora Harper … she seems very unwell …'

Clemency's expression was as glazed as the dead girl's. There was blood on her mouth. She had begun to stroke Mallory's hair. 'I'm so sorry,' she murmured. 'Sweet baby.'

'I can't take this,' said Annabelle abruptly. 'I just can't.'

As she turned to leave, Clemency looked up and for the first time registered her presence. '*You*,' she cried out, and lunged after her. Lorcan held her back, and Clemency began to shudder and moan. 'Leave me alone! *No*. Stop trying to take my baby. She's *mine*.' Now she was trying to haul the body onto her lap, though she was too weak to get very far. 'We need to get her out of here,' Lorcan panted to Lorenzo. As Clemency drooped in their arms, they debated whether they should take her to one of the bedrooms to recover.

Sirens could be heard, not far away.

'Go,' I urged. 'Try to calm her down. I'll stay here with the … with Mallory. The police will be here any moment.'

And then it was just me and Mallory and, through the gate to the canal, the slow suck and kiss of water on stone.

It was a simple story. It was late at night and the steps were slippery. Mallory had been drinking. Her cloak was too long, her heels too high.

Perhaps there was a coil of steel in Clemency after all, for she gave a credible account of hearing the scream and finding the body, even if her narrative was rambling and choked with tears. In the end, she had to be sedated and was taken off to hospital. Lorcan went with her in the water-ambulance.

And what was Senora Harper doing at the party? It was a gathering of students, was it not? I heard one of the kindly policemen ask.

Lorcan explained that Senora Harper had recently miscarried and had come to Venice for a short holiday to recuperate. Lorcan was worried about her. They were a close-knit family. He'd hoped if she came to see the palazzo and had a drink with him and his friends, it might raise her spirits a little. But to be witness to such a tragedy, after suffering her own loss … it was too much to bear.

I listened to this while watching the lights of the emergency vehicles through the water gate. The canal was bedazzled with flashes of red and blue. I listened, and I wondered. And I touched the ear of the gold cat in my bag.

In the aftermath, we girls mostly sat around crying. At intervals, we would enfold people into long, dolorous hugs. I held hands with Annabelle, hoping my nose wouldn't run (I was always a messy crier). The boys slumped against walls, staring broodingly into the middle distance. At one point Rocco had even kicked a chair over in a parody of impotent machismo. 'Poor Mal,' we kept saying. 'I just can't believe it. Poor Mal.'

'At least,' Kitty choked out through her tears, 'her last moments were happy.'

As proof of this, she was flicking through her picture gallery of the night's revelries. There were several of Mallory clowning about in fancy dress with Annabelle and Willa. Annabelle had the gold cat pushed back on the top of her head; Mallory was puckering up to a long-nosed *pulcinella* mask; Willa was wearing a black lace and diamanté visor. They were all laughing.

The whole time I'd been wondering where everyone else had disappeared to, they'd been upstairs, posing for photos in front of the Triumphs fresco. Mallory had apparently masterminded the costume changes. She had been drinking more heavily than usual, but although she must have been on edge, it was the kind of suppressed tension that shows itself as excessive high spirits.

'Can I see?' I asked.

Kitty handed over her phone. More gurning faces, more theatrical poses, becoming significantly wobblier as the party progressed. In the background of one group shot, I saw the blurred but unmistakable image of Mallory again. She didn't have the *pulcinella* mask in this photo. She was holding the gold cat. I looked for Annabelle, but she had moved away to take a phone call.

It was the work of a moment to delete the photo, both from the picture gallery and from Kitty's online storage. I'd had practice earlier that night on Mallory's phone. There were possibly other photos, on other phones, but never mind. I did what I could.

The mask in question was wrapped in a plastic bag in a rubbish bin on the Strada Nova. Nobody noticed me throw it away, just as nobody witnessed me pick it up in the courtyard in the few minutes I was alone with the body.

Even now, I can't be sure of my motivations in taking the mask. Looking back, I felt utterly removed from myself, watching my own actions unfold as if from a great distance. I was driven by an instinct I didn't understand. Yet I trusted it all the same. As my thoughts raced and skidded – making connections, calculating risks – I was possessed by a kind of serene urgency. It was time to stop watching. It was time to *act*. Whatever the consequences, this was my moment.

I was the *deus ex machina*, descending from on high.

Count Monegario arrived just after the police and medics. He was tall and deep-voiced, a naturally commanding figure. It was a relief to feel that somebody – a proper grown-up, somebody's dad – was in charge. He contacted the British as well as the American consulates and arranged for us to be put up in a hotel. The girls were put in the honeymoon suite, where we curled up together like a pile of puppies on the king-size bed. Soft sobs eventually gave way to the sighs and snuffles of sleep. Through the open doors to the living room, I could see where Annabelle lay on one of the day-beds that had been hastily provided. She too was wakeful, staring up at the ceiling, completely motionless. At 5 a.m., I sent her a message and watched as her phone glowed into life. *Can we talk? With Lorcan. It's important.*

The three of us met in the hotel dining room. The tables were already set up for breakfast but the few staff we saw kept a respectful distance, except for a housekeeper who brought us, unasked, tea and brioche.

We stared down at the cooling tea. As the silence stretched on, I realised the others were rigid with the tension of waiting for me to begin.

'How's Clemency?'

Lorcan grimaced. He'd got back from the hospital only just before I messaged him and was grey with exhaustion. 'Heavily sedated. Nate's on his way.'

I couldn't put it off any longer. So I turned to look directly at Annabelle. 'I think Clemency mistook Mallory for you.'

She wasn't the only one. When I first looked over the

balustrade, I had been sure it was Annabelle lying at the foot of the steps. It was only when my initial shock retreated a little that I'd seen the poor twisted body was shorter and stockier than it should have been. The dark hair wasn't silken; the out-flung hand was stubby, with bitten-down fingernails. And that pitiable toe, sticking out of the hole in the pop-sock … I felt tearful whenever I thought of it. Still, an indignity like that wouldn't have happened to Annabelle, even in death.

She and Lorcan remained silent. Still wide-eyed, still waiting. Still rigid. So I pressed on.

'That's why Clemency pushed Mal down the stairs.'

'*What?* No.' Lorcan began to shake his head. 'No, no, no, no, no, no.'

'It – it was an accident,' said Annabelle.

'Not an accident. A mistake. Clemency mistook Mallory for you. Clemency wanted to kill you, and Mallory died instead.' I waited a beat. 'And you both know it.'

'You're insane,' Lorcan said in a fierce whisper. 'Clemency would never –' the same time as his sister said, 'She thought Mallory was me? That's impossible.'

'Clemency knew you were wearing a gold cat mask. I heard somebody tell her.' I could never let on that was me. If I thought too hard about the part I'd played, I could feel my heartbeat stutter and a terrible pressure grip my chest. *What if, what if, what if* … 'But then Mallory picked up the same mask. It was dark outside. Mallory was taking selfies all wrapped up in a cloak, the gold cat hiding her face. She's the same height as you in heels. She'd straightened her hair, making it close enough in length and colour to yours. And it's not like Clemency was particularly rational at the time. For one thing, she'd drunk enough grappa to sink a ship.'

Annabelle folded her arms across her chest. She was very pale but I appreciated the way she'd kept her cool. 'An interesting theory.'

'A compelling one. Except for the fact no mask was found by the body.'

'What?' Her mouth fell open, into an almost comical O of surprise. 'I –' She looked at Lorcan, whose right leg had begun to jiggle insistently on the floor. 'I don't understand,' she said flatly. 'I don't understand any of this.'

He shrugged, helplessly.

It was strange, if gratifying, to be the one in control. It was time for them to hang on *my* every word. 'Here's the deal: I'll tell you what happened to the mask if *you* tell me about Clemency.' In the pause that followed, I sensed a telepathic negotiation between them.

'OK,' Lorcan said at last. 'Fine. Yes. You're right: Clemency phoned me and said there had been an accident, and Mallory was dead. And ... and that it was her fault.'

I let out a breath I hadn't realised I had been holding. 'She confessed?'

'Pretty much. When I got there, she kept saying, *I thought it was her*. And, *I didn't mean to do it*. Then ... well...' He wiped the sweat from his brow. All his fizz and fluency were gone. 'I didn't know about the mask – it was all so confused, so sudden – I didn't understand how it had happened. But it had.

144

Obviously. And then she collapsed, and you arrived on the scene only a minute or so later.'

'You told Clemency to say it was an accident.'

'My impulse was to protect her. Buy her some time.'

I frowned. 'Even though she'd wanted to murder your sister?'

'I was in shock. We all were. Christ, it's such a mess … I don't know. It's just … well, dragging Clem off in handcuffs … what good will that do? It certainly won't bring Mallory back.'

I understood. Of course I did. My own motives were similar. Clemency had said she despised pity, that she'd prefer indifference or hate. Yet I pitied her all the same. She had taken a life for nothing. I didn't think she was evil, but she was certainly damaged, perhaps beyond repair.

Annabelle leaned forward. 'Now tell us about the mask.'

'I'll get to that. First, I want to know why you're willing to protect someone who tried to kill you.'

A long pause. 'Because if Clemency is arrested, it will destroy Nate.'

I closed my eyes. Yes. Not only would Nate be married to a murderer, but his and Annabelle's affair would be exposed. His life as he knew it would be over.

I'd shown them I could be in control. Now it was time to be kind. I needed them to know they could be vulnerable with me, as well as open. I opened my eyes again and kept my voice gentle. 'Aren't you afraid? What if Clemency tries again?'

'I'm not in any danger. Not any more. I mean, you saw her, Ada. She's sick. More than that … broken. I just don't want Nate, our whole family, to be broken too.' Annabelle wrapped her arms round her chest. 'But maybe that's wrong. It's certainly selfish. What about Mallory, what about *her* family? Don't they deserve to know the truth?'

Lorcan shook his head. 'Letting them think it was an accident is the kinder thing.'

'It's not justice, though. Is it? I don't know ... Clemency would probably be treated lightly. Diminished responsibility and so on–'

'Think of the press, the intrusion, the *scandal*. C'mon, Ani. Think of Pa. And we can't do that to Clem. We just can't. It would be too cruel.'

She shook her head, wearily, but didn't answer.

'Ada ... what do you think we should do?' Lorcan had that blurred, uncertain look again. Annabelle had her eyes fixed on my face. She was waiting, and so was he. They were waiting for me to take charge. The realisation of this spread through me, warm and bright.

'Here's what I've already done.'

I told them about deleting the selfies on Mallory's phone and the photo on Kitty's. I told them about getting rid of the mask. I kept my account matter-of-fact; I wasn't looking for applause.

'The mask was the only aspect of the death that could raise questions, because it might suggest a case of mistaken identity. After all, nobody had any reason to push Mal down the stairs. That's why I got rid of it, and the pictures of Mallory wearing it moments before she died. It removes any potential for complications.'

'You did all that ... for us?' Annabelle said faintly.

'But *why*?' Lorcan asked. 'You barely know Clemency. You hardly even–'

'Because we're friends. And we look out for each other. It's the same with family – that's why your instinct was to protect Clem.' Saying the words aloud gave me confidence in their righteousness. 'Besides, why drag murder and scandal out of a tragic mistake? No. We're doing the right thing. It's going to be fine, I promise.'

Annabelle shook her head. 'I don't know what to say.'

'How about "thank you"?' I meant it humorously, though they immediately began to mumble expressions of gratitude. I raised a hand to stop them. 'Look, don't over think it. I was happy to do you a favour, that's all. A favour for my friends.'

A favour they would be grateful for – always.

The possibilities danced before me.

The unreality of the murder, and of the days that followed, rolled through and past me like a great wave. Its force was savage yet exhilarating. I was not dragged under, but borne upwards. It left me cleansed.

This might seem an odd way of describing the cover-up of a botched, half-accidental crime. But the inevitability of my involvement did not start with the moment I told Clemency of Annabelle's disguise. It was not for nothing I'd felt that snap of connection with Lorcan the morning we'd first met. It was not for nothing I'd divined Annabelle's secret based on little more than a hunch. It was not for nothing I had stumbled upon Clemency's miscarriage, which I now saw as the trigger for, as well as a foreshadowing of, the dreadful act to come.

It may be that my part in the drama was determined the moment I rested my hand on the Dilettanti Discoveries brochure and vowed that I'd become one of these people, whatever it took. Or maybe it went even further back than that. Ever since Garreg Las, I'd been searching for meaning and consequence, some grand gesture that would restore a little of my perceived loss.

I sincerely believed that covering for Clemency was a noble act. Destroying her would have dragged Lorcan's whole family, as well as Dilettanti Discoveries, into the kind of bloodstained sex scandal no one recovers from. That protecting Clemency meant Annabelle and Nate were free to walk away from the devastation they'd wreaked was ironic, but also fitting, because that was the kind of people they were. Similarly, it was Lorcan's innate reluctance to commit to one course or other that had enabled me to step into the breach. *A man's character is his fate.* And so poor Mallory was doomed to be the hapless stand-in, and Clemency was doomed to be haunted by the wrong murder.

And at the time, I believed that my own destiny was this: to be the taut, gleaming thread that bound all of us together.

The case was closed with very little fuss. Yes, we all told the police, Mallory had been very cheerful that evening. She hadn't quarrelled with anyone. There were no tensions, no love rivalries. She was not depressed. 'I guess that's something we can cling to, at least,' said her father. 'Mallory spent her last hours so happy. Italy really was everything she'd hoped for.'

Her parents had arrived the next day. It was Lorenzo's father, Count Monegario, who had made the call. They moved with the slow, blurred heaviness of people underwater. I myself felt as if I was looking at them through fog, or from very far away. Perhaps I didn't want to see them clearly. I don't think I was the only one, and this discomfort wasn't limited to those of us who knew the real circumstances of their daughter's death. Even as we murmured our shock, our sorrow, our love, it was an effort to meet their eyes.

Perhaps if Mallory had kept up her tweets or Instagram or Facebook posts, a sense of dissatisfaction might have leaked through. She might even have posted some cryptic remark about broken trust or the burden of secret-keeping. But Mallory was generally faithful to Dilettanti Discoveries' rules about social media avoidance. The few updates she gave were relentlessly positive. Her online presence was its own smiling mask.

And with time, those final photographs of Mallory became how we remembered her: the quirky, loveable American goofball. We gave this character credibility by inventing or exaggerating our reminiscences, which were frequent. Because in some respects, our toasts in the palazzo's *salone* did come true. Though we did not attend all the major markers of each other's lives, we reunited for many minor ones. And on such occasions, the spirit of this alternative Mallory was regularly invoked. We told others that we were marked by her tragedy forever. It is true that it was a deeply traumatic event. But to make it bearable, we had to airbrush our memory of Mallory, and also ourselves.

PART TWO

I Trionfi

CHAPTER ONE

I was treated like an invalid on my return. My mother, Brian and
Delilah spoke to me in gentle sickroom voices and kept the blinds
drawn. Our phone line was constantly engaged with gossipy
acquaintances calling to enquire if I was suffering from PTSD.
Although Mallory was American, her death still received a fair
amount of coverage in the UK press, which has always savoured
tales of gap-year hedonism gone awry. This story had all the
ingredients of a hit: public school kids, alcohol and a 'decadent
Venetian masquerade ball'.

By contrast, the event received very little attention in the
Italian papers, which I later heard was due in no small part
to Lorenzo's father, the count. We had him to thank, too,
for the speed and efficiency with which the official enquiry
was wrapped up. Naturally, he did not want the Monegario
name dragged into such an unfortunate business. No doubt he
was also concerned with how the incident might impact the
palazzo's retail value.

Meanwhile, Dilettanti Discoveries released a statement that
paid tribute to Mallory's 'joyous spirit and zest for adventure',
while carefully distancing itself from the circumstances of her
death. The tragic accident had occurred at a private event after the

course had finished and was wholly unconnected to the company and its staff. Dilettanti Discoveries made the safety and well-being of its students its highest priority, et cetera. Even so, I heard bookings took a hit that year.

In the weeks following my return, my mother regularly found me in storms of passionate tears. She naturally assumed that I wept for the loss of my friend. This is what I told myself, too. In truth, it took a long time for the implications of Mallory's death to become real to me. Instead, I think, I was in mourning for Italy, for a time in my life that had been as glorious as it was fraught, and because I was afraid I would never feel or experience anything so intensely again.

While I returned to the basement photocopier, the instant coffee and the daily commute, my fellow Dilettantes resumed their round of gap-year holidays. Lorcan went travelling around South America. Others were backpacking in South East Asia, yachting in the Caribbean and visiting friends in places like Cape Town or LA or the south of France. Annabelle's whereabouts were unconfirmed, though she had at one point mentioned going to see her mother's relations in Iran.

Petra, at least, was in London. She was working in the production office of the National Theatre, on a paid internship procured by a family friend who was on the board. She still managed to complain about having to 'slave away' all summer while everyone else she knew was off finding themselves in exotic destinations. 'What a pair of Cinderellas we are,' she sighed.

I met up with Petra several times. A recurring theme of our conversations was how Petra had felt everything about that night in the palazzo was somehow wrong, *sinister*, from the start. How she had sensed something horrible was about to happen. If only she had trusted her instincts … She became tearful every time she thought about it. Dutifully, I praised her sensitivity, reassured her that nothing could have been done and shared her lamentations, before moving on to the next inevitable topic of conversation: Lorcan. Obsessively, we hypothesised as to where he was, what he was doing, who he was with and whether they would still mean something to each other on his return. Mallory's death had brought them closer together, of that Petra was sure. Lorcan had been profoundly moved by the tragedy. It had revealed another, vulnerable side to him.

As Petra-centric as these conversations were, she listened respectfully whenever I spoke of Mallory. I had been one of the first on the scene, after all. Furthermore, Mallory's parents had greeted me with particular warmth, implying a closeness between me and their daughter that in times past I might have resented, but now gave my part in the narrative an uncomfortable privilege. I kept revisiting our last conversation together. I'd been brusque and dismissive, then sent her off to pester Annabelle, knowing that she'd be rebuffed. Mallory had trusted me and I had betrayed her. Firstly, by being mean. Secondly, by protecting her killer. There were times when both offences seemed equally unforgivable. These were the times when I woke up gasping and sweating in the night.

Above all, I wished I had been kinder. We all did, I think. But since our lack of kindness was not as bold as open hostility or scorn, it became increasingly easy to forgive, then forget.

My recurring nightmare was not, as one might expect, of Mallory's death. I didn't even dream of Italy. Instead, I dreamed I was home in Garreg Las, running barefoot over the front lawn, past the sundial and copper beech and down to the ha-ha. Ahead of me loomed the hills, even larger than in real life and swoony with the haze of our fleeting summers. In the dream, I was getting ready to leap – over the ha-ha and then higher still, above the tops of the murmuring trees – but as I did so, my foot slipped or the ground crumbled, and I was suddenly tumbling into a chasm that had opened before me. It was not the sheep-trampled ditch of the ha-ha, but a churned and oily trench that opened wider and wider, deeper and darker, dragging me irresistibly downwards until I woke up with a thump.

I dreamed a lot about Garreg Las that summer. Night after night, its landscape bloomed within my head, its presence more vivid and insistent than memory. I dreamed of following my father as he ambled through doors or along pathways, always just out of reach. I dreamed of the orchard and the voluptuous unfurling of spring. I dreamed of windows warm as syrup and of nights swarming with stars. I dreamed of the hills, and their lost horizon made my heart shake.

In July, almost as if she had been summoned by my subconscious, I had a visitor from home. Connie Rhys-Morgan's family had lived about ten miles from ours, in a house that was older, larger and even more run-down than Garreg Las. The Rhys-Morgans farmed, in addition to managing a couple of commercial properties in Swansea, and lived in a state of cheerful dilapidation. Connie and I had kept in occasional contact, and I was both surprised and touched when she messaged to say she was visiting London and did I want to meet up.

Connie was as stolid and easy-going as I remembered. She was quite happy to reminisce with me, though her own attitude to home was resoundingly unsentimental. She told me her brother Roly was taking over the farm and marrying an Australian 'who thankfully comes with a bit of cash. They're even talking about replacing the roof.' She herself was studying pharmacology at Newcastle and planned to stay on after graduation. 'Even my student digs are a cut above. Frankly, I've had enough of living in a house with mushrooms growing up the walls.'

'I've always thought fungal infestations add character.'

She smiled obligingly. 'You know, it's funny you never went back to visit. You and your mum left so suddenly. One moment you were there, and the next you'd gone.'

'How is the old place? Do you see anything of the owners?' I asked, as casually as I could bear to.

Connie told me that Mr Price was mostly away on business. By contrast, his wife had thrown herself into local life. 'Always campaigning to organise fetes and book clubs and so on. Not that she's got very far – we're not exactly *The Archers*. She's all right, though. A bit try-hard. I went to the younger daughter's eighteenth. They'd put up a marquee on the lawn and there was a band and everything. And a harpist!'

Jealousy stabbed through me.

'Sounds fun.'

'Well, they're doing B & B now.' She gave a cheery laugh. 'Maybe you should go snoop around.'

Over my dead body.

I had one other visitor. One workday lunchtime, the receptionist phoned to say a friend was waiting for me at the front desk. It was Annabelle. 'Would you like to get a coffee?' she asked.

Finally. It was now August, close to three months since the end of Italy. I'd spent the time in a state of suspended animation, trawling through Instagram to see what everyone else was up to, trying to keep the banter and the in-jokes going without letting my neediness show. I checked in with JJ to see how the fickle-hearted Georgie was behaving; I consulted Rocco about the Jeff Koons retrospective; I invented sexcapades to amuse Willa; I sent drivel laden with emojis and exclamation marks to Kitty 'n' Missy. With Petra, I speculated about Lorcan. I'd found a Tumblr blog called Ugly Renaissance Babies and sent Oliver a meme of a Gollum-like infant taking a piss. *I saw this and thought of you.* Lorcan and I had exchanged messages, but he hadn't responded as quickly or in as much depth as I would have liked. Mostly, I'd got bland updates about his travels. Annabelle had been silent, as well as invisible online. It was possible her relations in Iran were conservative and strict about social media usage.

Annabelle was scruffier than I had seen before, in a grey T-shirt and leggings. She had also lost weight, which gave her looks an arresting hawkishness. Otherwise, she was as composed as ever. She didn't waste time in getting to the point. 'I wanted to properly thank you for what you did in Italy. I didn't really get a chance before, so I owe you an apology as well as thanks. Everything was so shocking, so chaotic … But you kept your head, and as a result our family was spared some very unpleasant exposure and – well, *suffering*. I had my doubts, at first, but now I'm sure we did the right thing.'

'I think so too.' I cleared my throat. 'Have you heard how Clemency is?'

'Not very well, I'm afraid. She's gone on some kind of health retreat. The official line is she's suffering from exhaustion.'

Like a celebrity, I thought. 'Is Nate with her?'

'He's supporting her, yes.' Annabelle fingered the beaten-gold chain around her neck. 'Or so Lorcan tells me. Nate and I … we don't really talk any more.'

'I'm sorry.'

'Don't be. You know, Clemency wasn't a very stable sort of person, even before her pregnancy issues. I didn't know the extent of her problems until recently, but for what it's worth, I regret … well, I regret adding to her troubles. It set in motion what turned out to be a very tragic set of events.' Her voice went quiet. 'I will always bear responsibility for that.'

After that, conversation faltered. I wanted to ask about Lorcan, and how their father was doing, and when we were going to organise the first Dilettanti reunion. However, Annabelle was frustratingly reticent. She even glanced at her watch. It was as if, having said her piece, she thought her obligations discharged. *You've had a good run*, Oliver had told me. But my run wasn't over, not even close. Because Annabelle *owed* me, she'd said so herself.

Or very nearly. So did Lorcan. So did all their family. I realised I needed to set down a marker.

'It's funny,' I said, 'the things that bring people together. That was one of the big selling points of the Dilettanti course, wasn't it? Friends for life. But we could never have imagined it would be a secret like this that would bind us.'

Annabelle looked wary. 'I suppose. Maybe.'

'Definitely.' I smiled back confidently. 'So I'll see you soon. You and Lorcan.'

CHAPTER TWO

I embarked on my university career without particularly high expectations. My mother had – not very enthusiastically – suggested I commute from home for reasons of economy. It was true Dilettanti Discoveries had drained my meagre savings, and the pay cheques I'd accrued on my return had barely managed to clear my overdraft. But I couldn't face the ignominy of being a stay-at-home-student. Instead, I applied for a room in a purpose-built block of student housing near Tottenham Court Road.

The block resembled a vertical storage unit, with a scatter of yellow and green cladding that was presumably meant to scream 'Fun!!!' On my first night there, I stared at the walls of my cell and tried not to think of sandstone quadrangles and oak-panelled rooms. I knew my decorative centrepiece should be a collage of self-promoting photographs, but my only evidence of anything approaching a social life were my pictures from Italy. I supplemented the Dilettanti with a snap of Connie on her London visit and one of my parents drinking tea on the veranda at Garreg Las. A postcard of *The Birthday* completed the gallery.

Interestingly, the camera didn't capture any of Lorcan's quicksilver allure. He appeared narrow, slanting. Flimsy. By contrast, Mallory photographed surprisingly well. She was in most of the group shots, looking more vibrant than she ever had in life, and I found myself avoiding her eye. After a while, I took the pictures down and kept my room as bare as I found it. I wasn't much in residence, after all. I ended up spending most of my free time at Petra's house-share in Hackney or away on weekends in Oxford.

Without Petra, my time at UCL would have been entirely different. The friends I made there were mostly girls like me, who'd been mousy and industrious at school and were only just beginning to reinvent themselves, albeit in a tentative and modest fashion. But as an associate member first of Petra's 'set', and later Lorcan's, I had little need to separately establish myself. Perhaps my share of their social cachet was a spurious one, but I told myself it shouldn't matter. I'd earned my place, hadn't I?

Petra's digs were in a run-down Georgian town house festooned with tea lights and furniture salvaged from skips. It soon became an unofficial club house for the university's hipster brigade. In my second year, I moved into the house myself, even though the rent was more than I could afford, and I knew the invitation had been something of an afterthought, as the original tenant (an art student with an eating disorder) had suffered a nervous collapse.

I had become Petra's confidante of choice for all matters Lorcan. It helped that she knew he had little patience with most of her friends and an established liking of me. I doubt their relationship would have survived much beyond Italy, and certainly not through Lorcan's time in Oxford, had Petra not had an unexpected brush with celebrity. In our first term at university, she managed to secure a recurring role in the wildly popular Sunday-night costume drama *Highwayman's Wager*. As it turned out, it was both her first and last mainstream success as a 'grown-up' actor, but for a while she was on the cusp of small-screen fame. Though she and Lorcan were on and off over the next couple of years, and the relationship was tear-stained and tantrum-prone on one side and not entirely monogamous on the other, *Highwayman* kept Lorcan's attention where it might otherwise have wandered.

Even with the distractions of minor celebrity and her new showbiz friends, Petra proved more loyal to me than I would have expected. I came to be very fond of her. Underneath the posturing, she had a fundamental decency. 'I wish we'd been nicer to Mal, you know,' she said once, which was the most honest thing any of us ever said about the subject.

Petra was generous, too, in including me in her jaunts to Oxford for parties and balls. She fancied a whiff of condescension from Lorcan's 'ivory tower posse', whom she suspected of not being quite as respectful of TV stardom as they should have been. All the same, I knew I had to find a measure of independence from her and Lorcan's relationship. So when I bumped into a boy I recognised from school, waiting for the bus to London one dank Saturday dawn, it felt like serendipity.

Ethan had been in the year below and had won a place to read biochemistry at one of the smaller colleges. I mostly remembered him for his acne. His newly clear skin had a pink and tender look to it; behind the old-fashioned spectacles his eyes were clever and mild. I was visiting my mother, so we ended up making the journey home to South London together. I was very much aware of the impression I was making, or trying to make – to appear as the Dilettanti had first appeared to me. Ethan was still transitioning from gangling to rangy and was far better looking than he realised. But I'm not sure my feigned sophistication was as much of a draw as I imagined. Ethan was bemused by Oxford's pomp and circumstance and unmoved by its glories in a way I first found irritating and then rather impressive.

It was easy to fall into a relationship with him and even easier to get into the routine of commuting every weekend, usually in Petra's company, down to Oxford. And because Ethan had little interest in the wider social scene, and took his studies seriously, he was quite content for me to spend time catching up with my old art history pals. Unfortunately for me, this often included Oliver, who had several friends at Oxford. We contrived to be polite whenever we found ourselves in each other's company and so, for the moment, an unofficial truce held. I would occasionally catch him looking at me with a perfect blend of pique and perplexity. Perhaps this should have made me nervous; instead, I couldn't help but savour his frustration.

Ethan spent the holidays working in a lab outside Bristol, so we didn't see much of each other outside of term. At the start of our third year, he came to visit me a few times in London, and we ambled around Hampstead Heath and ate dumplings in China Town and took his little brother to the zoo. On neutral ground, I began to feel a rare peace. I realised that perhaps I'd been underestimating him, underestimating *us*. But just before Reading Week, Ethan broke up with me. He'd met someone else.

She was, he said apologetically, more 'emotionally available'.

It hurt, much more than I'd expected. Petra rallied round, but though she'd never explicitly said so, I knew she thought Ethan was a bit of a drag. 'Honestly, sweetie, you deserve someone *fabulous*. Lorcan knows buckets of eligible bachelors. I'll make sure he sets you up with someone properly exciting.'

Though I didn't admit it to Petra, I found a certain relief in turning my back on the dreaming spires for a while. Although I had got used to strolling confidently through the quads and cloisters, larking about in coffee shops and getting elegantly wasted at black-tie balls, I never forgot I was little more than a tourist. I was always quick to correct anyone who assumed I was studying there, however tempting it was to feed the fantasy. I knew that being exposed as an Oxbridge pretender would be a humiliation I'd never recover from.

(I once tried to explain this mix of shame and envy to Ethan. It was, perhaps, my one attempt at emotional availability. However, he told me not to be silly: I was at a good university, taking a good course. Once we embarked on our adult lives, nobody would give a toss where we got our degrees. But Ethan was a scientist through and through. It seemed to me his understanding of life could be wilfully prosaic.)

'Aren't you *lucky*,' Oliver once observed. 'All the perks of the Oxbridge experience and none of the slog.' Infuriatingly, Annabelle and Lorcan were there to see me squirm.

Although the two of them were friendly with each other's circles, they attended different colleges and ran with different crowds. Lorcan's style, which somehow managed to be swaggering and self-effacing at once, was as successful at Oxford as everywhere else. He was a particular favourite with the college porters and scouts, whose names he learned and family history he was intimate with by the end of his first week. A few people persisted in finding him obnoxious, which Petra attributed to anti-public school prejudice, though he won popularity points by baiting the more humourless of the college athletes. He worked hard without seeming to and assembled an entourage of interesting people as well as glossy ones.

Annabelle enjoyed a similarly high profile, though she was as understated and enigmatic a presence in Oxford as she had been in Italy. 'Oh, Annabelle Gilani,' the girls would say, knowingly or wistfully, according to their own position in the pecking order. And the boys would self-mockingly put hands on hearts.

I would see her at Lorcan's college balls or dinners, wearing a plain backless slip dress, her face bare. *She walks in beauty like the night* … Often there would be a boy accompanying her, and it seemed she had acquired a type, for they were always tall and assured, quick with the quips, the provocative statements and the roguish smiles. And although they were loud where she was quiet, dominating where she was discreet, it was obvious that they were the foil to her, rather than the other way around.

CHAPTER THREE

My mother had liked Ethan, but I was still surprised by the extent of her disappointment at the end of the relationship, which she persisted in thinking was my doing. It was a subject she'd bring up for many months afterwards. 'I do hope,' she would say with deceptive mildness, 'it's not something you're going to come to regret.' Otherwise she kept what she no doubt thought of as a tactful distance from my student life. She trusted me to be sensible, she said. Brian had moved into the Brockley terrace; the last traces of my father had been quietly removed.

As a result, I grew much closer to Delilah. I ended up spending quite a lot of time in her Hampstead flat, often in the company of Petra. From the first, she and my godmother got on so well that I sometimes felt slightly excluded. On the other hand, Delilah could be relied upon to talk about Daddy and the happy days in Garreg Las, relaying tales of my childhood that made me appear much more precocious and diverting than I had ever been in fact. She would throw chaotic cocktail parties, too, to which I invited the other Dilettanti; with Delilah, I was safe to blossom in a way I knew my mother wouldn't approve of.

Although I never told Delilah what really happened in Venice, she was as interested in and impressed by dysfunction as she was by glamour. When the two of us speculated about Clemency and Nate, Leo and Tess Holt or even Lorcan and Petra, it was almost as if we were discussing favourite characters in a novel. Delilah had the gift of elevating gossip to a branch of moral philosophy.

It was, admittedly, a little embarrassing to envisage how these people would react if they knew the extent of my interest in their affairs. With time, I came to acknowledge the part that accident and timing had played in the accomplishment of my insider status. But most relationships have tenuous beginnings. It didn't mean they couldn't grow into something steadfast and true.

In order to further this, I got into the habit of messaging Lorcan or Annabelle at least once a week – checking in, really, to see what they were up to and if they were in need of any support. In this respect, it was to my advantage that Mr Holt did not die when expected. He defied doctors to live for four years past his diagnosis – long enough to see his third child, Felix, emerge from babyhood. Family relations remained civilised but strained. Lorcan did not confide in me with the detail and depth of feeling he had shown in Italy, but I still encouraged him to share his complaints. I gathered more snippets of information from Petra. And of course I was free to make my own observations – Mr and Mrs Holt hosted a number of kitchen suppers and Sunday lunches that were designed to be family affairs, but which Lorcan and Annabelle adulterated by inviting their friends. It was, they said, less awkward that way. This meant that when I indicated I'd be glad to join them I felt I was being helpful rather than intrusive.

Mr Holt's behaviour on these occasions was much as it had been in Rome, alternating between domineering, mischievous and sentimental. I was never quite sure of his sincerity. 'That sweet little Jew,' he said to me once. 'The one who tumbled into a canal. What was her name?'

'Mallory,' I told him. 'And she fell down some stairs.'

'Terrible,' he said, screwing up his eyes. 'Terrible. It haunts me, you know.' But the next moment he was recounting a lewd joke to Lorcan and laughing uproariously.

Mr Holt always professed to be delighted to see me. Annabelle was, of course, popular, and the company she kept was appropriately rarefied, but she did not appear to cultivate close friendships. It is possible that in my occasional interactions with her father I gave the impression that Annabelle and I were confidantes; I might have felt uneasy about the exaggeration, except for the fact Mr Holt seemed pleased by the idea. 'She's the cat who walks by herself, that one,' I heard him describe his daughter once, a little plaintively. Whereas he and Lorcan often bristled at each other, there were flashes of affection between them too. Annabelle was always scrupulously polite to her father, yet every interaction came with a glimmer of disdain.

So although I was happy to be included (it seemed only right that I was treated as one of the family), these suppers and lunches were never particularly relaxed occasions. The Kensington house was stylish but sterile in character, a chilly monochrome space that seemed designed for its inhabitants' past rather than present lives. People tended to focus their efforts on the little boy, Felix, because he was the least complicated repository for affection, but faced with so much competing attention, he inevitably grew overwhelmed. There would be tears, screams, snot … a rampaging exit everyone was at pains to ignore, in the same way nobody ever acknowledged Mr Holt's increasing decline.

In spite of an army of nannies and nurses, the strain of caring for a small child and a dying husband had taken a visible toll on the third Mrs Holt. Lorcan had said his stepmother was desperate to ingratiate herself with him and his wider family and friends, but I saw little evidence of this. With Annabelle, indeed, she was noticeably cool. As we'd seen in Italy, Tess had taken it upon herself to reach out to Clemency; we suspected Clemency had told her Annabelle's role in her marriage troubles. 'In which case, she's a stinking hypocrite,' was Lorcan's verdict. 'It's not as if she was Snow White herself, back in the day.' Tess still possessed a hard-bitten sexiness, but once or twice I caught her glancing about with a kind of stunned incredulity. *This is not my place, these are not my people.*

I saw Clemency just one other time, during a summer weekend at Lorcan's home in Wiltshire, the year his father died. The occasion was Lorcan's twenty-third birthday and all of the Dilettanti attended, including Annabelle, which I found surprising, since Clemency and Nate were also going to be there.

It was sad to see Nate so much thinner and greyer, and Clemency was even more changed. She had put on weight, and her skin had the sallow sheen of someone who rarely goes outdoors. Her lips were smooth, her expression empty. I had been feeling as much dread as curiosity about our meeting, but Clemency's recognition of me was entirely impersonal. 'Lovely to see you again,' she said listlessly. *I know what you did,* I wanted to say, *and I saved you anyway.* I had the same impulse whenever

I looked at Nate. I had reminded him of where his true loyalties lay; I had saved both his wife and his reputation, and he was a better man because of it. It didn't matter that neither of them would ever know. The people who counted did.

Clemency spent most of the party sitting on the shaded part of the patio, wrapped in scarves despite the heat and sipping water very slowly and carefully. 'Drugged to the gills,' Petra told me. 'Poor thing.' But I noticed that her eyes followed Annabelle, and there was a glint of calculation in them.

At the close of the birthday meal, the Dilettanti made a toast, as was our custom, to Mallory; down the other end of the table I saw Clemency raise a hand to pick at her lip. It was the only time I saw her make the gesture.

The old vicarage was less grand and more chocolate-box than I expected, with roses around the door and faded chintz in the drawing room. Lorcan's mother, Chrissy, was elegantly faded too, and with a look of Nate as well as Lorcan about the eyes. She was one of those people who always speaks in a murmur, forcing those trying to hold a conversation with her to lean in deferentially close. Around Lorcan, she assumed an air of indulgent exhaustion. 'Oh! He's *too much*, isn't he?' she was apt to exclaim; in these instances, anyone could hear the pride in her voice.

Delilah and I discussed the Mrs Holts in some detail. Early on, we had worked out that my godmother had actually met Leo Holt some thirty years before. 'Terribly dashing with the most delicious hint of a scoundrel,' was how she remembered him. Had Lorcan and Annabelle's mothers failed to remarry because Leo Holt was

171

so awful he'd put them off men entirely or so dazzling that no other suitor could compare? Contrasting the three wives was an interesting exercise because, on the surface at least, they were so dissimilar. Their appeal was archetypal, like a trio of princesses in a fairy tale.

I only ever saw Annabelle's mother fleetingly, on a couple of visits to Oxford and once when she collected Annabelle from some event or other. Laila Gilani was a darker, more voluptuous version of her daughter, and although she was some years younger than Lorcan's mother, and chicly dressed in well-cut trouser suits and designer scarves, her looks were already beginning to coarsen. It was she who had kept Annabelle away from her father and also Lorcan during her childhood, and Mr Holt apparently held her responsible for Annabelle's continued failure to warm to him. Whether this was fair or not, I fancied Laila had a touch of the wicked stepmother about her in the way Tess, the actual stepmother, did not.

One time I suggested meeting with Annabelle at her mother's eponymous gallery. I was curious to see the place, which was in St John's Wood and specialised in antique Persian art. The showroom was a plain white space in which a small number of *objets d'art* were displayed. A turquoise glazed pottery bowl. A bronze horse's head. An enamelled cup. Each piece was exquisite yet somehow restrained, perfectly lit in their solitary alcoves. *So*, I thought, *that's where Annabelle gets it from.*

Leo Holt died that autumn, four years after Italy. All three wives attended his funeral, though Petra told me they kept a scrupulous distance from each other at all times. (I admit I was disappointed that I was not invited. It was one of the rare occasions when the hints I'd dropped to Lorcan were ignored.) The funeral was by all accounts a large and lavish affair which ended, as per Mr Holt's instructions, with a riotous party at his private members' club. 'How does it feel,' Delilah enquired the day after, 'to be friends with not one but two multi-millionaires?'

'It won't change anything,' I said, but laughed all the same, a little giddy at the idea.

CHAPTER FOUR

Post-graduation, I secured a job as editorial assistant at an independent publisher of military-themed paperbacks. I'd planned to work in fiction, but after reaching the final round of several interviews with no success, I asked Lorcan if he or his family knew anyone who might be able to help. My position at the indie publisher came about thanks to an introduction by one of Lorcan's mother's friends.

Publishing seemed a natural career choice for the daughter of a writer. If, like my mother, I was starting out in an essentially secretarial capacity, I was confident that, unlike my mother, this was only the first step in a glittering editorial career. To cement my new grown-up lifestyle I moved into a flat-share in Islington with two of Petra's friends. The rent was high and the space ludicrously cramped, but, as I told my concerned mother, there was no point living in London if you weren't in the centre of things.

My job was neither well-paid nor particularly interesting but I tried not to let this dishearten me. It was surely only a matter of time before I graduated from proofreading the indexes of military histories to launching the debut novels of brilliant, brooding literary pin-ups. In the meantime ... well, weren't your twenties *supposed* to be about crappy jobs, relationships and accommodation? For all our public cynicism, our mordant proclamations of despair, most of us couldn't really believe that this way of living could be anything but short-term. We were young, educated, attractive; somehow everything was bound to work out.

The few genuinely bohemian elements of Petra's set were the first to drop away – those struggling artists who lacked wealthy parents to cushion the garret lifestyle. The next people to stop posting status updates and absent themselves from social gatherings were at the other end of the scale: high-flyers who vanished into eighty-hour weeks of toil at the big finance and law firms.

I knew, and was grateful, that I wasn't one of the harried London masses condemned to live in a state of endless discouragement and financial anxiety. If disaster struck, I could always live with my mother; and for the moment, credit cards sustained my lifestyle. Ever since Italy, I had shunned synthetic fabrics and invested in cashmere knits, silk-mix blouses and shoes and bags of quality leather. I collected illustrated Folio hardback editions of my favourite books. My bathroom cupboard had the high-end face-cream range that Willa had used and the artisan shampoo that Petra swore by. Organic bronze-cut dried pasta and cold-pressed extra virgin olive oil were kitchen staples. I refused to think of these things as luxuries, but as an essential part of practising 'self-care'. They also meant I was perpetually at the end of my overdraft.

It felt as if I was alone in this. That first year after graduation, Petra secured a new American agent and went off to try her luck in LA; Annabelle was studying for an MBA; Lorcan was working for a prestigious centre-right think tank. The other Dilettanti had resumed doing the kind of things they had been doing in their gap years, which they had managed to turn, seemingly effortlessly, into full-time employment. Yet everyone's lifestyles stayed the same whether they were paid a pittance or not.

My friends helped where they could. The Dilettanti network frequently supplied free entry to shows or exhibitions or club nights. Lorcan always picked up the tab when we went out, and Annabelle regularly treated me too. On a couple of occasions when I'd been in crisis over some unforeseen expense, Lorcan had even written me a cheque. I wasn't embarrassed by this, for I never had to ask for any favours outright. Lorcan understood how hard it was to be the only person we knew with any significant debt. His and Annabelle's debt to me was of a different nature, and I was rich in friendship as a result.

Lorcan and Annabelle's wealth was, of course, in a different league to most people's. *It won't change anything*, I'd told Delilah with regards to their inheritance, and I wasn't entirely wrong. Lorcan had always had expensive tastes and now he was free to indulge them, but, like most of his class, he was fearful of anything that might smack of a rich man's vulgarity. He said himself that he'd got the wild-child phase out of his system at school. He was now a director on the board of his father's environmental charity and took his responsibilities there with surprising seriousness.

Annabelle, who had always been careful with money, was even more restrained, though I noticed her clothes underwent a subtle designer update, and her mother's gallery moved to a prestigious Mayfair address. Annabelle herself was working in an investment fund, with a view to becoming a venture capitalist. It was undeniably strange to think the two of them would be able to do exactly what they wanted, forever. (*Thanks to me*, it was tempting to add. By saving their family from scandal, I'd ensured their privilege was impregnable.) But though it would have been convenient to blame the slight, yet growing, distance between us on money, I didn't feel that it was the real cause.

With Petra largely absent in LA, one of my most direct links to Lorcan was gone. It was also true that Italy, and the tumultuous events there, was starting to recede into the past. The only time I felt any real guilt about the matter was on my birthday, since every year, without fail, Judith Kaplan sent a card in recognition of my 'special kindness' to Mallory. But since Lorcan and Annabelle never spoke of regret, let alone remorse, I kept this to myself.

Still, as the seven-year anniversary of Mallory's death approached, it seemed to me that the siblings' initial gratitude to me should have grown into something more dependable. So whenever they cancelled plans, or were slow to respond to a message, or failed to like one of my Instagram posts, I felt a prick of resentment as well as worry. And what made our diminishing contact really sting was my suspicion that it was being orchestrated by Oliver. He worked in private wealth management, which mostly seemed to involve schmoozing on expenses, and while his friendship with Lorcan had only got stronger over the years, his animosity towards me had sharpened.

Since Italy, his hostility was never overt. But once, when

we'd gone to a private view at the gallery Rocco worked for, I overheard him talking about me to Lorcan. 'Where's Loveless?' he asked. 'She went to get a catalogue,' said Lorcan, and I realised they were referring to me.

'Loveless?' I repeated as I came to join them, and felt a hateful blush burn my face.

'Love*lace*. As in Ada Lovelace, your illustrious namesake,' said Oliver, with his most guileless smile. Spoken aloud, the two words were indistinguishable.

And of course, I had to pretend I was amused, even flattered, because Ada Lovelace was indeed illustrious – the illegitimate daughter of Byron and a Victorian computing visionary. I knew who she was well enough, though I'd been named for my maternal grandmother, who had died several years before I was born. I also knew Oliver wasn't referencing Byron's daughter with the nickname. He was calling me unlovable, and Lorcan had colluded with him. How long had they been dismissing me like this behind my back?

I confronted Lorcan. 'I don't want you calling me Lovelace.'

'OK. No need to get het up about it.'

'I don't like it, that's all.'

'It's just a nickname.'

'Not an affectionate one. Oliver doesn't like me,' I said, feeling – and sounding – like a small child.

'Of course he likes you,' said Lorcan. 'You're a Dilettante, aren't you?'

'Well, yes …' I wanted reassurance. I wanted him to say, *I like you, Ada, and that's what counts*. But he'd already moved away.

And Oliver was in his place. 'Hm. What have you got on them, I wonder?'

'What are you talking about?'

'I just can't think why the likes of Lorcan and his sister would be so determinedly pally with the likes of you. And that designer bag on your arm … didn't Annabelle buy it?'

Defensively, I stroked the smooth leather. 'It was a late birthday present. I'm sorry – did she forget yours?'

'There must be *something*. Some sordid Italian escapade is my guess.' Oliver winked broadly. 'I'll winkle it out of you eventually.'

It was unfortunate, then, that seven years after our trip the Palazzo Monegario was in the news again. A leading Italian politician had been caught with two underage girls in one of its luxury apartments. All reports referenced Mallory Kaplan's death as a matter of course. 'Depraved Sex Den in Cursed Palazzo' was the headline of the *Daily Mail* article that Delilah cut out and sent to me. (Delilah did not believe in news she read online.)

I was staring at the cutting when I got the call.

'Did you get a postcard too?' Annabelle asked without preamble.

I picked up the card lying next to the paper. A grimacing man writhed out of a giant shell, a serpent wound around his arms. My hands shook a little. 'I did.'

'Are your flatmates out? We'll come over.'

They must have already been on their way, for twenty minutes later the three of us were sitting round my tiny kitchen table, staring at the postcards that had been sent, anonymously, to each of our work addresses. All had London postmarks. Lorcan had been sent *The Ship of Fools* by Hieronymus Bosch. Annabelle had *Lilith* by John Collier. Mine was Bellini's *The Falsehood*. All three cards had the same line of type pasted on the back:

I see you.

'Tacky, aren't they? Someone's been watching third-rate slasher films,' I said, trying to lighten the mood.

'It's creepy as fuck,' said Lorcan.

'Well, that's Clemency for you,' said his sister, giving her postcard a flick. Lilith was a naked woman lasciviously entwined with a snake.

'Are we sure it's her?' I asked.

'Of course. She's calling you a liar, Lorcan a fool and me a slut. She'll always hate me and now she hates the two of you by association.'

'But we protected her. *She's* the guilty one. It's hardly in her interest to go stirring this up.'

'Clemency's gaga,' said Annabelle, with a viciousness that, although understandable, was also disquieting. 'Everyone knows.'

I had in fact heard that Clemency's marriage to Nate had finally broken down, and she was living with her sister. It made sense that mention of Mallory and the palazzo in the press had triggered some kind of manic episode.

'But what if they're from somebody else who was at the

party?' Lorcan fretted. 'Somebody we don't know about who was watching from a window?'

I considered the postcards. They made for a strikingly loathsome set. Nonetheless, I wasn't entirely sorry for the opportunity for the three of us to be gathered around a table again, not making idle chit-chat but discussing a situation of real importance.

'Then why make a move now? No, it's most likely Clemency. Or –' I hesitated.

'What?'

'Oliver.'

'*Oliver?* What's he got to do with anything?'

'Just a few weeks ago he said something creepy about us being up to no good in Italy. God – he even tried to imply that you were buying me off.' I laughed. 'Oh, and he said that he'd "winkle" the truth out eventually.'

Lorcan and Annabelle exchanged glances.

'He said something along those lines to me,' Lorcan said reluctantly. 'I'm sure he was joking though.'

'He can't possibly know anything,' said Annabelle. 'He wasn't anywhere near the scene.'

I nodded. 'I agree. If it *is* Oliver, he's just fishing. You know what he's like – he likes to cause trouble sometimes, just for fun. It'll be a game to him.'

Clemency was, in every respect, the obvious culprit. Still, by suggesting Oliver I'd planted a seed of doubt that would be difficult to dislodge. If he was coming for me, I would be ready for him.

'I don't buy it,' said Annabelle, but she looked troubled. Lorcan too.

'Do – do you think there will be more?' he asked me.

'We can only wait.'

But there were no more sinister postcards, and a couple of months later Clemency was dead.

The official story was that Clemency was killed in a road traffic accident, crossing a busy junction into the path of a truck. For those who knew the family, the death was quietly assumed to be a suicide. It shook me more than I expected; I had always felt slightly uncomfortable about pitying Clemency. Mad and spontaneous as Mallory's killing had been, it was still a wicked thing. Her intended victim, Annabelle, hadn't deserved a violent death any more than poor blameless Mal. But Clemency's obvious wretchedness before and most evidently after the act had always made it hard to think of her as a villain.

It was Petra who phoned to give me the news of her death. Petra had recently given up on making it in the US, a failure she was trying to present as a triumph of artistic integrity – 'LA was *just* as ghastly as you'd expect. All glaring sunshine and crocodile smiles.' I'd been excited about her return to London. But though I hadn't forgotten how self-centred she was, I found I had less patience with her neediness than in times past. *Highwayman's Wager* had bought her a garden flat on the fringes of Notting Hill, and her parents were subbing the mortgage repayments while she cast around for her next acting gig. And, to everyone's surprise, she and Lorcan were giving it another go. It was astonishing to me that they hadn't exhausted each other.

Petra confirmed that Clemency had killed herself. She had suffered from mental health issues for years; it was common knowledge that Nate had only stayed with her as long as he had out of loyalty. Clemency had, apparently, left him a note. 'Lorcan's taken it very badly. I mean, it's only been three years since his dad died. He's shut himself up at home and won't see or talk to anyone, not even me. I'm starting to *really worry*.' And her voice caught. Meanly, I wondered if this was an acting technique as opposed to the choke of true emotion. Petra had always made much of Lorcan's supposedly depressive streak – his black moods, his anxiety – but I suspected that playing this up was all part of the melodrama of their relationship.

Lorcan had followed his stint in the think tank with work for a non-profit that campaigned for ecological and cultural diversity. The job involved a lot of rather glamorous travel – either helping to run conferences in places like Berkeley or Tokyo, or else going on research trips to India and Thailand. He blamed his elusiveness on work commitments, but though his campaigning zeal seemed sincere, I was growing tired of his cancellation habit. So I was both pleased and relieved when he messaged me a couple of days after Petra phoned and suggested a drink. It would be a good opportunity to remind him of all the times I'd been there for him, waiting patiently, faithfully, to offer my support.

We met in the dingy old man's pub around the corner from his apartment. I'd taken Petra's anxiety about Lorcan to be her usual posturing, but in truth he didn't look good – unshaven and bleary, all gleam gone.

'They had to practically scrape her off the road, you know. I can't get it out of my head. I mean, I've known Clemency for practically my whole adult life. She was *family*.'

I swilled the ice in my glass. 'Nate must be suffering dreadfully.'

'God, yeah. He's sick with guilt. I mean, he should have got out of the relationship years ago. It wasn't doing either of them any good. But he was at my mother's this weekend and it was awful to see him. Like he'd aged twenty years. And poor, poor Clem ... She was always so sweet to me, you know.'

I was glad to see this softening. In Italy, Lorcan had been a little brusque – callous, even – when it came to Clemency and his cousin.

'So you don't think she sent those creepy postcards?'

He shook his head. 'I don't know. She might have been crazy enough. And you could say those postcards got it right. The Liar, the Fool, the Slut ... None of it matters now, though, does it?'

He had a point. Clemency's death, seven years after Mallory's, had a certain tragic neatness to it. Justice was finally served: discreetly and scandal free. It also released Lorcan and Annabelle from any obligation to me. This wasn't necessarily a bad thing, I reasoned. The time had come for our loyalty to each other to be untainted by collusion. Instead, we'd share the joint enterprise of muddling through life as best we could. As team mates, not co-conspirators.

'I feel responsible,' Lorcan finally said, as they called last orders.

'How can you be?'

Lorcan didn't answer this directly. 'Clemency was a good person.' Then, as if I was about to dispute this: 'She *was*,' he

184

insisted, jabbing his finger at me with drunken righteousness. 'A good person, till she went crazy. Till Annabelle came along. That's what did it. That's what – *turned* her. It was all too much. Fucking Annabelle. Fucking Annabelle fucking Nate.'

I stared down at my hands.

'Come back to mine,' Lorcan said. 'Have another drink. It's early yet, and I can't talk about this shit with other people.' I had never seen him so vulnerable. Not even after Mallory's death. 'Don't leave me alone. Please?'

Post-inheritance, both Lorcan and Annabelle had splurged on property. Annabelle's place in Marylebone was not unlike her mother's gallery in feel; it was easy to imagine that at night, instead of going to bed, she curled up gracefully in a plain white alcove. She did not like to entertain at home, however, and so we generally met elsewhere.

This was the first time I'd been to Lorcan's penthouse in Spitalfields on my own. The apartment was in a former Victorian leather factory that had a rooftop terrace with views over the city and the kind of stylistic flourishes that were becoming a staple of interior-design magazines – feature walls of bare brick, polished concrete floors and mid-century furniture; artsy-industrial light fittings. These clichés were alleviated by a number of family antiques, sourced from Lorcan's mother and grandparents, of which the centrepiece was the portrait of a Regency dandy above the main fireplace. Lorcan had begun to collect art, too, including a Picasso print of a nude and a small Renaissance Madonna and

Child. What I particularly noticed this evening, however, was the smashed whisky glass on the floor. There was a corresponding dent on the wall. Lorcan picked it up without comment and went to fix the drinks. His mind remained fixed on the past.

'It's all such a bloody miserable mess,' he said thickly. 'Sometimes I think I'll never get beyond it. Never be free. Every time I think I'm done I can feel myself getting sucked back in.'

I'd rolled my eyes when Petra had said on the phone what a sensitive soul Lorcan really was and how nobody got to see his emotional side. Now I began to wonder if the problem was me, and that my relative ease in getting over Mallory's death and our cover-up of the circumstances was a sign of some deeper moral malaise. Lorcan's sadness was leaking out of him; I could almost see it overlay the scene, like a sepia wash.

'I do love her, you know,' he said abruptly, as if he'd known I'd been thinking of Petra. 'Truly. Madly. Ridiculously. All of that. I can't help myself, I suppose. But I know that's another bloody mess. Hopeless. I mean, what's the point, going on and *on* like this? We're just driving each other mad.'

'So maybe it's time to cut loose,' I wanted to say, and I may in fact have spoken aloud without realising it. By now I was fairly drunk too. We were sitting on the floor, our backs against one of the angular sofas. The edge of his hand was just barely resting against mine, so that it was hard to tell if the feel of his skin was anticipation or reality. Hot silk.

'Lovelace,' he murmured. 'Loveless. Are you?'

'Aren't we all?' I said, trying to make the remark light and throwaway, though my throat had constricted.

Now he looked grave. 'Such a terrible thing.'

His face was very close to mine. The sepia wash had receded; everything about him glimmered silver and bronze.

It seemed we were about to kiss. Was this inevitable, what everything had been leading up to all this time?

I think I pulled away first, but I can't be sure.

The silence afterwards was oddly peaceful. '*Hiraeth*,' Lorcan said. 'Maybe that's always been my trouble ... Tell me about your lost house.' Like a child asking for a bedtime story. 'Was it heaven?'

So I told him.

I told him about the scent of lilacs on the tennis lawn and the chatter of the rooks in the elms. I told him about the sundial with the broken gnomon and the bells in the bell room, rusted to silence. I told him about the cabinet of curios in the library, with slippers made to fit the bound feet of Chinese concubines, and a green glass witch-ball to keep evil spirits at bay. The scarred table in the dining room on which great-great-uncle George, the naval surgeon, had operated on people too poor to pay the doctor's fee. The old bake-house with its brick oven; the wash-house with its stone tub. The taste of the figs that grew along the kitchen garden wall. I told him all my lost treasures and, just for a moment, it was as if they were returned to me.

Lorcan fell asleep in the end, sprawled on the floor with his jacket under his head. He was still young enough for a drunken stupor to have a kind of innocence; his heavy breathing was more sighs than snores, and he looked flushed and rumpled as a little boy. I covered him with a throw from the sofa and let myself out.

I sent him a message later, thanking him for the evening. *Call me any time. I'll always be here for you.* But he didn't reply.

CHAPTER FIVE

Had Lorcan's whisky and self-pity revealed an essential truth? Or had we both simply embarrassed ourselves? I didn't know what to make of his proclamations of love for Petra. Lorcan's eye was prone to wandering, and it wasn't as if he lacked for female attention, yet he'd seemed sincere. Surely, though, I hadn't imagined the momentary tension between us.

I was relieved nothing irreversible had happened. I'd always been self-controlled in that respect, and it had paid off. It was part of the reason Lorcan trusted me. It was the foundation of my friendship with Petra. Still, a treacherous little voice had begun to whisper in my ear: *You've done all the hard work, you're where you always wanted to be. Why hold back? What are you afraid of?*

The next time we saw each other was at Oliver's engagement party.

I knew I was only invited because all of the Dilettanti were. We had already been introduced to the girl Oliver was engaged to, who was even smaller and more elvish than him. Davina hadn't gone to university and looked up to Oliver as a great intellectual, at the same time bossing him about to an astonishing degree. He seemed to find this adorable. I wondered what it would take for him to turn on her. It could only be a matter of time before he showed his teeth.

His relations with Annabelle and Lorcan hadn't suffered any obvious harm in the wake of the postcard incident. They still saw each other regularly. But a faint suspicion must have lingered, all the same. 'I'm glad Lorcan and Oliver aren't so tight these days,' Petra had said to me. 'Oliver's never been a good influence.'

Oliver's future in-laws owned a luxury resort in the Caribbean, which was where the wedding was to be, and so the engagement party was held at his family pile in Hampshire. According to rumour, the party was going to be almost as lavish as the main event, just without the actual marriage ceremony.

Petra couldn't attend, as she had an audition up in Edinburgh. 'Keep an eye on Lorcan for me, will you?' she said. It made me a little uncomfortable. I wasn't sure if my next encounter with Lorcan would be awkward or not. I wasn't a teenager any more and I didn't want to be dragged back into the teenage mindset – skittish and self-doubting. To bolster my confidence, I bought a new dress that was vaguely 1920s in style, in sea-foamy shades with a drop waist. Nothing could spoil the bloom of confidence it bestowed.

I caught the train from London with Kitty and Missy and their boyfriends, two amiable hulks working in property. The girls' double-act banter had an excitable edge, for attending anything wedding related was still a novelty. At twenty-six, Oliver was the first of our peers to get engaged.

The party began with a drinks reception, then dinner; brunch would be provided the following morning. Shuttle mini-buses had been arranged to transport guests to and from Horton Hall, picking up from the Travelodge I was staying in as well as the more picturesque local hotels. Everyone craned to see when our bus climbed the wooded hillside that overlooked the house. The Palladian mansion was built from a soft golden stone; the walls seemed to radiate the evening's gauzy light. As a setting it was ephemeral yet timeless, and I wanted – truly, madly, ridiculously – to believe in its promise.

The only disappointment was that the hall was roped off, with guests confined to a marquee on the lawn. Oliver's parents were genial yet aloof, like royals hosting a garden party, but his three brothers were seemingly everywhere. As a gaggle of small tow-headed boys, they must have been adorable. As adults, I thought their extreme fairness gave them a washed-out look. They all had the same watery slyness about the eyes. And Petra was right – Oliver was very much the runt of the litter.

Although the crowd of a hundred and fifty guests was much as one would expect, it was enlivened by a handful of outliers. I'd encountered most of them before, since they were part of Lorcan's set too. They included a rising black actor, whose degree from Oxford was always mentioned in the same breath as his childhood entanglement with South London gangs, a transgender model currently fronting Burberry menswear, and the daughter of a single-parent dinner lady who'd graduated with a double first in physics and was now raking it in at Goldman Sachs. I had once heard Annabelle refer to them as 'Lorcan's pet exotics', and it was probably true to say that their success was not the principle reason he and Oliver courted them. But I still envied them, because among these people they had nothing to prove.

'Enjoying yourself, Lovelace?' Oliver had suddenly materialised by my side. I'd wandered away from the main throng to view the scene from under the shade of a spreading oak.

'Yes, thanks,' I said warily. 'Congratulations. It's a great party.'

'Everything you ever wanted, I'm sure. Perhaps I should be the one congratulating you.'

I decided to ignore this.

'Your persistence is remarkable. Lorcan and Annabelle can't shake you off. They won't even admit to wanting to.' He took a leisurely sip of champagne. 'I was going to leave you off the guest list, as it happens. But Lorcan insisted you come. "More trouble than it's worth" was the line he used.' A pause. 'Now what does that mean, I wonder?'

I didn't believe Oliver. I refused to. *I can't talk about this shit with other people*, Lorcan had said. He'd practically begged me to stay and drink with him. We'd almost kissed. And Annabelle – Annabelle had pointed me towards the boutique where I'd bought my dress. *Mention my name and they'll do you a discount*, she'd told me. That's what friends did. Oliver was just trying to mess with my head.

'Well, I'm sorry to be such a thorn in your side. But you invited me to that party in the palazzo, and you invited me here too. Some people might wonder what *I* have on *you*.'

He frowned. It was hardly the world's best parting shot, but it enabled me to leave the conversation with a little dignity.

Our exchange brought back a painful conversation with my mother that I'd been trying my best to forget. I'd gone to hers and

Brian's directly after buying the party dress. When she'd peeked into the bag, the incriminating price tag was clearly visible.

'It's for Oliver's engagement party,' I said, more defensively than I wanted to. 'Annabelle got me a discount.'

'Mm. Very pretty.' My mother fingered the soft drapes. There was a pause, and I thought I'd got away with it. 'You know,' she said, in entirely conversational tones, 'the thing about toffs is that, although they pride themselves on being all chummy with the working classes, it's the aspiring bourgeoisie they really look down on.'

'And you'd know all about this, would you?'

She looked amused. 'Anthony was hardly a toff. But he and I came from very different worlds.'

'Evidently. You've made it very clear you want nothing to do with his. Or mine, apparently.' And I'd snatched the dress away.

After leaving Oliver, I felt grasping, snobbish, small. My worst self. And yet my impulses were only natural – beauty and power and wealth are attractive for a reason. I shouldn't be ashamed for wanting this, I thought, looking at the courtly figures milling about under the stately trees, the golden walls. I should have been perfectly at ease here.

The old resentment flared. My mother had cut all of Daddy's old friends, except stubborn Delilah, out of our lives. She'd taken me as far away from his – my – roots as possible. She had tried to stop me going to Italy. If everyone has a defining period in their lives, unique to their sense of self, then Italy, along with Garreg Las, was mine. And my mother had done her best to undermine both. No wonder I clung to them so hard. No wonder Oliver despised my doggedness.

'Are you feeling all right, Ada?'

Lorcan, this time, looking at me with concern. I hadn't wanted him to see me like this. Oliver's insinuations had been more upsetting than I liked to admit.

'Sorry. Yes. Just some mother–daughter shit that's caught up with me.'

'Sounds rough.' He cleared his throat. 'Look. I feel I should probably apologise for the last time we hung out. I … I really hope I didn't say or do anything, you know, weird.'

'God, no. Of course not. Everything's fine.'

'Good. That's good to know. Sorry all the same.' Lorcan sounded genuinely relieved, just as there had been a thread of genuine nervousness beneath his breezy tone. I didn't know what to make of this. Was he embarrassed by his behaviour or mine? Did he think his attentions were unwelcome … or was he trying to warn me off?

What are you afraid of? I'd asked myself. Well, here was my answer: of having the perfect understanding between us spoiled.

'Don't mope over here on your lonesome,' he said, linking arms. 'Come and meet some people.'

Lorcan led me to where Annabelle and a few others were in conversation. Annabelle, as usual, managed to make every other woman there look overdressed, wearing a petrol-blue jumpsuit and flat gold sandals. She was talking to someone I vaguely recognised as one of Lorcan's old school friends. Nico, I thought his name was.

'Nice pearls,' he said to me with a grin. I felt the fizz of returning confidence as I smiled demurely at him over my coupe of champagne. The magic of the dress was working again. The evening was still there for the taking.

From there on it was a lucky night. All around us, the ripening sweetness of the countryside breathed out from hedgerows and flower beds. A string quartet played on the terrace as we filed in to dine in the marquee, where food was served on tables crowned with flower-wreathed silver and crystal. The hum of talk and laughter had intensified to a dull roar by the time brandy and cigars were passed around.

Afterwards, as the indigo sky deepened to black, avenues of Roman candles were lit, creating inviting new paths around the gardens. A swing band took over from the string quartet. People went barefoot, the better to dance under the stars, and I too kicked off my heels, greedy to feel the velvet lawn beneath my feet. I was happy to be there, among friends, feeling as pretty, *apt*, as I was ever likely to be. I spent a lot of time with JJ, still the most laid-back of the Dilettanti boys, and also Lorenzo Monegario. Nobody referenced that other party in that other grand house, even though it was the first time we'd seen each other since that fateful evening, seven years before. 'To the triumph of love!' Lorenzo proclaimed, raising his glass. '*Salute*!' And it seemed to me that the gesture, and his presence there with us, in such a place, had to be healing; a resolution of some kind.

Although I had a lot of champagne, I was careful, too. I made no obvious effort to seek out Lorcan's old school pal, contriving to make our repeat encounters appear entirely happenstance.

Nico was lean and freckled and dusty-fair, with a reassuringly ready laugh. In the course of the evening, I pieced together that he was a solicitor, 'grinding along', as he put it, in a city law firm; that he came from a doctor's family and was a regular at Henley and Glyndebourne. 'Come find me after,' he said, with a lingering look, as I headed off to the midnight bacon-butty bar with Kitty and JJ. But then I lost him in the party's final throes, when he was bundled away by a couple of friends having been sick into a rose bush.

I wasn't unduly disappointed. I knew I'd made an impression, one that would hopefully stick. *An eligible bachelor*, I remarked to myself with a tipsy giggle, for it was a night where thinking along the lines of an Austen novel seemed perfectly fitting.

The next morning, I woke up early, the better to luxuriate in an unusual sense of optimism. I got the first of the shuttle buses that had been laid on to return guests to the hall for brunch, only to find my fellow passengers were mostly the middle-aged-cousin contingent; everyone else appeared to be sleeping off their hangovers. I hoped this didn't mean I'd have to spend the next hour dodging Oliver.

Instead, I was collared by his fragrant fiancée, Davina, as I collected coffee in the marquee. 'Hello, hello. You're friends with Lorcan Holt, aren't you? Do you know where he's got to? He's not answering his phone.'

Lorcan, who was to be one of the ushers, was apparently scheduled for a suit fitting before brunch. He was among the select group who had been given accommodation in the house; we'd passed his room in the converted stable block during an unofficial tour of the grounds.

'I can always go knock on his door,' I offered.

'How heavenly of you. Poor Ol's still in bed and I've a million and one things to manage.' She bustled off, aglow with the pleasures of bridal martyrdom.

I set off for the stables at a more leisurely pace. The morning was dewy, the air still, and my route was solitary enough to indulge the fantasy that I was mistress of the place.

Lorcan was staying above the former tack room. I rapped on his door, but got no response. 'Hello?' I said, giving it an experimental push. It wasn't locked. I caught a glimpse of a smooth naked leg, the swirl of disordered sheets. There was a muffled female exclamation and masculine swearing. The sudden creaking of bed springs and the slam of an interior door suggested Lorcan's companion had taken refuge in the bathroom.

A moment or so later, Lorcan was glowering at me through a crack in the door. 'What?'

I was mortified. No doubt he was well aware that Petra had told me to keep an eye on him. I resisted the urge to peek over his shoulder for the mystery girl. I thought the most likely candidate was Maisie, the Goldman Sachs prodigy. They'd had a fling at Oxford, and her mane of platinum hair – even thicker than her Geordie accent – had lost none of its shine.

'I – uh – um. Sorry to intrude. Your phone was off and Davina asked me to find you – something about a fitting?'

'Shit. I totally forgot. Yeah, OK ... tell her I'll be there in five.'

The crack in the door was already closing.

I was more thankful than ever that I'd retreated from the idea of Lorcan as a romantic possibility. Even so, I wished I could erase the whole encounter. The best policy, I decided, was to act as if nothing had happened.

It was still awkward, though. As part of last night's rapprochement, Lorcan had offered me a lift back to London. But he didn't appear at brunch, and I wondered if he was regretting the offer.

When I got to the prearranged meeting point by the clock tower, however, he and Annabelle were already waiting by his Tesla. Annabelle was tapping away on her phone, looking sleek in a crisp white shirt-dress. By contrast, Lorcan was sour faced, his eyes hidden by dark glasses.

'Thanks again for the lift.'

'No problem,' Lorcan said tersely.

'Rupert is staying on, by the way,' said Annabelle, glancing up at me from her phone, 'so if you can think of anyone else who might like a ride ...'

'I'm not a bloody chauffeur service.'

His sister raised her brows but didn't say anything. I thought it politic to get into the car without further comment.

For the first twenty minutes or so, the drive passed in silence.

'So ...' I began, drawing breath, 'Nico.' Much to my disappointment, he had not been at brunch either.

Lorcan grunted. 'What about him?'

'He's a good sort, is he?'

'He's all right. Bit of a lightweight.'

I wasn't sure if this referred to Nico's intellect or his drinking. 'Well, I liked him. We got on.'

I waited. I'd thought the impression I'd made on Nico was obvious. But the expected teasing and banter weren't forthcoming.

'So …'

'So what?'

'So I'd like to see him again.'

'Then why didn't you get his number?'

'I would have. But he spent the last hour of the party vomiting in a bush. It didn't seem the right moment.' I was beginning to get exasperated. 'Look, I'm not asking for you to set us up on some elaborate date or anything. But since we're both friends of yours, it shouldn't be too hard for you to help us cross paths again.'

'Is that a fact?'

I was annoyed. I'd never chased after any of Lorcan's friends before. And now the lingering luckiness of the dress, and the dreamy atmosphere of the star-spangled evening, was evaporating. All because I'd interrupted Lorcan's grubby little hook-up.

'Fine. Forget I asked. I thought it was a pretty small favour in the scheme of things, but never mind.'

The silence prickled.

In the front passenger seat, Annabelle sat up straight. I thought she'd dozed off, but now she turned to look at Lorcan.

'Ada has a point. We do *owe* her, after all.' Her voice was laced with irony. I was taken aback. Was she implying I was blackmailing them in some way? The idea was grotesque. Friendship involves give and take, and surely *I* was the one who'd done the majority of the giving. It was true they'd opened a few doors, or at least smoothed my way, on a couple of occasions. And, yes, Lorcan had helped me out of a little financial embarrassment once or twice. But he'd always offered. I'd never had to ask.

Though I couldn't help but remember Oliver's insinuations.

They can't shake you off.

And *more trouble than it's worth.*

So when Annabelle's words had an effect, I was not as pleased as I thought I'd be.

'Fair enough, fair enough,' said Lorcan, with a hollow sort of heartiness. 'I can play cupid. Leave it with me, Lovelace.'

CHAPTER SIX

Back in London, I decided that it wouldn't do any good to keep second-guessing Lorcan and his sister. They'd been hung-over and tetchy, that was all. My mother was always telling me I had a tendency to read too much into things. I mustn't let Oliver rattle me. I mustn't give him the satisfaction.

A new relationship would be an opportunity to win over a whole new group of people and compel me to be my best self again. I went into work the Monday after the party determined to focus on the positive.

This was easier said than done at Bricklesmith Press. A veneer of respectability was supplied by a handful of decent popular history titles, otherwise our books ranged from vanity publications by amateur enthusiasts to the lurid Nazi-themed titles that kept our finances afloat.

In the beginning, I'd felt that working for an independent publisher carried a certain intellectual cachet. We were specialists, *artisans*, among a swamp of soulless corporate behemoths who cared only for the bottom line. Now that I had inched up from editorial assistant to assistant editor I was, of course, actively seeking to join said corporate behemoths, or anything that might provide escape from the likes of *Nazi Sex Cults in Combat*.

Still, I made the best of it. Lorcan was true to his word and stage-managed some initial matchmaking with Nico. On our early dates, I represented my editorial apprenticeship in the world of warfare as evidence of an independent spirit, as well as a certain intellectual rigour.

Nico's law firm was not a big name, but long established and respectable. He was fairly ambitious, though not energetically so, perhaps because he was accustomed to things coming easily to him. I soon realised he thought I was the kind of girl similar to his sisters and their friends: unassuming and uncomplicated, cheerily employed in 'the arts' or charitable sector in roles that suggested a certain accomplishment, while also providing decorative benefits – good dinner-party chat and an office uniform of florals and ballet flats. Meanwhile, Nico listened sympathetically to the story of Garreg Las and, when shown a photograph of Aunt Laetitia's portrait (the painting was in storage), said that he could see the family resemblance.

His parents liked me, and I got on particularly well with his father, who was a World War II buff and thus disproportionately impressed by my job. My mother was unfailingly polite to Nico and was always sure to ask after him. She did, however, see fit to ask if I'd heard from Ethan at all. Some light cyber-stalking revealed Ethan was doing a DPhil at an American Ivy League university and had acquired a very pretty Californian girlfriend, but I was not about to share this information with my mother. I focused on the pleasing idea that people might look at me and Nico and assume a natural fit.

Petra often remarked on this, though I found the assumption less satisfying when it came from her. 'How lucky you are to have found someone so reliable,' she'd sigh, in a way that suggested she was commiserating a little too. Things with Lorcan had crashed and burned for what both swore was the final time. 'My main feeling is relief,' she avowed. 'I was in danger of throwing away the best years of my life on him. And, honestly, he could be *so bleak*. You have no idea.' A series of doomed affairs with unreliable thespian types inevitably followed.

As a matter of fact, Nico was not always as straightforward as he seemed. On the subject of Annabelle, he was notably unenthused. 'She's a cold fish, that one,' he said. And he once described our time in Italy as 'finishing school for people who failed at STEM'.

This slight edge was one of the things I most appreciated about Nico. Likewise, in bed he could sometimes be unexpectedly assertive, even aggressive. Did I like this too? It was deliciously hard to judge.

For a while, I was nervous that Oliver would find some way of sabotaging us. Nico was not part of Oliver's inner circle but they'd known each other since childhood. 'Congrats, Lovelace,' said Oliver the first time our paths crossed after Nico and I became official. 'You got Lorcan to pimp out his mini-me.' Otherwise he left us alone. Marriage must have mellowed him, I thought.

Or else he was just biding his time.

'How's your muse behaving?' Rocco asked me one evening, over drinks at his members' club in Soho. Now assistant director at his gallery, he had exchanged the grubby fedoras for designer tailoring and statement glasses, and the fragrant gallerinas for a video-artist boyfriend. Of the old Rocco, only the tattoos remained. 'Done any writing lately?'

'Not really,' I confessed. 'I've been stuck. Or maybe just distracted. But I do have some new ideas kicking around. Maybe it's time to put them to the test.'

Rocco nodded politely and I realised he was only making conversation. Nobody seriously believed I was a writer any more.

For some years, I'd dropped self-deprecating hints about the novel I was working on, or the poetry I was 'fiddling about with', but the truth was, I was blocked, and always had been. I was bookish, well-educated, bright, with a job in publishing. Writing should have come easily to me. I was still a little baffled as to why it did not. But it was clear I couldn't keep trading on aspiration alone. At least when Kitty described herself as a jewellery designer, she had something material to show for herself – even if it was only a few bits of turquoise strung on a chain.

I was currently flat-sitting for Delilah while she was abroad for a three-month 'sabbatical'. Living rent-free in the rarefied air of Hampstead, while surrounded by rare books and collectors' editions, might be just what my muse required. So the next time I had an evening to myself, I got out pen and notebook and waited for inspiration to strike. When it did not, I reviewed my existing oeuvre. This mostly consisted of character sketches of people I knew or musings on my favourite pieces of art and landscape. Most of my best work, I realised, was in some way related to Italy or Garreg Las. I must be one of those writers whose creative energy has a strongly autobiographical streak.

To this end, the next time I was at my mother's I went to my old bedroom (now Brian's study) and looked for the box of Daddy's writing notebooks. It had survived my mother's various purges, though she had donated his manuscripts and earlier jottings to the National Archive of Wales. I didn't know whether she had kept this box back for sentimental reasons or because the contents didn't relate to any of his published work. I took it to Delilah's to browse at my leisure. Anthony Howell's six novels and assorted short stories were all written before his return to Wales. From then until his death, the only thing he published were two slight volumes of poetry. Yet the box was stuffed with dusty paper covered on both sides with his distinctive spiky hand. The last time I'd looked through the box I'd been a teenager. I'd been intimidated by the density of the writing and assumed Daddy's creative thought processes would be even more impenetrable than his books.

It was different now. I was older and wiser, and a better reader too. I felt a tightness in my throat as I flicked through these relics of abandonment and frustration. Whole pages had been crossed out with emphatic black lines, the force of the pen so savage that the paper was sometimes torn. Other passages just had 'NO' scrawled across them. Why had Daddy kept these rejects, rather than throw them away? Had he had second thoughts? Or did he want to create a kind of monument to his failure? I wished, desperately, that I'd been able to talk to Daddy about his work as an adult. Maybe I could have helped coax him out of whatever creative hole he was in. The more I read of the notebooks, the more I was puzzled by what had gone wrong. There were so many lovely fragments – pin-sharp epigrams, striking and subversive metaphors, sketches for stories and characters that fizzed with dark life.

I put the box to one side, sad but also energised. I felt the benevolence of Daddy's spirit in a way I hadn't felt since we left Garreg Las. There was one seed of an idea I especially liked: about a girl who metamorphoses into one of her lover's running shoes. I decided to use it as my starting point.

I entitled the final story 'Atalanta in Enfield'. Whenever I flagged, I'd dip into my father's notebooks again, and it was almost as if we were throwing around ideas together. I knew he wouldn't mind me drawing inspiration from his unfinished work. It would have tickled him to think of us as collaborators.

I sent the story to the same family friend of Lorcan's who had helped find me the job at Bricklesmith. She was a retired non-fiction editor but also a respected poet. Her response to the story was so encouraging, and her editorial suggestions so astute, that I felt able to submit the story to the literary journal she recommended. When the acceptance email arrived, I didn't even feel particularly surprised. It felt *right*. As if all the different pieces of my life were finally falling into place.

I had written under a pen-name and, after some debate, decided against telling my mother. Her support of Daddy had been purely practical; I never heard them discuss his work. At least not in my presence. However, I didn't want to risk any potentially awkward questions. If the story turned out to be a one-off, it was hardly worth troubling my mother with it. If I wrote more, I would obviously move away from Daddy as a source of inspiration. Perhaps helping me to find my creative voice was to be part of his legacy.

CHAPTER SEVEN

Only a month later, I had a second story accepted for publication. This time, I drew on Daddy's notes about the *gwyllgi*, the monstrous dog that haunts lonely roads in Welsh folklore. I worked it into the tale of a mother–daughter road trip to a series of strangers' funerals. The title was 'Another Black Dog'.

The first journal to accept me had been a feminist publication for women writers; the second was higher profile and more established. Whether it was thanks to the confidence this gave me or the achievement itself, I found a job at a fiction publisher soon afterwards. It was another independent press and, like Bricklesmith, paid a comparative pittance, but I had high hopes of finally working with interesting people on prestige projects.

To celebrate the new job, and my recent literary success, I threw a party in Hampstead the week before Delilah was due to return. She'd told me to think of her flat as 'home from home' while she was away, so I took her at her word.

It was a small crowd – the Dilettanti and their partners, a couple of university friends, my former flatmates and some of Nico's circle – but I was determined to do things properly. I hadn't thrown a real party before; for my twenty-first, I'd taken the easy way out and hired a bar. I knew exactly what the evening should look and feel like, however. There were two acceptable aesthetics: minimalist and contemporary, with white linens and maybe a decorative branch of driftwood or two. Or there was the boho look: big on twinkly lights, wild flowers and colourful vintage glassware. Every party I had attended with the Dilettanti had been one of the two.

Delilah's flat naturally favoured the boho aesthetic. Petra helped me get the place ready, while Nico assembled the playlist. Annabelle had sent over a box of luxury candles that promised to scent the air with 'Italy in the shade of lemon groves'. Delilah's fridge was crammed with the crate of champagne Lorcan had presented me with on news of the job. Even so, the costs stacked up.

I'd planned to put the saving I'd made on rent towards paying off my credit cards. But by the time I'd hired a barman and bought the ingredients to keep everyone in negronis for the evening, plus invested in catered canapés (so many arancini balls!), my stash was seriously depleted. Those antique glass goblets I'd found on the Portobello road hadn't been as much of a bargain as I'd expected. And sourcing branches of greenery and bundles of wild flowers wasn't, as I'd blithely assumed, a simple matter of foraging on the heath. In the end I had to get them from a florist. And after putting all this effort into creating the right ambience, it didn't make sense to skimp on my dress. So I bought another frock, vintage this time, made of crushed black velvet with embroidered poppies on the hem. I deserved it, didn't I?

'Looking good, Howell,' said Nico, as I checked my back view in the hallway mirror.

'Same to you.'

I'd persuaded Nico to wear his hair a bit longer and had upgraded his wardrobe by encouraging him to visit the same tailor as Lorcan. Tonight, he was wearing jeans with an open-necked shirt and a dusty pink linen-blend jacket I'd bought him. Pastel tailoring is a look I've always found attractive on men.

'Hello, Lorcan,' said Oliver, as soon as he came through the door. He did a theatrical double-take. 'Oh, I'm sorry, Nico. My mistake.'

'Poor Ols. Are you losing your eyesight along with your hair?' I raised my glass to him. '*Salute*.'

I'd had to invite Oliver as a matter of course, but he hadn't RSVP'd to my handwritten invitation card, so I had hoped he wasn't going to come. No such luck. He didn't have Davina with him either, which was a bad sign. He generally behaved better in her company.

I anticipated the moment that conversation turned to my writing with a mix of excitement and anxiety. The second story had yet to be published, but copies of the magazine in which 'Atalanta in Enfield' appeared were laid out on one of the coffee tables. I'd felt self-conscious about this act of self-promotion, wondering if it was tacky, but both Nico and Petra had urged me not to be bashful. 'If this was a book launch, everyone would expect to see stacks of your novel,' said Petra. 'We're here to celebrate your first appearance in print, so what's the difference?'

It was Willa who first picked up a magazine. 'You know, I went to school with an Atalanta,' was all she found to say on the subject. Willa worked at a talent agency, though not the highbrow kind. Still sexy, if increasingly thuggish, she was apparently much in demand among the celebrity clientele.

'It's really good, Ada,' said Lorcan seriously. 'I mean it. Metamorphosis is tricky to pull off.'

'Thank you,' I said. He would look at me differently now; maybe they all would. I wasn't just another well-spoken English graduate with a job in the arts. I was an actual *artist*.

'Is your father an influence on your work?' enquired Rocco's somewhat severe boyfriend.

'I guess. I like to think I inherited his love of wordplay.'

'Yeah, the puns were cool,' said JJ. He'd brought his own crumpled copy of the magazine for me to autograph. 'Very clever. And also learning about shoes. Tongue, throat, welt ... who knew they had so many parts?'

'"My sole, cradling your cracked and tender flesh; the sweet stink of you, thick in my throat ..."' Nico read aloud. 'That's my girl. Not only a shit-hot wordsmith, but a *dirty* one.'

Petra gave him a friendly swat. 'Stop it, you're making her blush.'

As a matter of fact, my discomfort was because that particular line was mostly my father's.

'Why not write under your real name?' Annabelle asked, from where she was lolling against Oliver.

A good question. Howell is a common enough surname, yet I was still wary of people in the book world making the connection. I didn't want to be in the position of having to formally clarify my and Daddy's relationship. 'I want to be judged on my own merits, not compared to my dad. And I don't want people to think I've used some family connection to get into print.'

'But you were happy to use Lorcan's,' said Oliver.

This stung, mostly because I didn't like the idea that Lorcan had told him about me asking for help. 'Well, *you'd* know all about family favours,' I replied. Oliver's father had lately been in the press regarding an expenses scandal in the House of Lords. 'Go on, tell us how much your brother was paid to be your dad's intern. Enough taxpayer's money to fund twenty duck houses, or just fifteen?'

My gibe was met with tolerant chuckles. *Just Ada and Oliver doing their schtick.* Nobody took our antagonism seriously. One day, I determined, I would laugh it off too.

Either way, nothing was going to spoil my evening. Right here, right now was everything I'd dreamed of. A handsome man by my side, champagne in my hand; my dearest friends, gathered together in candlelight and surrounded by the lustre of lovely things. That all this was in celebration of a new, brighter stage of my life was almost too much happiness to bear.

The time had come.

'To Mallory,' I said, raising my glass in toast, as was our custom.

'To Mallory,' my friends obediently chorused. And, as was my custom, I looked to see if I could catch Lorcan or Annabelle's eye.

A couple of weeks later, Nico announced he'd organised a surprise weekend in the countryside. By now, we'd been on several mini-breaks as well as a more extensive holiday in Croatia. This felt different, however. Nico said he would arrange all the details. I'd

212

be attending the Frankfurt book fair the week before, so he would pick me up from the airport and we'd go from there.

'Oh, my ever-loving God, he's going to ask you to move in with him!' Petra gasped, hand placed on heart.

I denied this steadily. I was too superstitious to trust the pleasurable flutter I got from the idea. Petra, however, was confident Something Was Up and that it could only be good. She'd lately begun to talk of 'retiring' from the fame game, which had coincided with her meeting a somewhat older fund manager called Alistair. He was indulgent of Petra's wild-child affectations in a way that suggested he was quietly confident they wouldn't last. I suspected that he was right and in a few years' time she would be comfortably installed in a commuter-belt farmhouse, with two photogenic children and an Aga. I found the idea amusing, but was not inclined to mock. Petra and Lorcan were back on friendly terms, and she seemed happier than she had been for a long while.

Our country jaunt came at the end of a long week. My first time at the book fair had been considerably less fun and more slog than I'd anticipated. Funds being tight, I and another editor had to share a cheap rental room. After a long day manning our stand in a neglected corner of the least popular exhibition hall, we'd go and drink ourselves silly, then stumble back to our twin camp beds. Less than an hour after Nico collected me from the airport, I fell asleep.

October is my favourite month, and I was hoping for blue skies and bronze leaves. London, however, had been chilly grey for weeks and I woke, in darkness, to find rain flinging itself on the car windows. It was just after nine. 'Know where we are?' Nico asked. He'd angled the satnav away from me.

I peered out of the window groggily. The car smelled of cheese sandwiches and stale air. I saw dripping hedgerows, a narrow country road. 'No. How exciting,' I said, trying to sound like I meant it. Nico was looking quietly smug. I comforted myself with visions of a boutique hotel, replete with squashy velvet sofas and open fires and artisan gin. Finally, I glimpsed a road sign.

'Hold on, are we in *Wales*?'

'Crow-esso why cimroo.'

'Har-har.' Then I had a moment's doubt – perhaps Nico's mangled pronunciation of *Croeso y Cymru* hadn't been intentionally comic.

'I've always thought your alleged Welshness was a bit suspect, to be honest,' he said cheerfully. 'I mean, you hardly sound it.'

'Welshness isn't just about watching rugby and waving daffodils. My ancestors have been running around these hills since the ninth century. At least.'

'Settle down. I'm sure your inner sheep-shagger's alive and kicking.'

To be honest, I did feel a bit of an imposter. I had not been back to the Land of my Fathers since Daddy's death. I looked out of the window again and felt a wrench of homesickness. The hangover wasn't helping. Nausea was followed by a shiver of unease.

'Nico … where are we going?'

'Wait and see.' The satnav gave some instructions. 'Honestly, I'm surprised you haven't worked it out yet.'

Here and there, a sprinkle of lights shone out from across the

214

fields. Rain gusted; the headlights briefly illuminated a wind-swept stand of trees. I knew the huddle of those trees, the curve of that ridge. They were embedded in me, like the lines on the palm of my hand. The root of my heart.

Home.

Home.

'Can you stop the car please? I – I think I'm going to be sick.'

CHAPTER EIGHT

I had very deliberately avoided looking into Garreg Las's fate. I knew from my old friend Connie, of course, that the place was being run as a B & B, and though I'd had a brief moment of schadenfreude, I mostly found the idea a distasteful one. The house had already been usurped by strangers, now it was overrun by them. And I was going to be one of their number. *A paying guest*.

What was almost worse, Nico thought I'd be entertained by the idea.

'I'm surprised you haven't been down here before, curling your lip at the soft furnishings. How could you resist the chance to throw shade on their poached eggs and make unreasonable demands as to the quality of the loo roll?'

We would be there in less than ten minutes. Then five … My gut twisted with every familiar turn of the road. Finally, the stone entrance posts loomed into view. There was a new sign to point the way: *Garreg Las Mansion* it proclaimed, in a curly gold script that reminded me of the Dilettanti Discoveries brochure. As we turned in to the avenue, I didn't so much feel that I was in a dream, as that all future dreams would be coloured by this moment. The lower branches of the limes were tangled and swaying eerily in the dark.

I'd known every lump and bump of the old avenue. Now the potholes were smoothed over with fresh tarmac. The gates at the top weren't mouldering painted wood, but wrought iron, in the same overly ornate style as the sign for the house. I didn't know if it was more or less disorientating not to be able to see the view. Somewhere out there were the Black Mountains and the craggy hump of the ruined castle that gave the house its name. But for now they were swallowed up in the rain-swept night. So was everything. The rest of the world might as well have been spirited away.

I clambered stiffly out of the car while Nico went to get our bags. His face was set: he was annoyed with me. After recovering from my attack of nausea, I'd been almost silent for the rest of the drive.

We'd parked by the side door, under the shadow of the beech hedge. Only a few windows were lit. A new fear clutched at me.

'These people … they don't know that I used to live here, do they?'

'I don't think I mentioned it, no. I thought you'd like–'

'OK, then don't. Please.'

He frowned. We waited in silence for someone to answer the bell as the beech leaves shivered in the wind, and the rain, which had finally begun to ease, misted our faces with clammy damp.

Our host was the lady of the manor herself, wearing a bobbling pink jumper and too-tight jeans, with a determinedly perky smile. 'I'm Tania,' she said. 'Welcome to Garreg Las!'

All I knew of her was the newspaper feature from when her husband first bought the house, where she'd been drivelling on about what a dump it was before her interior-design savvy had 'brought the Sleeping Beauty back to life'. I was ready to loathe her, but as she fussed about with our bags I found it harder than I expected.

As she showed us in, she asked the usual questions – where we came from, what we did, had we been to Wales before, et cetera. I left it to Nico to reply.

'I'm from Manchester myself,' she explained. 'So I'm hardly a real country girl. But I do love it here. After me and my husband split last year, all my old mates were, like, great, now you can come home! But I told them how this house feels like a friend. Like family. Sounds silly, I know, but we've both been through the wars and come out smiling.'

By now, she'd brought us through the library and into the main hall, pausing expectantly for the accustomed sounds of admiration. 'Really nice,' I said feebly.

Nico was looking at me in concern – or possibly irritation. 'Mm. Super old place.'

People always say that when you go back to your childhood home, everything seems smaller. This wasn't the case here. The house was, if anything, lovelier and more expansive than I remembered. It was surprisingly easy to look past the fussy little brass sconces, or the splashy abstract rug, or the library's overblown botanical print wallpaper. The bones of the house, like that of an ageing beauty, endured.

And there, hanging in the stairwell, was the portrait that had been far too big for us to take with us and that nobody wanted to buy – great-great-uncle Toby, the army doctor who'd served on Lord Robert's famous march from Kabul to Kandahar. In the end, my mother had thrown him in with the house. A job lot. I fancied I saw reproach in his painted eyes.

'Ah, that's the colonel. Splendid old fella, isn't he?' Tania said, with proprietary pride.

We followed her up the stairs. The fifth step from the top, where I used to sit after creeping out of bed to listen to my father tipsily play the piano in the drawing room, had the same creak of old. There was still a grandfather clock, too, in the alcove on the landing. But its tick was wrong: brisk and tinny.

We were in what had been the second-best guest bedroom, the one that looked out over the lilacs around the tennis lawn. The colour scheme was anaemic pink with charcoal grey accents. Our hostess informed us the bathroom was just across the hall. The rooms with en suite, she said apologetically, had already been booked. (I had to admit this was an improvement; in the old days, the house had barely managed to provide hot water.) Finally, after an excruciatingly prolonged chat about breakfast options, she left.

'I'm sorry,' I said, once we were alone, 'but this is very strange for me. I'm finding it quite hard.'

'Yeah, I can see that. Maybe doing this as a surprise was a bad idea.' Nico looked impatient, all the same. 'You obviously need some time to get your head around it.' Then he sniggered. 'You're not the only one. Those porno pixies are going to haunt my dreams.'

He gestured to the painting above the fireplace, in which naked elves gambolled in a singularly unconvincing Pre-Raphaelite style.

I stared at him. Didn't he know me at all? And shouldn't it be obvious – a place with so many memories – where my father died – the home I loved, which was forever lost – wasn't it obvious that coming back here, as a stranger who paid for the privilege, wasn't something to be undertaken lightly? How could he have thought this was an appropriate venue for a dirty weekend?

It was abominably careless, no – *callous* – of him.

Somehow, though, I managed to tamp down my rage.

'Never mind. I know you meant well.' That came out wrong. 'I mean, it was a lovely idea. I'm sure we'll have a great time.'

All the same, we went to bed in silence, both prickling with suppressed resentment. I lay awake for hours as the unbearably beloved quiet of the house settled around me, like the embrace of a longed-for ghost.

I woke up determined to do better. It was unfair of me to blame Nico for not anticipating the effect the visit would have on me. I'd been careful to outline The Fall of the House of Howell in a light-hearted manner. I'd talked about Garreg Las, and Daddy, in a way that was meant to establish my origins as romantic and interesting but didn't suggest I was trying to trade on past glories. Don't be morbid, my mother used to say. Don't *wallow*. So it was possible I'd gone too far the other way. Maybe Nico had assumed my feelings for the house were akin to those one might feel towards an aged and eccentric relative. Affectionate, appreciative, but involving no great emotional investment.

I came back from my shower to find Nico reading in bed. He was not much of a reader, and there was something a little ostentatious about the way he was holding the book. Dutifully, I asked him about it.

'This? Oh, it's an anthology of short stories by Welsh writers. Your dad's in it.'

Delilah had mentioned something about a forthcoming collection; although my mother was Daddy's literary executor, in practice she often offloaded the admin to Delilah, who found genuine pleasure in answering the rare fan letter or copyright enquiry. Nico passed the book to me: it was a nicely designed but flimsy publication from a Welsh press.

'I remember now. I think there are some proof copies waiting for me at my mother's. Is it the story about Ceridwen?'

'There's something about a witch and a Japanese tourist lost in Swansea … and an ingrown toenail that talks. I have to say, most of it's over my head.'

'I suspect Daddy sometimes set out to baffle.' I was touched Nico had made the effort to look it out and felt a rush of remorse, as well as affection. 'How did you get hold of it?'

'Oliver gave it to me, actually. Said it might be of interest.'

'Oh? That was thoughtful of him.' I set about getting dressed as the pages rustled, trying to dismiss the creep of unease.

'Huh,' Nico said. 'The biographical note.'

'What about it?'

'It says that Anthony Howell is survived by his wife and *step*daughter. That's not right. Is it?'

I felt as if I'd missed a step on the stairs.

My first instinct was to dismiss it as, yes, a minor biographical cock-up. But then there was the brutal fact that Oliver had put the book into Nico's hands. And Oliver would have checked his facts. Since it would be far worse to be caught in a lie, denial was not an option.

'No … I suppose that's right. Technically.'

A variety of unpleasant thoughts were racing through my mind. Who had given the publishers of the anthology the biographical information – Delilah or my mother? Oliver must have gone to considerable effort to look for dirt on me. I was shaken. He must hate me even more than I thought.

'So who's your real dad?'

'Anthony Howell is – was – my real father, as far as I'm concerned. He raised me.'

I hoped the wounded vehemence in my voice would be enough to shut down the conversation. It wasn't.

'OK, put it another way … who was your sperm donor?'

'I – he – just some guy my mother knew. Basically, it was a one-night stand, and he died in an accident soon after. Before she knew she was pregnant. Look – I really don't feel comfortable talking about this. I'm Anthony Howell's daughter. He was the only father I ever knew. He might not have made me, but he *chose* me.'

My voice choked. Surely Nico would be abashed and apologetic for his crassness. But he was still staring at me, face scrunched up in what seemed like excessive bewilderment.

'And you're not even a little bit curious about your other relations – about where you really come from?'

'No,' I said through gritted teeth. 'As I keep telling you.'

'You must see why this has come as such a surprise. I mean, you always say you got your writing talent from your dad. And you're so hung-up on this house. All the family portraits and stories of princes. Your so-called ancient Welshness.'

'What's your point? That I'm claiming to be something I'm not? Putting on airs? You think I'm some kind of *fraud*?'

'No, of course not. I'm sorry if it came across that way.' He didn't sound particularly sorry. He sounded aggrieved. 'I just thought we shared personal things with each other, that's all.'

We had breakfast in the dining room, which had been relocated to the former servants' hall, presumably because of its proximity to the kitchen. The walls were a deep salmon colour, and the room had acquired a new marble mantelpiece as well as an incongruous plaster relief of classical garlands and urns.

Two other, older couples were staying at the same time, and both seemed happy to chat with our host. Listening to their exchange, I gathered that the stable block now contained self-catering accommodation and that Tania was in the process of applying for a licence to hold weddings at the house. Mentioning this, she shot Nico and me a brightly mischievous glance, which we studiously ignored.

'So what do you want to do today?' he asked, without looking up from his scrambled eggs.

I stared out of the window into the lime-washed service courtyard. It wasn't raining, but the sky was oppressively dark. 'I don't know. What do you want to do?'

223

'I thought you'd be bursting with ideas. We're here to visit your childhood haunts, aren't we?' His face was studiously neutral.

'OK. Well, there are some nice walking trails. One's to an iron-age fort. Um. Or there's always the castle ...'

I didn't want to see any of it. Just looking at the swell of the hills made my throat ache.

We ended up going to the local market town, whose Georgian centre had had something of a makeover since my time there. Afterwards, we walked around the deer park attached to the neighbouring National Trust pile. It didn't rain. The views were pretty. It was ... fine. I tried to compensate for my earlier despondency, but my thoughts were already filled with dread of returning to the house.

Garreg Las had clearly benefited from some serious investment. There was fresh tarmac on the drive, a new roof. All the old stains and cracks and chips had gone. But in the light of day, the interior décor didn't look like it had been updated since the original renovation and was showing signs of wear. Although the lawns were mown and hedges clipped, the garden was a little ragged too. I thought Tania looked tired. The reception rooms were littered with silver-framed photos of her two daughters. They were close to my age; I wondered what they were doing and how often they came home. It was hard work running a bed and breakfast. Tania's eagerness to chat came out of neediness, I thought, as much as her role as gracious host.

I mentioned this to Nico as we were getting out of the car. But he misunderstood the motivation of my remark.

'Christ, give the poor woman a break. There's really no pleasing you, is there?'

'I didn't mean–'

'I don't understand you, Ada. You're always banging on about this place. How it will always be a part of you. *Hiray, hooraeth* – was that the word? I thought that by bringing you here, it would bring us closer. Oliver said –'

Oliver again. Oliver, who'd somehow sniffed out my step-daughter status and turned it into an offensive weapon, because Oliver was the kind of person who had an unsavoury reverence for blood purity. I sensed that had I been an actual confidence trickster, someone who'd hustled and schemed their way out of an actual gutter, he might have found it amusing. But my lesser kind of effort was – in his eyes – a far more shameful affront. And he wanted to punish me for it.

'What's Oliver got to do with anything?'

'I met him and Lorcan for a drink the other day.'

'You never mentioned it.'

'So? I don't have to tell you all my social engagements,' he said coldly. 'Anyway. They said you'd love it. That it would be the perfect surprise. Oliver sent me the book afterwards.'

'Then you've been played. Oliver loathes me.'

I'd gone too far. Nico's coldness turned to ice. 'That's news to me. We met at his engagement party, if you remember. And Lorcan's supposedly this great pal of yours.'

That gave me pause. Lorcan knew how much Garreg Las meant to me. Lorcan, of all people, understood – he'd lost his grandparents' beloved family house in similar circumstances. He couldn't have thought this was a good idea. Was it possible he knew about Nico's book, too? Had he and Oliver been laughing at what a phony I was the whole time? To my horror, I felt the beginning of tears.

They only made Nico more infuriated.

'God, Ada. There's no need to look so tragic. Like I said to Tania, your Garreg Whatever's a nice old place. But it's hardly Horton Hall, now, is it?'

He ran his hand through his hair, then turned impatiently on his heel.

'Wait, Lorc–'

He whipped round. '*What* did you call me?'

'Nothing – I – it was a slip of the tongue, OK? I'm upset.'

'*You're* upset? I'm the one who's been played here. You said so yourself.' Nico gave a hard little laugh. 'Really, I should have known when you bought me that ridiculous pink jacket. What a fucking idiot.'

'Nico, no. *No.*'

'I see it now: you make-believe people into who you want them to be. I'm the same as your so-called father in that respect.'

'This is ridiculous–'

'Spare me. Please. The only person you're still fooling is yourself.'

We went back to London that same afternoon, sitting in silence for the duration of the five-hour drive. Something had come up, we told Tania. A family emergency. I hugged her on parting, which took us both by surprise.

That was the last I saw of Nico. I didn't miss him in the way I

226

had missed Ethan, but because the break-up had been so much uglier, the fallout felt much worse. Sometimes I thought that part of him had enjoyed taking me down a peg or two, both about the house and Daddy. Certainly, that's what Oliver would have wanted. And Nico had always had a slight and unexpected edge. But if that was true, how had our relationship started to sour without me noticing?

I'd always prided myself on being unusually perceptive as to people's motivations and needs. I was, I believed, a privileged observer of different worlds. Now my faith in my own judgement was shaken. I began to wonder if I'd been reading people wrong the whole time.

CHAPTER NINE

My mother was unrepentant.

'Yes, I signed off on the biographical note. It was a statement of fact. I don't see why you're so upset about it.'

'Because *Daddy* would be upset about it. You know he never looked on me as just a step-kid. He *adopted* me. *Officially.* I have his *name*. So your fact is wrong. Write to the publishers, and tell them to make the correction in the reprint.'

'I think expecting a reprint is a little ambitious, darling. Oh, Ada – are you actually crying? For goodness sake. Come on, now.'

'*Why don't you want me to be his daughter?*'

'I do. You are.' She was infuriatingly placid. 'I just don't think it would kill you to acknowledge that you have more family out there. Actual living relatives, who I'm sure would be more than happy to connect with you.'

Around the time she married Daddy, my mother had reached out to Tim Franks' parents in Australia to inform them of my existence. Over the years, she kept them updated as to my progress, though health complications meant they did not travel back to the UK to make good on their expressed wish to meet me. Their other grandchildren also lived in Brisbane, which made it easier to assume I was surplus to requirements. I was an indifferent recipient of their birthday and Christmas cards, and wrote sparse thank-yous to 'Dear Pam and Bob' for the book tokens inside them. On their one visit to the UK – the year after Daddy's death – I became hysterical at the idea of an introduction. At the time, I saw any association with my birth father's family as an affront to Daddy's memory.

This hadn't changed. Eating eggs in Garreg Las's servants' hall, under that tacky faux-classical relief, had only reinforced the injustice of my exile. Screw Nico, screw anyone who tried to tell me my birthright was a lie. I knew exactly who I was meant to be.

But a week after Wales, I had a visitor, and everything changed.

I was back at my mother's, sleeping in the tiny guest bedroom, since Brian had failed to relinquish the study. With Delilah home from her travels, it was time for me to find a new flat and flatmates again. But none of the Dilettanti were on the market, and I'd put off looking further afield because part of me had hoped Petra was right and that Nico was going to ask me to move in with him. Now, thanks to Oliver, I'd never know. And it was Oliver who rang the Brockley doorbell, one Sunday afternoon in November.

I was deep in the post-break-up fug of unwashed pyjamas and angry crying. Oliver, by contrast, was irrepressibly puckish. My mother and Brian were out, so I showed him into the sitting room. If he was here to gloat, I might as well get it over with.

He looked around, hands in pockets, rocking gently on his heels. Lord of all he surveyed. 'Well,' he said. 'Isn't this *nice*.'

My mother's furnishings were perfectly tasteful in that everything matched and looked like new. Naturally, the likes of Oliver would think this hideous.

I folded my arms. 'Let's not pretend this is a social call.'

'No? Perhaps we might call it a literary salon, instead. You're a lady of letters, after all.' He batted his lashes. 'Though whose letters they are is an interesting point.'

I went hot and cold all over. No. There was no chance Oliver could have found Daddy's notebooks. The only time he'd been anywhere near them had been during my party. The box had been stashed under the writing desk in Delilah's bedroom, where I did most of my work. But the bedroom door had been locked.

'"My sole, cradling your cracked and tender flesh; the sweet stink of you, thick in my throat …" It's hardly immortal prose, but a nice turn of phrase nonetheless. How did you come up with it, I wonder?' Oliver got out his phone. 'Ah, yes. Here we are.'

He held up the screen. It was filled with a photograph of Daddy's inky scribbles.

'How – how –?'

'During your ill-fated attempt to go stargazing on the heath.'

That had been Lorcan's idea, at the exuberantly drunken stage of the party. We didn't get very far before turning back: it had started to rain; the girls were hobbled by impractical shoes; there was talk of muggers and perverts. Oliver had stayed behind in the flat, saying he needed to phone Davina. I remembered, with excruciating clarity, how I'd left the key to Delilah's room in a bowl on the sideboard.

I licked my dry lips. 'Look,' I said, very weakly, 'Daddy and I ...'

'Your stepfather.'

'My *father*. My father would have done anything to help me. He wanted me to be happy. To be successful. To create–'

'That's very touching,' Oliver cut in, 'but the thing is, I don't.'

I had a flash of what Clemency must have felt the moment she pushed Annabelle/Mallory down the stairs. But I had no opportunity. No weapon. My fury wasn't even righteous. I was entirely defenceless.

'I'll admit I got lucky with those notebooks. I wasn't expecting to find anything particularly incriminating. I was being nosy, that's all. Your social rise, not to mention resilience, has always been a mystery to me. Because at the end of the day, all you've got to offer is a degree of emotional intelligence and a raptor-like tenacity in going after what you want.

'Now, this here is some fairly tin-pot fraud. What's a little bit of plagiarism between friends? But there's no denying it could make a splash. "Adopted Child of Semi-Famous Author Rips off Old Man's Legacy" – I'm sure you can see how *that* would play out.'

I could. Quite apart from the public humiliation, I would most likely lose my job. The stench of scandal would follow me wherever I went, whatever I did. Whoever I met.

'What do you want?'

'I want you to leave us alone.'

And even though I'd been expecting it, my limbs turned to ice water all the same. 'Why do you hate me so much?'

'I could ask the same of you.' His eyes narrowed. 'There's

231

something rotten about you, Lovelace. I can smell it. I always have. I know you tried to cause trouble between me and Lorcan and Annabelle. Some sick fuck played a practical joke on them about Mal's death and Lorcan straight out asked if it was me. Didn't take a genius to work out who'd given him the idea.' He shrugged. 'Still, I wasn't too concerned. People like you always overreach themselves in the end. But this isn't just about your pathetic attempts at sabotage. Mainly, I'm just *tired* of you. Always turning up. Always tagging along. Always organising reunions and jollies and jaunts. Always *there*. I'm tired of how my friends tense up whenever you're in the room, yet somehow don't seem able to shake you off. I'm tired of your jibes and your pretension and your lying, and I want it all to stop. I. Want. You. Gone.'

I was crying now.

Oliver cocked his head, pursed his cherubic lips. 'Chin up, Lovelace. One day you'll see I'm actually doing you a favour. Even poor old Mallory knew when she didn't belong.'

I reached a deal with Oliver. He wouldn't tattle about the plagiarism. In return, I'd make a gradual, seemingly natural withdrawal from everyone else's lives. I had no idea how far I could trust him. It was quite possible he'd already gone straight to Lorcan and Annabelle with what he'd found in Delilah's flat. But he put on a good show of being magnanimous in his victory. He even shook hands on parting, in a caricature of public school gentlemanliness. As if this had ever been a matter of fair play.

I still didn't know how much Lorcan knew but his failure to reach out to me spoke for itself. Some days, the bad ones, I believed that Oliver was right and he and Annabelle had become tired of me, that without Clemency's secret to bind us we would never have been friends. (Was it conceivable that Lorcan had proposed the stargazing trip to the heath just so Oliver could search the flat? Had I been betrayed as well as entrapped?) On others I refused to be swayed by Oliver's spite. Maybe Lorcan was confused by what he had heard about me; maybe he was waiting for me to explain myself.

But I wasn't sure I could bear the pain of such an encounter. In truth, I had written those fraudulent stories for his sake. I'd wanted Lorcan to be dazzled by me, just a little, as I had been dazzled by him. So Annabelle was the one I went to in the end.

I waited for her in the expensively dull lobby of her bank and remembered the time she came to see me at work the summer after Italy and thanked me for what I'd done. After twenty minutes, she emerged from the lift. Her heels clicked efficiently across the floor. She was wearing a soft charcoal pencil skirt and an oyster-coloured silk blouse, her face bare, smile professional.

'Ada, hello. What can I do for you? I'm afraid I'm a little stretched for time.'

This wasn't how she'd greet an important client or trusted colleague. No, I was the troublesome office junior whose work required more supervision than it was worth.

I had rescued her, once. But the need for rescue was long gone.

We perched ourselves on a couple of greige chairs, the ones furthest from the reception desk. I got straight to it.

'I think Lorcan's pissed off with me.'

'Oh? Why?'

'I … I suspect he thinks I've been pretending to be something I'm not.'

'Aren't we all.'

'But I didn't set out to fool anyone. Not deliberately. I hope Lorcan understands that.'

'Then why aren't you saying this to him?'

Up until that moment, I suppose I was nursing a faint hope that Annabelle would tell me not to be ridiculous: that whatever our ups and downs, the bond the three of us shared was unbreakable. I would confess all, and we would blacken Oliver's name together. *Don't worry,* she'd say, *together we can work anything out.* Instead, I had an unwelcome flashback to Mallory in the Palazzo Monegario, wringing her hands over Annabelle and Nate's affair. 'Why not talk to Lorcan yourself?' I'd said. And Mallory had blushed and squirmed. And I'd been impatient, just like Annabelle was now.

'I think he's probably had enough of my drama. I mean, *I* have.' I tried to smile. My face, my words, my heart … everything hurt. 'Just – let him know I'm sorry and that I've decided to do things differently now.'

'You sound as if you're breaking up with him.'

'I'm trying to break up with a lot of things.'

It proved insultingly easy to fade away. I was late responding to messages, if I responded at all. My cancellation of plans was

234

always last minute. I stopped issuing invitations and excused myself from those which came my way. Quite soon, they stopped arriving. I maintained an occasional online presence, which at least enabled me to see what people were up to. But before long, my only remaining link to the Dilettanti was Petra. She had also distanced herself from the old days. I think she found it hard to be around people who primarily knew her as the quirky starlet with the theatrical patter.

The logistics were simple. The fallout was not. Some days I would pace about for hours in furious shock. On others, I was too limp with self-loathing to get out of bed. Everything I had schemed and struggled for, everything I had dreamed of – gone. I had worked my way into a life filled with treasures, I had been surrounded by things to celebrate and to cherish. And now ... nothing. No one.

My twenty-seventh birthday fell a few weeks after Oliver's visit. It would have been miserable in any case, but it began in the worst possible way – with an envelope with US postage, brought to me in bed by my mother. A birthday greeting from Judith Kaplan. They were always sugary Hallmark offerings, speckled with glitter like a toxic rash and addressed in her familiar looping script.

I'd got in the habit of putting Mrs Kaplan's unopened cards straight in the bin, but this year even the sight of the handwritten address was unbearable. Why me? I thought piteously. Mallory's mother wasn't sending Lorcan and Annabelle birthday cards laced with glitter and guilt. No. Those two didn't waste any time feeling remorseful about Mallory or Clemency. Small wonder they'd already forgotten me. And I was suddenly breathless with rage.

That night, and for countless nights afterwards, my dreams were plagued by night terrors of bloody staircases, grinning carnival masks and monstrous black dogs. Then there were the nights I didn't sleep at all. Only a few months into my new job, I was signed off work with depression.

I deserved this. I deserved everything.

My mother assumed the break-up with Nico was to blame. She threatened to send me to a therapist. Perhaps the threat worked; at any event, my misery eventually dulled to a manageable ache. I moved out of Brockley to a flat-share in Streatham and found an editorial position at a large educational publisher's. My flatmates were quiet and tidy-minded and liked to bake. My work was dull, but paid better than anything I'd done before. I didn't trust myself around fiction.

I didn't trust myself around anything to do with my former life. It took a concerted effort to stay away from plush and shiny things. I decided to think of it as a detox. I even had to withdraw a little from Delilah. While my mother approved of my new lifestyle in every way, Delilah was apt to lament it. 'Sometimes I worry about you, Ada, darling,' she sighed. 'I can't quite put my finger on it, but you seem to have lost a *soupçon* of your spark.'

And she would ask, endlessly, about the Dilettanti. 'Those divine boys! Those adorable girls! You hardly mention them any more. What happened?'

'Everyone's busy, that's all. Growing up, getting on with our lives. Moving on …'

I reasoned it had been too easy to imagine I belonged to a group apart from ordinary life and that this gave me dispensation to float along without any real commitments or purpose. I couldn't dwell on the past forever. It was time to grow up.

My one throwback to the Dilettanti days was an unhappy one. It happened about a year after Oliver's intervention, when I was walking to Charing Cross on my way home from work. I caught the eye of a woman passing in the street, and we both gave a slight start of recognition.

'Ada?' she said tentatively. 'How strange. You've been on my mind lately.'

It was the third Mrs Holt. I was surprised that Tess recognised me, let alone remembered my name. I'd only ever been a very marginal presence in her life, at a time when she had a great deal to cope with. Yet as it happened, I'd been thinking of Tess, too, because I'd recently heard from Petra that there had been a mysterious bust-up between Annabelle and Lorcan and their former stepmother. Relations between them had never been warm, and Petra suspected this latest rift was another inheritance-related squabble.

It must have been six or seven years since we'd last met. Tess had the same choppy dark crop and pared-back sexiness, but was lightly tanned and looked younger than I remembered. Possibly she'd had work done, or perhaps it was just that the weight of her husband's slow death had finally lifted. She'd acquired a new tattoo, I noticed, under her collarbone. It was of a swallow. I wondered what it signified.

'How are you?' I said. 'How's your little boy?'

'Oh, we're both doing great, thanks.' She paused, obviously trying to make her mind up about something. 'It's so weird, bumping into you like this … Do you have a sec, or are you in a hurry to get somewhere?'

'I'm in no rush.'

'That's good.' She bit her lip. 'Great. It's a small thing, really … and I don't want to cause any upset, but it's to do with – well, I'm sure you know that Clemency, Clemency Harper, she was married to Lorcan's cousin, Nate –'

'Yes, of course. I was terribly sorry to hear about her death.'

'Thanks. She and I weren't family, except in the most roundabout way, but we'd become close. She was a very special person. You know it was a suicide?'

I nodded.

'Well, although she left a note for Nate, what's not generally known is that she also wrote a letter to me. You were mentioned in it.'

'Really?' The words came out with difficulty. 'How odd. What did she say?'

'Little of sense. Clemency had become very … mixed up, let's say. She was on all this medication, and then she'd started drinking, too. It was a crazy letter, to be honest. A lot of rambling about Italy and art. And that poor girl who died.'

My voice had rusted in my throat. 'Mallory's accident affected Clemency very badly, I remember. I mean, it affected all of us –'

'Right. Yeah. I mean, I get it. That's partly why I kept the letter to myself. I didn't want to cause any more trouble. Because the note Clemency left for Nate was rather loving, see … And this letter was different. It was so angry. Bitter. Full of wild accusations and, OK, *violence*.'

238

'Towards who?'

Tess knit her brows. 'There wasn't anything specific. That's what I wanted to ask you about. Clemency wrote about how, uh, observant you were. "Watchful", she said. So I just wondered ... if maybe you were aware of anything that might have set off those dark thoughts? Could there've been some other trauma in Italy, something connected with the dead American?'

Clemency herself had been dead over two years; I couldn't understand why Tess was returning to the letter now. Lorcan had been fairly sure Tess knew about Nate and Annabelle's affair, but this conversation suggested otherwise. I suddenly wondered if this was what the recent argument had been about – had Tess seen or heard something that revealed their distant romance had been the start of Clemency's unravelling?

If so, I didn't see the point of dredging all that up again. And Tess didn't have the air of somebody fishing for scandal. She looked genuinely troubled. 'Italy was a long time ago,' I said carefully. 'But the Clemency I remember from then was grieving, not angry or ... or disturbed. I mean, she hinted at her fertility issues. Otherwise, we talked about art a bit, that's all. Art and Plato. She seemed a very gentle person.'

Unbidden, Clemency's face flashed before me: ice-pale and red-eyed, her blood-flecked snarl.

Tess nodded. 'Thanks. I'm sorry to have bothered you. I can see I probably need to let this go.'

'What do Annabelle and Lorcan think about it?'

'They ... they haven't ... we're not on good terms at the moment. I would have thought you knew.'

239

'We've rather lost touch, I'm afraid.'

'Oh. I see. It can happen.' Tess looked away. 'Perhaps these things are for the best.'

And that was the last I heard from the Holts and those connected to them until a year later, when the invitation arrived.

PART THREE

Pentimento

CHAPTER ONE

The envelope was sent to me care of my mother's address and had been forwarded by the Dilettanti Discoveries office. The card inside was from Judith and Ari Kaplan, inviting me to Venice for a weekend in August to mark what would have been Mallory's thirtieth birthday.

I stared at the invitation, without moving, for a long time. My pulse sounded loudly in my ears. It was a lavishly printed card with a photograph of Mallory in the centre and the date of her birth. There was a typed letter attached.

Dear family and friends of Mallory,

As you know, our darling girl should have turned the big 3–0 this year. Our pain at her passing never fades, but as the years go by, the light of her spirit continues to shine in our hearts. To mark the occasion of this special birthday, we wanted to find a way in which we could all come together to remember our lovely and loving girl, whose short life brightened everyone she encountered.

And so we'd like to invite you to join us for a weekend of great food, wine, fun and laughter – and maybe some art too! – in the beautiful city of Venice, Italy. Mallory had been so excited to visit this amazing place, and we feel the time has come for us to honour her memory there. We can't think of a better opportunity to celebrate her life and the things she loved best in the world.

We do so hope you can join us.

Peace and blessings,

Shalom v'berachot,

Judith, Ari, Toby & Danielle

Underneath, Mallory's mother had written by hand – 'Dear Ada, Mallory always spoke <u>so</u> warmly of you. We'd really love for you to be there!!! ☺'

The bulkiness of the envelope had led me to believe that Dilettanti Discoveries was spamming me with marketing material. Instead, the envelope was stuffed with various schedules and brochures that attested the Kaplans would be paying for accommodation, food and 'optional excursions'. The only thing their guests were expected to sort out for themselves was travel.

Eventually, I picked up my phone and called Petra. 'Did you get an invitation to Venice from Mallory's parents?'

She had. So, apparently, had all of the Dilettanti.

'It's a bit creepy, isn't it?' I said. 'Holding a party in the place she died? If it was me I wouldn't want to set foot in Venice ever again.'

'Maybe it's part of the mourning process. It's possible they feel this is the only way they'll get closure – to make good memories there, instead of bad ones.'

244

'I wonder how many people they invited. Imagine the cost! I mean, I knew Mal's family were rich but this … this is something else.'

'Are you going to go?'

'I don't know. Are you?'

'I think we have an obligation to, actually. I think we owe it to her family.' In the old days, Petra's voice would have throbbed with tragic portent. Lately, however, she'd acquired an unusual briskness. Sometimes I fretted that *I* was turning into the needy, self-aggrandising one.

Our meetings were infrequent in any case. Petra had given up treading the boards for marriage with Alistair the fund manager and had settled into exactly the kind of life I had once predicted for her: a Sussex 'cottage' that was in fact a sprawling farmhouse, with actual honeysuckle around the door. She was expecting her first baby in June, but even before this was announced had relaunched herself as a designer of children's clothes. Her range, Aphra & Behn, was stocked in a couple of local boutiques as well as online.

'I'm going to wait and see,' she said, as the Venetian weekend drew nearer and her bump grew yet bigger. 'It will likely be too hard with the baby so little. But you should definitely go. For one thing, Mallory's family want you there. For another, everyone would love to see you. They've been asking after you. They miss you. They can't understand why you've apparently dropped off the planet.'

Petra accepted that the responsible, frugal new me was incompatible with the Dilettanti lifestyle. But I knew she didn't really understand. 'Nico hurt you badly, didn't he?' she said on more than one occasion. Perhaps she thought a broken heart was the kindest excuse for my lameness. I had also implied that my depression was due to writer's block – 'Just like your father!' she exclaimed, brimming with artistic sympathy.

However, she wasn't letting me off Mallory's anniversary reunion. 'Come on, Ada. The only other person not going is Oliver, and that's only because his mother-in-law is dying.'

My ears pricked up. It had been three years since our confrontation in my mother's sitting room, and Oliver and I had both stuck to our agreement. Surely Mallory's memorial was an exceptional circumstance.

So I sent him a message.

Mallory's parents particularly asked me to come to her memorial. I hope this is not going to be a problem.

He left it three days before replying.

Pay your respects. Just don't get comfy.

It was loathsome to have to ask his permission. It was even more revolting to feel relieved when he gave it.

Was I relieved, though?

The reunion posed several kinds of risk, not all of which I

246

could prepare for. Did I really want to see these people again? Was my new life secure enough to withstand the lure of my old one?

I liked to think so. Petra aside, I had a handful of singleton sidekicks. Although there had been no one serious since Nico, I'd had a couple of enjoyable flings. With my mother's encouragement, I had reached out to Tim Franks' family – there had been an awkward but friendly meeting with my biological aunt. I'd been promoted at work, and thanks to an offer of a loan from Brian, I could now save for the deposit on a small flat of my own. For the first time in my life, I was living within my means. It was unexpectedly liberating.

In fact, I thought the real proof of my new-found better self was the news – via Connie Rhys-Morgan – that Garreg Las had been put on the market the previous year. Tania was selling up and had already had two offers. The old me would have tormented myself by obsessively viewing the estate agent's listing. Instead, I had undertaken to put it out of my mind entirely.

I would be ready for Venice's ghosts too.

CHAPTER TWO

Preparations for my second trip to Italy had some undeniable parallels with the first. Here I was online, well after I should have gone to bed, scrolling through the feeds of shiny, pretty other lives.

The lack of Oliver more than compensated for the loss of Petra, who had elected to stay home with her baby girl, Antigone. Otherwise, I knew from Missy's group email (every bit as cluttered with exclamation points and emojis as her first communication with us) that everyone else would be there, including tutors Yolanda and Nate. Partners had also been invited, which added to the intrigue.

I wondered if any of the other Dilettanti had been attempting to look me up in the same way as I was researching them. I had to acknowledge it was unlikely. The biggest Instagram junkies of the past were now far less active, presumably because they had better things to do with their time. Rocco was busy brokering multi-million-pound art sales; Willa was now a junior partner at her talent agency. I reassured myself with the thought that, except for a few flashy engagement rings, none of the others had anything especially impressive to show for themselves since our paths had last crossed.

Lorcan and Annabelle were the inevitable exceptions. Over the years, Lorcan had become something of a poster-boy for environmentalism, and on the back of his research for the biodiversity campaign group, as well as his work for his late father's charity, had published a number of high-profile articles on the subject. Recently, he'd taken up a post to review the government's environmental policies. Petra said it was only a matter of time before his place on the roster of parliamentary candidates was announced. 'Prime Minister Holt, God help us. I mean, can you *imagine*?'

I couldn't, actually. Lorcan had always had a self-admitted playboy streak. He had always photographed poorly, the camera somehow making his face look beakier than it did in person, and I wondered if this actually worked to his advantage in PR terms, making him appear a more plausible heavyweight. But I was less impressed by how seriously other people apparently took him than by how seriously he now took himself.

In a recent profile in the *Guardian*, he'd made much of his father's self-made origins and how he and his sister had been raised with the expectation they'd 'contribute to society in a meaningful, as well as productive, way'. Annabelle's contribution was a little less clear – she was still working as an investment banker, albeit one who managed an ethical fund. When compared to Lorcan's ascent, I found this unexpectedly underwhelming.

Still, Annabelle was an undoubted high-flyer, and she'd acquired a fiancé to match: Peter Masterton, dubbed 'the silver-fox-about-town of broadcast journalism' by *Vanity Fair*. The two of them made regular appearances at worthy cultural events and charitable fundraisers. Lorcan would sometimes pop up too, along with his latest girlfriend, a lissom brunette who worked for an eco-conscious fashion label. I felt a certain bitterness, yet there was an undeniable frisson in catching sight of their names or photos in the social diary pages.

While both Lorcan and Annabelle were bringing their partners to Venice, and Dr Nate Harper would be accompanied by his wife of three years, nobody else was bringing their plus-ones. I wondered if this was significant, and if the inclusion of partners suggested a certain nervousness felt by their other halves. I wondered if the new Mrs Harper knew about Annabelle, or if Lorcan and Annabelle's intendeds would ever be told the truth about Clemency and Mallory and that night in the palazzo. I couldn't imagine wanting to burden a relationship in this way. But then, what would I know?

In deference to Oliver, I'd arranged my own, separate accommodation and would be arriving on the Wednesday before the welcome dinner on Friday night. I deserved a mini-break, I reasoned. The idea of exploring the canals and campos of Venice, unfettered by obligation and free to gather my thoughts, was enticing.

At one point during the packing process I glanced at the box that held my grandmother's pearls, which I had put aside a while back. Aged nineteen, I'd expected my life at thirty to be fully formed. This assumption now seemed laughably naïve. But I had to believe that not being the person I'd expected to be was primarily a hopeful state. Nothing was fixed. I might wear the pearls again, I might not.

'How do you feel about seeing Mallory's family again?' my mother asked. We were having dinner together the evening before my departure. 'I know the spirit of this weekend is supposed to be celebratory, but I can't help feeling it's a rather morbid thing to do – commemorating her life in the place where she died.'

Her question was unwelcome, as I'd been doing my best to avoid it, largely by recasting the trip as a more intense version of a high school reunion. I had to acknowledge that my obsessive repacking, my rehearsed summary of relationship status and career prospects, even my new haircut, were displacement activities of the crudest kind. I did not want to think about Mallory except in the most abstract terms. She needed to stay like the icon of a saint: flat and otherworldly, her sorrows nothing but ancient dust.

'It will be a bit strange, yes. As well as sad. I don't know how much interaction there will be with her parents, though. There'll be other guests – school friends and family – who knew Mal a lot better than we did.'

'Goodness, what a crowd. The Kaplans are being extraordinarily generous.'

'Mm. They're very wealthy.' Mallory's father had struck it big in tech, and so in the last few years the family had graduated from comfortably well-off to seriously rich.

I could feel myself growing irritated with my mother's questions, which only made me annoyed with myself. It wasn't her fault the conversation made me so uncomfortable. I fought the urge to shut it down. I didn't want to leave for Italy on a sour note.

We were both grieving, in any case. Delilah had recently died. Her heart attack had been as unexpected as it was sudden; I'd assumed she'd be one of those uproarious old troopers who'd still be overindulging in vodka martinis and unsuitable eye make-up until well into her nineties. My godmother was my last real connection to my father, as well as many of my former aspirations. I wondered if Delilah had been disappointed that I'd put so many of them aside; I wondered if she had been disappointed in me. I didn't want my mother to feel the same. She was all I had left.

Tonight, my mother had the look of a pretty little bird, bright eyed and sleek feathered. She had grown into the person she wanted to be, I realised. Her true self. I wondered what the secret was. Was it simply a matter of time? Luck? Brian?

Perhaps she was thinking along the same lines. She took a careful sip of wine. 'I realise I might not have appeared as positive about your time in Italy, and the friends you made there, as you would have liked. I know that it had a very profound impact on you.'

I gave a non-committal shrug. 'I suppose it did.'

'That's what I was afraid of, you see.'

'Afraid?'

'Of you finding something else that would take you away from me.' She ran a finger along the rim of her glass. 'You were always so determined to be a daddy's girl. Almost as soon as you and Anthony met ... It was love at first sight, it was, really.' She swallowed. 'These people – the Dilettante set, Delilah, that boy

Nico – well, I can see the attraction. Of course I can. It made me a little insecure at times.'

I reached across and put my hand over hers. But the very next moment, she ruined it.

'I'm so glad you're finally learning to manage your expectations.'

CHAPTER THREE

I had not expected it to be so hot.

After a typically British fits-and-starts summer that was more overcast than not, the row of sun icons on the weather forecast page for Venice had inspired nothing but optimism. I had a suitcase full of floaty frocks, sunscreen and strappy sandals. Highs of thirty degrees Celsius were, I thought, exactly what my pasty, vitamin-D-deprived skin longed for. What I had not taken into account was the humidity.

Stepping out of Marco Polo airport and into the queue for the water-bus was like being swaddled in damp fur. I was sweating in moments. Both the cityscape and the lagoon looked flat and sallow, heat blurred.

The hotel the Kaplans had booked out for their party was situated on the Zattere, the wide pavement on the Venice side of the Giudecca canal. The website suggested it favoured the frumpy red-brocade-and-Murano-glass style of Venetian furnishing. It also had air-conditioning. The studio flat I was renting near the Frari had the authentic appeal of ancient beams and whitewashed walls. But four flights up, and under the roof, it was an oven. I never took more than two steps onto the *altana* where I'd pictured myself sipping a spritz among the chimney-pots and campaniles.

Devoid of shade, the terrace had become a graveyard for pots of dusty twigs, and its baking hot tiles threatened to burn a hole through my flip-flops.

Instead, I ventured out to a neighbourhood bar and ate a plate of forgettable *cicchetti*. Then I went back for a cold shower and sat in front of the single creaking electric fan with the bottle of prosecco my kindly landlady had left for me. The calle below buzzed with the scuffle of sandals and trundle of suitcases and tourist chatter grown slurred and sleepy with heat. By the time I hauled myself into bed, I was considerably drunk. I spent the night in a syrup of sweat. My dreams were sticky, dark and cut through with a distant whine that nagged me with the intimation of something lost or forgotten ...

In the morning, this neglect was all too apparent: I'd omitted to reapply mosquito repellent before going to sleep and was now covered in red welts. My rusty head seemed to clang in time with the church bells.

Eventually, I forced myself outside and mainlined espresso, followed by several pastries filled with some sort of custardy-rice confection. It was already mid-morning and the streets were a heaving swelter of sightseers, grimly shuffling through the fug. For a while I let myself be carried along within the crush, waiting to see something I recognised. 'All paths eventually lead to St Mark's or the Rialto,' I remembered Ben telling us. 'You can always reorientate yourselves from those points.'

On my first visit to the city, its churches had been uninvitingly chill caverns. Now I slipped into their shade wherever possible. Some had softly rounded walls of faded pink plaster or else were handsomely angular in marble and brick; others had brooding barnacled frontages grown sooty with neglect. But whether they outwardly resembled a pagan temple or royal palace or stout stone barn, every interior had the same underwater feel: cool and dimly light-dappled. Noise was half-drowned too. Murmured talk and footfalls lapped against the stone, accompanied by mysterious booms and muffled clangs, like the echo of distant ships docking. I paid no attention to the gleam of their sunken treasures, I simply let myself drift. *For she hath suffered a sea-change, into something rich and strange* … I felt emptied out, wholly untethered from my usual self. Was this how Stendhal syndrome started? Was I about to collapse in an ecstatic faint, overwhelmed by the glories of my surroundings?

After a late lunch of pizza, I decided I was merely suffering from dehydration plus heat exhaustion and should stop being so ridiculous. The problem with being in Italy, I thought, was that it was naturally conducive to melodrama. I ordered a second iced-tea, and inched further under the shade of the café's awning.

'Sorry to intrude, but are you by any chance a Dilettante?'

Lorcan was grinning down at me.

And then: 'Cheer up, Ada. You look like you're going to a funeral.'

I suppose I must have been looking rather morose. Although we both laughed, I still felt ambushed. It didn't help that I was sun- and bite-blotched, my feathery new haircut sticking up in sweaty tufts. Lorcan and the girl he was with both had a film of sweat on them too, but it somehow looked deliberate – like the sheen sprayed on models in perfume ads.

Lorcan was sporting a slim white shirt, pistachio green chinos rolled up over the ankles, loafers and a straw fedora. It was a look my new friends would have relentlessly mocked but, I had to admit, had a certain élan. His girlfriend's hat was wide-brimmed, and her sun-dress's retro poppy print was the same colour as her lipstick. The tourist uniform in Venice tended towards the dowdy or the garish, and I noticed the lone natives – a gondolier touting for business on the bridge, a cassocked priest – surveying the two of them with approval.

I stood up, chair scraping awkwardly, and introductions were made. Yes, we'd all had the same bright idea – a couple of days in the city before the main event, wasn't it hot, weren't the crowds hideous, what a shame it had been so long, so difficult to keep up, great fun to see everyone again, very sad about the circumstances, et cetera.

'You here with anyone, Lovela– er, Ada?'

I had rehearsed a variation of 'it's complicated', hinting at some torrid but exciting entanglement I was on a temporary break from. Caught in the moment, however, I found the equivocation was beyond me. 'No,' I said.

'Me-time is so important, I always think,' said the girl, Suki, with a well-meaning smile. She was pretty, of course, but approachably so; in times past Lorcan had generally gone for glitziness with an edge. I wondered if she was part of his relaunch as a Serious Person.

'Is Annabelle with you too?' I asked Lorcan.

'She's in town, but she and Peter are doing their own thing. We're renting on the Grand Canal (fabulous old place – you'd love it); they're at the Cip.'

The Cipriani. Of course.

'Peter's her fiancé, by the way. Peter Masterton. I don't know if you'd heard?'

'No,' I lied. 'How marvellous.'

Suki glanced at her watch. I thought everyone relied on their phones these days, but hers was small and gold, the better to showcase her slim tanned wrist. 'Darling, I told the man in the antique shop we'd be back by three …'

'Sure, sure. You go ahead. I'll catch up in a minute.'

'So nice to meet you, Ada.'

'You too.' We watched her go. 'She's lovely,' I said dutifully.

'Mm. She's a great girl. Perfect, really.' Lorcan was still looking after her. I couldn't tell if his gaze was calculated or simply preoccupied. 'I hope this reunion thing won't be too tedious for her.'

'I'm sure she'll see it as good practice for chatting up the constituents.'

He laughed. 'Oh, Ada. Someone who looks as demure as you has no right to be waspish.'

I felt, despite myself, the glow of flattery.

Lorcan sprawled into a neighbouring chair, put his hat on the table and rumpled up his hair. The gesture was unsettlingly familiar. 'Christ, it's filthy hot. D'you mind?' He glugged down the remains of my iced-tea, waving off the waitress with a genial flap of his hand. 'I know it's Mal's birthday or whatever, but surely they could have chosen a more civilised time of year for their fake-wake.'

'I'm surprised you and Annabelle came,' I said bluntly.

He raised his brows. 'Well, why did *you* come?'

'Obligation, I suppose.'

'You didn't want to reconnect with people again?'

I thought of Oliver, in the Brockley sitting room. *One day you'll see I'm actually doing you a favour. Even poor old Mallory knew when she didn't belong.*

'Not really. It was time to move on a while ago.'

'I hear you,' he said soberly. '"To everything there is a season" and all that ... Neither I nor Annabelle wanted anything to do with it, but we got roped in just the same.' He moved his chair towards me, speaking in the confiding tone of old. 'Now that they're rolling in it, Mal's family are setting up this scholarship fund in her memory – it's a European study-abroad thing, it's going to be announced over the weekend. Seems a bit perverse to me. I mean, it's not like studying abroad worked out so well for Mal, did it? Anyway, they got in touch with Dilettanti Discoveries, asking if they'd help with some UK contacts, and Nate – who still freelances for them – got involved. So bloody *Nate* said what a nice gesture it would be if we got Dad's trust on board. He's still clueless, of course. But Annabelle and me could hardly say no, could we?'

'Isn't your family charity all about the environment?'

'Which, coincidentally, is what Mallory was going to major in. Conservation biology.'

'I didn't know that.' I'd probably never asked.

'Yeah, well, the Kaplan scholarship will be for US kids who are going to study the same sort of thing. Which is all well and good but, frankly,' he continued, slumping back into his chair, 'I think this whole weekend is going to be beyond ghastly. You

259

know how corny Americans are. It'll be endless group hugs and execrable poetry readings and laughing-through-tears.'

I considered Lorcan again. He was lightly tanned, which, I now saw, deflected from how tired he was looking. There were deep circles under his eyes and his fingernails were bitten to the quick. Although his words were flippant, I sensed the effort behind them. He, too, was displacing his own tangle of feelings about Mallory and Clemency and how they died. Watching him frown to himself, I remembered the evening spent drinking whisky in his apartment, how the sadness had leaked out of him, like rusty ink.

'Her family are still looking for some kind of closure. I can understand that. I want that for me, too. Unlikely as it seems, it's possible we'll all feel the better for it.'

'Hm. Wise words as ever, Ada. Wise words.' Lorcan stretched widely, sending the surrounding pigeons flapping upwards in a dirty grey flurry. Then he got to his feet and repositioned the fedora at a suitably jaunty angle. 'You *have* been missed, you know.'

It was a politician's observation. The passive tense, the ambiguity of who, exactly, had been doing the missing. But as the birds whirled above our heads, I felt something in me lift too.

Now that I knew Lorcan and Annabelle and perhaps others were in the city, I could no longer afford to indulge in light-headed idling. Venice is a small place and seemingly designed for chance meetings. I returned to the state of vigilance I'd felt on my first trip to Italy, consumed by the same vague fear of not wanting to be caught out. I spent most of the next day in the Accademia, where I half-expected to glimpse Nate's tweedy jacket or hear Willa's braying laugh.

My attentiveness paid off, for I actually caught sight of Annabelle as I was making my way back for a shower before dinner. She was getting out of a motorboat near San Trovaso. Peter Masterton was helping her disembark; I would have recognised his handsome jutting profile anywhere. Annabelle was wearing a terracotta linen sheath, only faintly creased, with her hair piled high. She stumbled a little on the quay, and her fiancé steadied her. The way she looked back at him shook me. Her smile was open, her face bright ... bedazzled, almost. I had never seen her look at anyone like that. With Nate, she had always seemed ineffably adult, in contrast to the boyish eagerness she aroused in him. But in that moment, Annabelle looked far younger than she had then.

I remembered how I'd stalked the lovers through Florence, and how my initial satisfaction at finding them out had curdled into resentment and shame. I felt the same twist in my gut now. The skittish optimism I'd felt with Lorcan had evaporated; I knew for certain it had been a mistake to come.

CHAPTER FOUR

Mistake or not, I was committed all the same. The programme began that Friday evening, at six, with drinks and dinner at the Kaplans' hotel.

I stared into the mirror before I left, trying to work up my courage. I was in a favourite green halter-neck dress, enlivened by dangling gold earrings. The mosquito welts were starting to fade; I had even acquired a little bit of a summer glow. What was my problem? I was certainly far better equipped than a callow teenager to put a convincing gloss on the unremarkable particulars of my life. *I'm so glad you're finally learning to manage your expectations ...*

One of the hardest parts of the reunion was already over. I had seen Lorcan and kept my composure. I wasn't engulfed with bitterness or burning regret. I had, more or less, moved on. Seeing the rest of the Dilettanti would be easy in comparison. It was facing Mallory's family that was the real test. I'd thought having nearly three days on my own would have readied me for this. Instead, it had only increased my dread. I didn't believe what I'd said to Lorcan about achieving closure, though I'd meant it at the time.

'*Buonasera*,' I said to the hotel receptionist, as I exchanged my flip-flops for heels and fanned my sweaty cheeks. 'I'm here for the Kaplan party?'

'*Certo*. But you are a little early, yes? It is not to start before seven.'

I frowned. It was 6.15. I'd rechecked the invitation before going out, and it had definitely said six. Timings had evidently changed but, not being part of the main party, nobody had thought to get a message to me. It was possible Lorcan, Annabelle and co. would be under the same misapprehension, though somehow I doubted it. I hadn't wanted to be the last to arrive, as that might involve making an entrance. Being the first would be even worse. Yet I couldn't face leaving the air-conditioned cool for the swampy heat outside.

To kill time, I visited the bathroom and splashed water on my face, before reapplying my make-up. Then, as the receptionist had suggested, I went to wait at the hotel bar. Only one other person was there, a man in a rumpled shirt reading the *Herald Tribune*. I ordered a spritz, reminding myself to take it slowly. Alcohol would make the evening more bearable, but only up to a point. When I tried to pay, the bartender waved me off.

'The Kaplans are taking care of the tab,' my neighbour at the bar explained. 'Harry Geffen,' he said, reaching out to shake my hand. 'Old family friend.'

I should have known that he, and everyone else in the hotel, would be part of the same gathering. I stuck on what would doubtless be the first of many fake smiles that evening.

'Ada Howell. I was on the art history course with Mal. Mallory, I mean. I got a little confused about what time we were to meet. I thought the invitation said six.'

'Yeah, there was some screw-up with the caterers so they changed it last minute. Art history, huh? It's great that so many of you guys made the effort to show up. I know it means a lot to Judy and Ari. You still involved in painting and such?'

'Not really. I'm an editor, I work in non-fiction for now. Educational magazines ...' I trailed off. Harry Geffen was looking at me with new and disconcerting interest.

'Ada. Wait a minute – I just figured why I recognised your name.' He lowered his voice. 'Weren't you one of the first on the, uh, scene?'

It was unsettling the way people seemed to think this gave me some kind of creepy prestige. I nodded tersely and took a long gulp of my drink, hoping he'd get the hint. Instead, he moved closer.

'I'm sorry. It must've been a helluva thing to deal with. I mean, you were pretty much a kid.'

'Mm.'

'You have any counselling afterwards?'

This struck me as intrusive. Or maybe he was just being American. Harry was not more than early forties, and not unattractive, either, with a creased, lively brown face and curly dark hair. But I was in no mood to try and turn the encounter into a flirtation. 'No. My mother wanted me to but – Look, it was fine. I had support.'

'That's good. The other girl who found her – Clementine, was it? I heard she killed herself.'

'It wasn't connected,' I said sharply. 'From what I understand, Clemency had a lot of issues, going back a long way.'

264

He grimaced. 'I get it. I'm being an insensitive prick. My apologies.'

'That's OK. It's only – well –' I channelled Petra at her most pious. 'I thought we were all here to remember the good times. To celebrate Mallory's life. Not dwell on … You know.'

'You're very right.' He beckoned the bartender to refill both our drinks. 'I'm starting to think this city brings out the morbid in me. With all the sunshine, I expected it to be more, uh, sparkly, I guess. Carnival and coloured glass.'

Mallory, I remembered, had thought Venice 'beautiful but kinda poky'. And I'd mocked her for it. 'I know what you mean. Have you been to Italy before?'

'Coupla times. My mom's Italian, as it happens. From this dusty little hill town in Calabria. Pretty place, not much of anything going on.'

From here on, the conversation stayed safely bland, though it still came as a relief when the other guests began trickling in.

This relief did not last. My first, highly discomfiting reaction was the realisation I was overdressed. Everyone else was in casual holiday mode. As soon as I could, I slipped off the dangly earrings and put them in my bag. But it still put me on the defensive. Even worse, one of the first people to arrive was Oliver. Oliver, who was supposed to be sequestered by his mother-in-law's sick bed. 'Lovelace! What a *treat*. And how fancy you look! I hope you didn't go to all that effort just for me.'

'I – I didn't know you were coming.'

'Maybe I wanted to surprise you.' He had thinning hair and the beginning of a paunch. Less elf, more goblin. 'Davina's mother is still clinging onto life by her talons. It seemed a shame to miss out on the party. Or is it a wake? The invitation wasn't clear.' He pulled a sad face. 'Is that why you were confused by the dress code?' Then he put his mouth to my ear and whispered moistly, *'I've got my eye on you.'*

Seeing Oliver again was still preferable to being welcomed by Mallory's mother, Judy. I had only the vaguest memories of her and her husband from the terrible day following Mallory's death, when they had been in a trance of grief and shock, and we'd been in a stupor of our own. Then there had been all the birthday cards, of course, which I'd done my best to ignore. Was now the time to mention them? Yet another thing to feel guilty about … I barely recognised the stout, bustling woman with the expensive haircut who pulled me into an embrace. She was saying my name with a catch in her voice. 'I'm just so happy you're here. Mallory told us how the two of you were set to be fast friends.'

My mouth felt sticky from the cocktail; my hands were damp. I murmured something inane about how the feeling was mutual. The next moment I was hugging Mallory's father. He was bald and compact, vibrating with energy. 'It's going to be so great to reconnect with you,' he was saying. Others were crowding around: Mallory's softly spoken younger brother and then her older sister, who had eerily similar features to Mallory, but prettier, enlivened by a confidence that was all her own. Or perhaps, I thought with a pang, I was looking at the kind of woman Mallory might have grown into.

More introductions to more smiling strangers followed. I was disconcerted to find that the Dilettanti made up the majority of the guests who were not family. As such, we could hardly keep a low profile.

It had been over three years since I'd seen any of them. Despite my nervousness, my overwhelming feeling was nostalgia. *Hiraeth*. JJ was as cheerfully shambolic as ever, and proudly showing off photographs of his two-year-old mini-me. Kitty and Missy sported matching baby bumps, while Willa flashed an engagement ring that would have been the height of garishness if it had not been an old family heirloom. She herself was starting to look jowly. I was rather sad to see that the last of Rocco's tattoos had been lasered off; it was a crude reminder of how much time had passed since we'd shed our teenage skins.

Yolanda appeared exactly the same, though she had given up working for Dilettanti Discoveries after our course and was now a fairly established art critic and cultural commentator. I heard her pass on Ben's apologies to the Kaplans; he was away at a conference. I was sorry for this: Ben's uncomplicated good humour would have been a comfort. Nate was accompanied by his unexpectedly dumpy wife and for much of the drinks had a squirming toddler attached to each leg. He seemed quite at ease. If he and Annabelle were unsettled by each other's presence, they hid it well.

Annabelle and her fiancé, together with Lorcan and Suki, had arrived about twenty minutes after everyone else. The Brits in the room took pains not to look impressed by Peter Masterton's celebrity cameo, but it was hard not to turn at the sound of his voice, more usually associated with the lethally polite skewering of politicians or talking heads. He had the affable, ever-so-slightly

267

weary air of someone all too used to being the most interesting person in a room. I was surprised to see that Annabelle was wearing make-up for once. Discreet as her lipstick and eyeliner were, I felt obscurely disappointed that she'd resorted to the embellishment.

Oliver, I noticed, coloured a little when they exchanged a kiss.

The hotel bar opened into the breakfast room, where a local restaurant had set up an informal buffet supper. The Kaplan family did their best to mingle and introduce but, given the choice of seating, people naturally gravitated towards those they already knew. I noticed Harry Geffen was the one exception. He was here, there and everywhere, chatting to everyone. I found myself faintly annoyed by this, and annoyed with myself as a result. It wasn't as if I had welcomed his initial interest in me.

To my relief, there was little in the way of formal speeches, though Mr Kaplan gave a welcome toast at the start of the meal. Perhaps Lorcan was wrong, and it wasn't to be a weekend of sentimentality and grandstanding after all.

It was not possible to relax, and I barely tasted my food, but my carefully scripted account of the last few years seemed to be well-received and I felt I made a decent job of feigning reciprocal interest in everyone else's activities. I even remembered to send some updates to Petra, who responded with a slew of baby photos.

I had hoped to be unmoved by seeing the Dilettanti again. Yet I was still mesmerised, despite myself, by their absolute confidence in the rightness of their place in the world. Had they missed me? They proclaimed so, fervently. They were delighted, *thrilled*, to be reunited. I used to be able to tell the difference between sincere and feigned warmth, but I'd lost the knack. Nobody asked about my writing. Was this because Petra had told them my writer's block was a sensitive issue, or was it simply because they'd forgotten?

Given the circumstances, everyone was making an effort to keep their conversation subdued. As the evening went on, however, and the wine flowed, people began to loosen up. Some of the more outrageous reminiscences were aired. The laughter grew a little more raucous. Our invitation had stressed this was to be a weekend of celebration, and we were taking it at its word. I looked round at the Dilettanti, so garrulous and animated, and thought that maybe their consciences were, in fact, entirely clear. Maybe they'd genuinely forgotten what a nuisance Mallory was and how we punished her for it. 'Poor Mal,' we kept saying in the hours after her death. 'I just can't believe it. Poor Mal.' 'Poor you,' said everyone else – parents, police, teachers, press. And we came to believe them. We were traumatised. Scarred. Innocent.

Of course, some of us were more innocent than others.

I went to get another glass of wine. Yolanda was standing by the bar, watching Missy talk to Mallory's sister, Danielle. The sister looked emotional. Missy's face was shining with sympathy. One hand cradled her bump; she put the other, tenderly, on the sister's arm. Next to her, Oliver nodded along gravely. I thought Yolanda's expression had an ironic slant.

'You're judging us, aren't you?' I'd had more to drink than I'd realised.

Yolanda turned to look at me but didn't reply. Her brows knit.

'Hypocrites, that's what you're thinking. You always judged us. You judged *me*. All these years later … you can't let it go.'

'Goodness, Ada. In all these years, I haven't really thought of any of you. Except for Mallory, of course.' She said it kindly, which made it worse. Then she touched my hand. 'Are you all right? You don't look very well.'

I mumbled some inanity. I had a mad but fleeting impulse to unburden myself to her. To anyone. It was now urgent that I escaped the confines of the hotel. Under the pretence of taking a phone call, I went out to the little corte, only to find Peter and Harry smoking there, in the company of Annabelle, Suki and Lorcan. It felt like I was intruding, but Harry waved at me to join them. 'At least our toxins will keep the mosquitos away.'

Harry should have been the odd man out in this group, but he and Peter seemed to have gravitated towards each other, perhaps simply because they were closer in age. I decided to stay only as long as wouldn't seem rude. The Kaplan grandchildren, two boys of about six and seven, were running in and out, making the manic most of being up long past their bedtime. More than once, Harry marched them inside, but they proved resistant. Trying to hold a conversation among the shrieks and giggles was an uphill struggle.

'It's like social media imposes its own mourning rituals,' Suki was attempting to say when I joined them. 'Whenever there's some tragedy – the death of a pop star, a terrorist attack – the public response has become so predictable,' she said predictably. 'Everyone's recycling the same old clichés.'

'What I find slightly creepy is how nobody ever really dies in cyberspace,' said Harry. 'Mallory's Facebook page is still live. Her brother is posting updates on it from tonight–'

'Boo!' shouted one of the small grandchildren, springing out from behind a potted oleander.

I felt a lurch of horror – a golden cat mask was grinning up at me in the dark. It was stupid, really: I'd already passed plenty of these masks in the souvenir shops, and this one was likely taken from the little carnival display in the lobby. The child was only playing dress-up. None the less, it was hard to maintain my equability.

'You look like you've seen a ghost,' said Suki, amused, and it took a moment for me to realise she was talking to Lorcan.

'Hey – Dani!' Harry yelled in to the doorway. 'For the love of God, restrain your infants!'

Amid much protest, the children were dragged inside by their harassed mother. Harry had held on to the mask and was regarding it thoughtfully. 'You know, I'd rather the Kaplans didn't see this. It's kind of an unfortunate coincidence.'

'How do you mean?' asked Peter Masterton.

'Well, wasn't Mal wearing something like this when she fell? Posing for photos, wasn't she?'

I didn't hear the rest of what was said. I was concentrating too hard on keeping my expression neutral. All the same, there was a rushing and roaring in my ears. Because Mallory had not been taking selfies out on the stairs. Not officially. To maintain the fiction of her accident, and avoid awkward questions, we hadn't wanted anyone to entertain the possibility of mistaken identity. After all, both Clemency and I had confused Mallory with Annabelle because of their superficial resemblance when masked. That was why I had deleted the pictures of Mallory

271

posing in the cat mask from her and Kitty's phones. That was why I had removed the mask from the crime scene. So how, then, had the official narrative of her death changed?

Either Harry had misremembered the story and accidentally got it right ... or he was trying to trip us up. Deliberately. The implications were horrifying.

I didn't dare look at Annabelle and Lorcan. It was enough to feel how the air between us had rippled, then stiffened.

'It's not uncommon, I'm afraid,' said Peter Masterton's illustrious voice, as if from a great distance. 'Only last week, an Australian broke his back after falling off some rocks in Portugal, mid-selfie.'

Suki chimed in with another cliché, and then conversation moved on as people drifted inside. I said my goodbyes as soon as was decent.

But walking back to my apartment, my phone pinged. It was Annabelle. I didn't even know she had my number. 'Let's meet for coffee – 8 a.m.?'

Not a social invitation. A summons.

CHAPTER FIVE

I barely slept that night. I'd been the one to get rid of both the mask and the photos. I remembered very clearly that I'd erased the incriminating photos from the trash, then deleted the online back-up. The real-life mask I'd put in the real-life trash. At the time, I thought I'd been exceedingly clever to tie up any possible loose ends. But what did I really know about the dark arts of data retrieval?

I had been trying to prove myself indispensable to Lorcan and Annabelle. As I tossed and turned in my sweaty sheets, I saw my actions for what they really were: reckless and self-promoting. Criminal.

So what if anyone had thought to wonder whether Mallory could have theoretically been mistaken for Annabelle? It hardly suggested a murder had been committed. Nobody had uncovered Nate and Annabelle's affair, let alone suspected Clemency's vengeful response. I was beginning to face the fact that my intervention had been entirely redundant. Masked or not, Mallory's death would still have looked, from every angle, like an accident. And now a loose thread had come undone, bringing the mask with it …

If I was suffering from night-time paranoia, I wasn't the only one. Annabelle's texts had been so minimal that I knew she was taking this as seriously as I was. It was as if she was already anticipating a time when our personal communications might be examined.

I met her and Lorcan at a café near San Francesco della Vigna. This corner of the Castello neighbourhood was relatively empty of tourists and tourist traps, but only a short walk from where we were due to take a boat for a tour of the lagoon. At eight o'clock the temperature was mild, but it was shaping up to be another brutally humid day, with a harsh, bright glare that cast everything – sky, air, stone – in the same baleful light.

As I took my seat, I got the distinct impression I'd interrupted a sibling disagreement. Both of them were sitting very upright and looking away from each other, tight-lipped.

'So,' Annabelle said, as soon as the waiter had delivered my espresso, 'Harry Geffen. He's a private investigator.'

My mouthful of coffee turned to acid. 'What? *Shit*. He told me he was in software development.'

'Indeed. Anti-spyware. His business also offers private security consultation and investigation on the side. We did a little research last night. Family friend or not, I very much doubt his profession is incidental.'

'Shit,' I said again. It struck me, with horrible clarity, that it had been no accident I'd arrived ahead of schedule to find Harry waiting in the hotel bar. 'In that case, it's possible I … I think I was set up for an interview with him.'

Lorcan scrunched up his hair with his fists. He let out a low moan.

Annabelle merely frowned a little. 'Tell us exactly what was said.'

I related our conversation. 'It was hardly stuff to set the world alight,' I finished, trying to find comfort in my own words. 'And I obviously didn't say anything incriminating.'

'Sounds like he was just testing the waters,' Annabelle conceded. 'But that ridiculous performance with the mask was a deliberate ambush. He must have set the whole thing up to test our reaction because he knows the three of us were among the first on the scene. It's a little unfortunate we're the only ones who aren't staying at the hotel, you know ... Of course it's coincidental, but it's something else that sets us apart from the rest.'

'We don't have to put up with this bullshit,' Lorcan growled. 'I'm not hanging around to have my chain yanked by some two-bit private dick. I say we get the first flight out of here. Fuck 'em.'

'Yes,' said his sister, 'because *that* won't look at all suspicious. Christ, Lorcan. If you're serious about going into politics, you're going to have to grow a spine at some point.'

I wasn't used to Annabelle being bitchy; I'd assumed it was beneath her – like wearing make-up. It shook me more than I liked to admit. So did her newly brittle tone.

'I don't understand,' I said. 'Mal's been dead ten years. Why would her family want to hire an investigator now?'

'That,' said Annabelle, 'is a very good question. Something has obviously changed. Or been discovered.'

I took another gulp of coffee. 'OK. We shouldn't panic. I realise that getting rid of the mask and the photos may have caused more trouble than it was worth—'

'*No.*' Lorcan threw up his hands in mock surprise. 'Could it be you aren't such a great criminal mastermind after all?'

'Leave it, Lorcan,' Annabelle snapped. 'You're the one who first covered up for Clemency.'

'Well, forgive me for wanting to protect your lily-white reputation, sis. Let's not lose sight of who set off this whole shit-storm in the first place.'

I hadn't seen the two of them openly argue before, but it didn't surprise me that Lorcan was the one to lapse into a sulk. What I wasn't expecting was for Annabelle to come to my defence. I had braced myself for her scorn, if not actual recrimination. She'd been the only one of us who wanted Mallory's family to have justice, I remembered. Yet she'd thanked me afterwards. *I had my doubts, at first. But now I'm sure we did the right thing.*

'Let's not lose perspective on this. At the end of the day, we didn't, you know, *kill* anyone,' I said.

Annabelle laughed shortly. 'No. We merely allowed a murderer to get off scot-free. Perverted the course of justice. Concealed evidence of a crime. Gave a false statement.'

'None of which can be proven. Maybe Harry went through the old statements or whatever and noticed some random witness said they saw Mallory pick up a cat mask. So what? That's not evidence of anything. It's not like he can interrogate Clemency again.' I remembered how Annabelle and Lorcan had looked at me in that hotel dining room: waiting and hoping for my direction; the intoxicating feeling of being needed by people. Their faces were fixed on mine again, but this time I couldn't read their intent. To cover my disquiet, I spoke with a confidence

276

I didn't feel. 'Our actions may have been morally questionable. But I still believe we acted for the best.'

'Really?' Annabelle sounded genuinely curious. Her gaze moved to the white horizon. 'Does that mean, given the chance to do things over, you'd do it all the same?'

Luckily, the waiter returned at that moment and, thanks to the distraction of settling the bill, I didn't have to answer.

The Kaplans had laid on a choice of activities for their guests: a guided tour of Venice's greatest hits or a boat trip around the lagoon and its islands. Most of the Americans opted for the former, though Harry Geffen and Mr Kaplan were among those who had chosen the lagoon. The prospect of being confined on a boat with them made me feel sick to my stomach, though the trip would have been a chore even before the latest revelation. Unlike Lorcan and Annabelle, I didn't have a partner to buffer me. Every interaction with those I had once considered close friends had curdled into platitudes or evasions or lies.

As for the Kaplans … I had entirely underestimated them. Their calculated display of folksy American warmth. Their bogus hugs and bribery. Didn't anyone else realise how dangerous they were? Showering us with hospitality while conspiring to entrap us. And Harry was once again everywhere, with everyone, always with a ready laugh and a crinkle-eyed smile, as he asked his questions, made his calculations …

I should have known better. I *did* know better. Yet, like a fool, I'd still fallen for the bait.

Our boat departed from the Fondamente Nove, not far from the stop for the Palazzo Monegario. Nate – unencumbered by wife and children, who had elected to stay behind, along with Yolanda – gamely stepped into the role of tour guide, though his voice faltered slightly when he pointed out the cemetery island of San Michele. Scenic as the view was, nobody was moved to take a photograph of its fairy-palace walls. The weekend was full of unmentionables, even though Mallory was spoken of often enough. Or rather, two Mallorys were recalled: the adorkable, fun-loving party girl of Dilettanti memory, and the more rarefied soul invoked by her family and friends. The real girl I remembered, stolid and unprepossessing, with a too eager smile, had vanished.

As we took in the sights of Murano, Burano and Chioggia, I felt I had wandered onto the stage of a play I hadn't rehearsed for, improvising my unconvincing lines among an even more unconvincing parade of doll-like houses in primary shades. Burano seemed especially toy-like, with its tiny canals and miniature bridges. I couldn't think how I had come to be in such a setting. *This is not my place. These are not my people.* The plummy drawl of the Dilettanti, the excitable chatter of the Americans, seemed equally foreign. I took refuge in the company of a girl called Heather, Mallory's best friend from high school. She still bore the hallmarks of an awkward adolescence with her acne scars and frizzy hair, but her conversation was filled with happy boasts of her family back home and her work in pharmaceutical research. After a while, her words took on the hum of background static.

Our final stop was Pellestrina, a somewhat ramshackle settlement perched on a sandbank. We followed the walkway along the lagoon, where a fleet of dilapidated fishing boats was moored, before clambering down the steps in the sea wall to find the Adriatic on the other side. Locals had set up encampments of parasols and deck-chairs on the scrubby beach but it still felt a desolate place, littered with driftwood and seaweed. It was agreed to return to the little town for ice-cream before taking the boat home.

I hung back from the others, half-heartedly taking photos of the swollen grey sea. At least I could excuse myself from the evening's pizza supper. Escape was near. Closing my eyes, I finally allowed myself to think of Garreg Las, translating the sigh of the waves into the murmur of wind in trees. Using the house as a mental refuge was a habit I had worked to break, but today the images came too easily to be denied. The house was empty of Nico, empty of Tania Price and her knick-knacks, empty even of my father. I wandered through cool bare rooms brimming with pale light and climbed the stairs, feeling the silken length of the bannister glide beneath my palm–

'You having a good time, sweetheart?'

Mr Kaplan. Even worse than Harry.

I managed to dredge up the expected remarks about the charms of getting off the beaten track, seeing the real Veneto. So grateful. Et cetera.

'Mallory would have got such a kick out of these hidden corners, I think. My girl was adventurous that way. Curious about the world.'

'She was very special.' *Lie. Deceive. Mislead.*

Everyone else was queuing at the gelateria. The first in line had wandered back to the sea wall with their cones, but showed no inclination to come down and join us. Mr Kaplan's bald domed head was shiny with sweat, which he occasionally mopped at futilely. Even with the sea breeze, I could feel the same slickness on me. My armpits were damp and sour.

'We have our little memorial tomorrow. I thought I was ready for it, but now … ach.' He shook his head, grimacing.

I nodded in what I hoped was a sympathetic manner. The service was to be held in one of the Ghetto synagogues and would be followed by lunch. Then it would be over. Or not, I thought, panic scratching at my chest.

'I heard how the Venetian Ghetto was the first – leastways, it's the one all other ghettos are named after. Oldest in the world. But the Venetians didn't treat the Jews too bad, considering. Did you ever visit it, back in the day?'

'No,' I said uncomfortably. 'I … I suppose there wasn't room on the itinerary.'

'Mal managed to slip off and take a look. She said there wasn't much to see, and I guess she was right. It's more about atmosphere, memory. I mean, there are hardly any real live Venetians left in the city, still less any Jews. The soul of the place died a long time ago, anyone can see that. Whole damn city is a boneyard.'

He suddenly burst into tears.

I was appalled. The desolate beach, the lurid light and the heaving sea … The two of us could have been shipwrecked here, alone at the end of the world. My own eyes pricked with tears. I put out a useless hand, mumbled my useless words. 'I'm sorry. I'm sorry. I'm so, so sorry –'

'No,' he said, shoulders heaving. His voice was raw. His nose and eyes ran and he let them, unselfconscious as a child. 'You're all right, sweetheart. It's me who's sorry. I wanted this to be a happy weekend, in spite of everything. Whole thing was my idea. Judy – she wasn't so keen. She thought it would be too strange. Too painful. She thinks I'm going about this all the wrong way. Stirring stuff up that shoulda been laid to rest a long time ago. But how can I not?' He thumped his chest, a gesture that might have been theatrical but was of a piece with the snot and the sobs. 'Mallory was my baby girl … How can I let things go? There are *questions*.'

'What do you mean?' The ice-cream eaters were meandering about in the distance, taking photos or else perching on the sea wall. I could see Annabelle and Lorcan looking over at us. But nobody was coming to the rescue.

'Maybe I shouldn't be telling you this. Harry would be against it.'

'Harry?'

'Harry's been helping us. He used to be police, you know. He's a good friend. Maybe I shoulda asked him to take a look in the first place, but we were in shock, you know. Reeling. And it seemed so simple. Open and shut.

'But Harry, he says the original investigation was rushed, sloppy. There are these nagging little details, you know. Like how there was a boy at this party, an Italian, how he said in his statement that he saw my girl trying on this mask in the mirror, right around the time she went out onto those stairs. A golden cat, he said. And that would make sense because it was in other pictures, OK, and you guys were playing dress-up, weren't you? Like a carnival? But if my girl went outside to take selfies in that mask, how come there wasn't any sign of it when you found her?'

'I … I don't know. I mean, there might have been a mask lying around. I didn't look. I was so shocked. Horrified, really. The confusion. Then all the people. I –'

Mr Kaplan clutched at my arm. Afterwards, I found his grip had left red welts. 'I'm not blaming you, sweetheart. And even Harry says most likely it means nothing at all. The boy who said he saw her with it, well, he was high as a kite. There were drugs at the party – that's something else we only just found out. Nobody told us at the time. That bugs me, too. Because how reliable were any of those witnesses in the end?'

'None of us – the Dilettanti – were taking drugs.' I spoke vehemently, though in fact I couldn't be sure this was true. I'd seen Oliver, for one, wiping his nose outside the dining room. 'We didn't need to. We were drinking, yes, but we were happy.' Was this true, too? 'So happy,' I said again, with even more emphasis.

'That's what me and Judy keep telling ourselves. It's a comfort, the only one, to think of Mallory with her friends, having this amazing time, this magical experience she was so excited for. Her mom was nervous about letting her go to Europe. God forgive me, I told her not to fret. It was time to let our baby go, I said.' He put his hands over his face. 'God forgive me.' A long shuddering sigh. Then he looked up. Deep in their puffy creases, his eyes were bright and shrewd. 'Look, I'm not deluded. There's no smoking gun here, not yet. These are small things. Small and stupid, most likely. And if it wasn't for …'

I held my breath. Now, I sensed, we were coming to the heart of it.

'For the letter. Somebody showed us a letter, see.'

My stomach dropped.

'A *letter*?' I repeated stupidly.

'From that other poor girl. Woman, I mean. Nate's first wife, the one who walked in front of a truck. It was passed on to us last year. I won't go into it – I've probably already said too much – but there was stuff in there I just can't get out of my head. Dark stuff, you know?'

'Clemency was very troubled.' My voice sounded weak and distant. 'She had … a lot of problems. Nate'll tell you. You should speak to him.'

'Sure, sure. Nate's a stand-up guy. He's suffered too – you can see it on him. And now it looks like he's found his peace, and here we are, stirring old troubles up again …

'But before the letter, there was this. Look here.' Mr Kaplan brought up a picture on his phone: *The Painter's Studio* by Courbet. It was a picture of the artist at work, watched by a studious gathering of onlookers. 'I got this postcard sent to my office. Anonymous. You know what it said? "Look closer." And the date of my girl's death.'

Oh God. Oh God. 'That's … terrible. Somebody … I don't know … a cruel joke …'

'Sure. That's what we thought, at first. You get struck by a tragedy like this, it brings all sorts of creeps outta the woodwork. We got some of this shit right after it happened. Nutters and psychos, hoping to cash in. But this *and* the letter? Together, that's too much. Together, they're saying the same thing. Art, students. My baby's death. *Look closer.*

'I'm sorry, sweetheart. I've said too much. Rambled on, probably upset you over nothing. But the fact is, I know how Mallory liked you. Looked up to you, even. One time I spoke to her, she said how you'd been looking out for her. Giving advice on your English customs and so on.'

Did he mean the morning in Florence when I'd told Mallory not to be such a pain in the arse? I remembered how she'd thanked me afterwards, as if I had genuinely been trying to help. Her guileless smile. *All that stiff-upper-lip stuff … it's just not in my nature.* At least Mallory had always been true to herself. I was only now beginning to understand the courage that took.

'So if anything more or different about that night occurs to you – anything at all – you'll come to me, come to Harry? You'll talk to us? Please? Total confidence. You have my word.'

Of course, I said numbly. Of course. I promise. Anything I can do. Anything for Mallory.

We walked back up the beach, and by the time we caught up with the others Mr Kaplan had straightened himself out and wiped his face clean. His outburst of grief had been unforced. But I had to keep in mind that his kind of success was most likely built on a certain ruthlessness as well as smarts. I'd put my hand on his upper arm, in a feeble attempt at comfort, and had felt hard muscle, not flab. I knew from Tess Holt that I'd been directly named in Clemency's mysterious letter. Why, then, hadn't Mr Kaplan mentioned that?

'Do we need to talk?' Annabelle murmured, as we waited

to get on the boat. Her fiancé had left at lunchtime, taking a water taxi directly to the airport. From his seat inside the boat, Lorcan – with Suki wrapped around him – was staring over at us, hollow-eyed. In the background, Harry was deep in what looked like a serious conversation with Nate.

I shook my head. 'I think it's fine. He was just reminiscing.'

The only person I wanted to talk to was the third Mrs Holt.

CHAPTER SIX

The long-forecast thunderstorm was finally coming. On the journey back to Venice, the lagoon's waters turned muted and muddy, choppy in the sudden breeze. Bruise-dark clouds were massing, though heat still crawled, damp as a slug, over the skin. Sludgy canals and overflowing bins sweated with competing stinks.

My route from the boat to my apartment was long and convoluted. I was back in the stupor that had descended over my first days in the city. At one point, I found myself in the church of San Zaccaria, standing before the Bellini altarpiece. I hadn't ever consciously believed in an afterlife, let alone a Christian one, but if I were to acknowledge what my idea of heaven was like, I realised it was an improbably literal pilgrimage through the landscapes of Italian Renaissance art. In my imagining, the souls of the saved inhabited a kind of celestial advent calendar, framed in gold, in which one could pass serenely from scene to scene.

In these holy vistas, the instruments of torture were laid quietly by, like toys children have grown out of. Cherubs swam through the sky, birds strutted, fruit hung like jewels and flowers bloomed like stars, all to the accompaniment of an angel-strummed harp or lute. Behind the marble arbours – fragments of temples or palaces transposed to Eden – the hills held their blue silence. Ultramarine: the same shade as the Virgin's robes. Whether the slopes of an imagined Palestine, an Arcadian idyll or even my own soft hills of home, blue was the colour of heaven, and also of loss … I used to imagine how Mallory might be found in such a setting; Clemency too. They would be kneeling in homage a little way apart, like the donors of old, their faces peacefully upturned to the Divine, and anything foolish or vicious or sorrowing smoothed away.

I hadn't really interrogated this vision before and I was ashamed it had only just struck me how inappropriate it was – the Jew in worship of Madonna and Child, the murderess in the company of saints. I had even lit candles for the two of them, recklessly stuffing coins into collection boxes. Even now, I struggled with the implications, and resisted the diagnosis, of such gestures. *Guilt*.

As I left the church, my prissy self-justification to Annabelle came back to haunt me. *Our actions maybe have been morally questionable. But I still believe we acted for the best.*

I'd come to see the fatal entanglement of Annabelle, Clemency, Mallory and Nate as a series of unfortunate events, whose attendant passions were both distasteful and clichéd. This reassessment had seemed a sign of maturation. Back in Venice, however, it was easier to understand how I'd once viewed the affair in a different light. Tragedy here was lauded, magnified and robed in gorgeous hues. So which was Mallory – sacrificial lamb or hapless stooge?

'Hello, Lovelace.'

Oliver.

'Are you *stalking* me now?'

'Don't flatter yourself. I was curious, that's all. You seem more than usually furtive these days.'

The walls of the dank little cul-de-sac seemed to close in. 'What do you want from me? You won. I've done what you asked, I'm out of your and Lorcan's and Annabelle's lives.'

'Moved on to bigger and better things, have you?'

'I've grown up.'

'Mm. And found God, apparently. You were so long in that church I thought you were doing confession.' Dirty chuckle. 'You girls … Any excuse to get down on your knees.'

I rolled my eyes. It was crucial I kept our encounter as breezy as possible. Oliver had always had an unerring instinct for my weak spots. And now that my weak spots had become a matter of crime and punishment, Oliver wasn't just disagreeable. He was dangerous.

'Speaking of confessing one's sins … that Geffen chap told me he's a PI. Which is funny, don't you think? I mean, pretty much all of us had moments when we'd've cheerfully pushed Mal down the stairs.'

So Harry had broken his cover. Presumably, he wanted to see which of us turned green at the news. It was hardly surprising. *Art, students. My baby's death. Look closer.*

Look closer.

I tried to look as amused by all this as Oliver was. I knew that if he saw how much this line of questioning disturbed me, he'd scent blood. Rivulets of sweat were now snaking down my back.

'Imagine if it turns out we've had a murderer in our midst this whole time! Perhaps Geffen's going to gather us all round for a big post-kaddish reveal, Agatha Christie style.' He twinkled up at me. 'I'm surprised he hasn't interviewed you yet, Lovelace. I mean, you were practically the first on the scene.'

'After Lorcan and ... Clemency.' Could he hear the quiver in my voice? *Pull yourself together.* Oliver didn't know about Nate and Annabelle. He didn't know about the mask. It was all one big joke to him.

'Ah, yes, the madwoman in Nate's attic. She wasn't quite right in the head, I gather. That's what happens to women who can't breed.'

'My God. You really are a vile little shit.'

He giggled. It was the giggle that did it. I snapped.

'Mal's death isn't a punchline, you know. And Harry Geffen isn't a joke. He's officially reinvestigating her accident.'

Oliver blinked, and I realised my recklessness had paid off. Far better to go on the offensive. I would shock the smugness out of him. 'Yes. I've been helping him and Mr Kaplan with their enquiries. You see, it turns out that Mallory was probably masked when she fell.'

'What difference does that make?'

'It means her death could have been a case of mistaken identity. Mal could have been mistaken for Annabelle. And that raises the possibility she didn't fall by accident – for one thing, the mask wasn't by her body when we found it.'

Oliver gave a tight little laugh. 'In what possible universe could Mallory get mistaken for Annabelle? And why –?'

'It was dark on those stairs. The two girls were the same height. Same hair – Mal had straightened hers for the party.

She was all wrapped up in a carnival cloak, wearing the same mask that Annabelle had on for most of the night. I'm sure *you* remember. *You* always remember everything about Annabelle.'

He gaped at me.

'Marriage hasn't changed anything, has it? Your limp little dick's still pining for her. It's obvious, and more than a touch sinister.' I shrugged. 'Who knows – maybe *you* pushed Mal down the stairs because you mistook her for the girl who rejected you.'

For the first time in my life, I had got Oliver on the back-foot.

'That's – that's insane … absurd … Annabelle never –' He licked his lips. 'I was with Lorenzo when it happened anyway.'

'Mm-hm. Doing lines of coke together in the dining room. Great alibi, Oliver.' I blew him a kiss as I turned to go. 'Enjoy the rest of the weekend.'

My skin shivered as the first raindrops fell. They were fat and warm, bouncing off the paving stones. Flocks of birds swooped upwards in manic agitation; at ground level, amidst the dash to wind down awnings and pack away tables and chairs, an infectious giddiness took hold. People laughed loudly, drunkenly; the stones echoed to the slap of sandals and running feet. The sky shuddered and groaned. As the streets emptied, a different percussion took over: the creaking rattle and bang of shutters closing or else flapping, untethered, in the wind.

The horizon cracked then pulsed with a deathly violet-blue. Finally I began to run too, sliding and slipping through the gritty puddles in my cheap flip-flops. I had never been in a storm like it: water falling in sheets as the clouds churned black, almost volcanic in their density. I was soaked through in moments. It was epic. Biblical. I should have been frightened, but instead felt a strange kind of exultation. Perhaps my sins were about to be washed away. Perhaps we were all about to be purged in holy fire.

This self-aggrandisement vanished as soon as I was back in the apartment and wrestling to close the shutters. Wind and rain tore at the windows, but it felt claustrophobic rather than cosy to be shut up inside, in dimly lit rooms that were still muggy from weeks of stewing in heat.

I got out my phone and tried to collect my scattered thoughts. My first act was to message Petra:

Hey, strange question, but do you have a contact
number or email or anything for Tess Holt? Just
following something up – will explain later xx

I wasn't hopeful. For one thing, Petra was probably either asleep or tending to the baby. More pertinently, it was highly unlikely she'd have the contact details for her ex-boyfriend's stepmother after all these years. While I waited for her to respond, I tried a search engine, but nothing came up for the right Tess or Tessa or Theresa Holt; she must have taken steps to erase her online profile. However, Petra responded more quickly than I'd expected.

Think T went back to work – has PR company
under her maiden name, Burton. Must be a hobby
job cos it's not like she needs the money!!! Worth
trying there?

I ignored the inevitable flurry of follow-up questions and
typed in 'Tess Burton PR' with immediate success. The website
for her boutique firm even provided a contact email. It was late
on a Saturday evening but, hobby or not, there was always a
chance Tess checked work emails over the weekend.

It seemed evident that Tess must have sent a copy of
Clemency's letter to the Kaplans at around the same time we
bumped into each other outside the tube, just over a year ago.
At the time, she'd given me the impression that she hadn't
shared the letter with Lorcan and Annabelle. I'd assumed this
was because they weren't on speaking terms. Now I wondered
if it was the letter that had precipitated their estrangement.
If it contained some muddled part-confession, hinting at her
stepchildren's role in the cover-up, then Tess might well have
confronted them about it.

But I soon dismissed the idea. It didn't explain why Tess had
held the letter back until two years after Clemency's suicide.
And if the three of us were indeed implicated, then Lorcan and
Annabelle would surely have told me about the letter too – if not
when it first surfaced, then certainly this morning, when we were
speculating as to why Mr Kaplan had reopened the investigation
into Mallory's death. It was clear they were caught off guard, and
deeply shaken, by the turn the weekend had taken.

Seeing the letter for myself was now a matter of urgency. Whatever Clemency had confessed to could not be obviously incriminating, otherwise Tess would presumably have acted on it sooner, and the results would have been much more dramatic. But even if its contents raised more questions than answers, I needed to know exactly where I stood.

Although his stepmother was far from being the common-as-muck bimbo of Lorcan's sneers, she had always been something of an odd fit in the Holt–Harper–Gilani world. It wasn't just her bitten-down nails and hardscrabble past. I remembered Lorcan's baffled retreat whenever his flattering overtures failed to have the usual effect. She wasn't oblivious: she just didn't care.

Tess's motives were the most obscure of all. Right now, however, I had no choice but to trust her.

Dear Tess,

My apologies for contacting you in this way. It's been over a year since we met near Charing Cross, and you told me about Clemency Harper's letter to you, in which I was apparently mentioned. I'm sorry to bring up what must be a very distressing subject. However, the letter has come up again, in rather troubling circumstances, and I'm hoping you might be able to shed a bit of light on the issue.

You may be aware that tomorrow (Sunday) is what would have been Mallory Kaplan's thirtieth birthday and that her family have arranged a memorial weekend for her in Venice. I'm emailing from Venice now. Nearly everyone who attended the art history course with Mallory is here, including Nate Harper and, of course, Lorcan and Annabelle. It's become apparent that the Kaplan family are dissatisfied with the original investigation into Mallory's death, and Mr Kaplan confided that he reached this conclusion after receiving a letter written by Clemency. Although he didn't want to go into details, I assume this is the same letter you discussed with me.

As you know, I was one of those who found Mallory's body; a discovery that haunts me still. My own memories of that night have always been somewhat confused, as well as traumatic, and now I'm beginning to second-guess myself, wondering if there was something I somehow missed, or misunderstood, relating to Mallory's accident. I have promised to help Mr Kaplan however I can and hope very much to be able to set everyone's mind to rest.

However, I feel I need to know exactly what Clemency wrote about the night in question to understand why Mr Kaplan feels the way he does. I don't want to press him further – he's already upset enough as it is – and so I'm writing to ask if there is any chance you could send me a copy of the letter or, if not, provide a little more detail about what Clemency said about Mallory, and indeed myself? I hope this isn't too much of an imposition. Returning to Venice after so many years, and in such circumstances, has stirred up deep emotions for everyone concerned.

With best wishes,

Ada (Howell)

I was far from satisfied with this. The email was dishonest, it was craven and – I feared – unconvincing. However, it had taken me at least twenty overwrought drafts to get to this point, which was at just after two in the morning. My eyes were red, I was rimed with stale sweat and my legs were flecked with dirty puddle-water. The storm was over, leaving a damp chill in its wake. I pressed 'send'.

I went to bed expecting hours of insomnia, but instead lost consciousness almost at once. I dreamed the old dream of running through the garden at Garreg Las and the ha-ha widening into an oily trench into which I fell, helplessly, again and again. And when I was at last able to find refuge in the house, I entered it through a portico of soaring columns and under a mosaic dome, only to find the familiar rooms expanding and contracting before me as the hills pressed against the windows and doors, their shadows blue as loss, their echoes answered by my heart's lurch.

The first thing I did on waking was check my phone. Nothing from Tess. Although it had stopped raining, clouds still lowered overhead, and the streets were ashen; the city's crumbling facades took on a particular griminess when patched with damp. I ran through the puddles in my unsuitable shoes, already panicking I was going to be late.

The Ghetto was, as Mr Kaplan had said, short of obvious sights. The squares were anonymous, the high-rise tenements a little frayed and forlorn. In the central campo, memorial plaques to the Holocaust gleamed on a wall, below the barbed wire left by the Germans. If the Kaplans had hoped for Mallory's memorial to have a celebratory feel, I couldn't help but feel that the weather and the scenery were conspiring against them.

The synagogue, however, was lavishly appointed with marble and carved wood. For this event, at least, I wasn't overdressed. 'Hello,' said Annabelle as I slid, slightly breathlessly, next to Kitty in the pew behind. 'You're wearing your pearls again.'

'Oh.' I looked down, as if surprised to find them there. 'Yes.' Better to fidget with the necklace, I thought, than continually put my hand in my pocket to feel for the vibration of my phone. As a further diversion, I looked around at the congregation, and saw that Rex Whitelaw, the recently retired director of Dilettanti Discoveries, had also flown over for the occasion and was seated next to Yolanda. Sitting at the back, very upright, was Lorenzo's father, Count Monegario himself. I noticed that Nate was looking particularly sombre and wondered again what Harry Geffen might have said to him yesterday on the boat. Harry himself was sitting just behind the family. His eyes as he scanned the gathering were bright and quick, and when he saw me looking, he gave a small nod.

'I think you've made a bit of an impression there,' Kitty whispered in my ear. 'He was asking about you on the boat trip yesterday.'

I smiled weakly.

'He's quite attractive. And so interesting – the investigation work, I mean. He mostly deals with boring business stuff. But he hinted he's worked on darker things too. Murders, even. Isn't that cool?'

God, how I envied her cluelessness.

My only consolation was that Oliver was not present. I overheard Willa tell Annabelle that his mother-in-law had taken a turn for the worse, and so he'd had to leave late last night.

I spent the service trying to fill my head with white noise. I didn't want to listen to the eulogies or be seduced by the unfamiliar melancholy of the Hebrew prayers. The memorial was only bearable if I treated it as another act of theatre, like our tour of the lagoon toy-towns. *I was only trying to help*, I told the God of Israel. *Forgive me*. But there were no graven images, no wise angels to console me.

We straggled out of the synagogue to find the sun close to breaking through the clouds. The air tasted fresh; people's mood visibly brightened. Clothes were shaken out, shoulders straightened, smiles eased. Cooking smells from neighbouring houses were sniffed appreciatively. Lorcan sidled up to me en route to the restaurant. 'What time's your flight?' he muttered. 'Can you come round to the apartment beforehand? Suki will be out at four. Annabelle thinks we need to get our stories extra straight, just in case.'

'Fine,' I said distractedly. My flight wasn't until relatively late that evening. Maybe Tess would have been in contact by then. But first, there was still an interminable lunch to get through.

Food was served alongside more toasts and speeches, including a graceful few words from Rex Whitelaw and – as Lorcan had predicted – assorted tributes of the laughing-through-tears variety. The study-abroad scholarship in Mallory's name was formally announced; we toasted this and her birthday with champagne. I applauded, smiled and sighed on cue, all the while trying to keep my checks on the phone as discreet as possible.

There was only one moment where I came close to losing it. Heather, Mallory's school friend, got up to say her piece. She told us that she and Mallory used to swap corny jokes. When Mallory went on the course, Heather had texted her jokes with an Italian theme.

'I never got the chance to pass this one on to Mallory,' she said. 'But I know she would have laughed and laughed:

'What do you call a fake noodle?

'An impasta.'

People tittered obligingly. I did too. Mallory had a good laugh, I remembered. Her teeth were very white and straight – American teeth, the only glamorous thing about her – and when she was laughing, she'd throw her head back, mouth open wide, her delight loud and generous. I felt the shock of tears. The impulse to weep was so violent, I thought I'd have to leave the table. But I scrubbed at my eyes and the moment passed.

My jaw ached from the effort not to grit my teeth. The champagne burned in my throat. My fingers left clammy smudges on the glass. The constant refrain running through my head was *I want to go home, I want to go home, I want to go home*. But home didn't mean what I wanted it to. It meant the flat-share in Streatham. The internet dates I had no interest in pursuing. The work I trudged through so dutifully.

It meant ordinary life, where things were difficult and familiar, and always perilously close to disappointment.

Though disappointment was the least of my worries.

Perverting the course of justice. Giving a false sworn statement. Tampering with evidence.

How could I have been so stupid? A stupid, reckless, self-sabotaging fool …

At the final goodbye-gauntlet, Mr Kaplan held on to my hand an unnervingly long time. 'We'll keep in touch, won't we?' With Harry smiling blandly behind him, this felt as much a threat as an invitation.

They have nothing, I told myself. No witness. No evidence. No motive. Nothing to prove a crime even took place.

Or did they?

What's in that fucking letter, Clemency?

It came to me that I didn't want to spend my last hour in Venice locked up with Annabelle and Lorcan, stewing over our sins. Let it wait until London and after I'd heard from Tess. I hurried after Lorcan to tell him I'd misjudged my departure time and that I couldn't meet them at his apartment after all. But it was Nate, not Lorcan, who turned his tall back, and I realised that Lorcan, Suki and Annabelle had already gone. Fatalistically, I decided I might as well keep our appointment. For what else was there to do? Mope in front of more altarpieces?

Then my phone buzzed. I had received an email with an attachment from Tess Burton.

CHAPTER SEVEN

Hi Ada

So here we are again. At some subconscious level, I suppose I've been expecting to hear from you one way or another, ever since that day on the Strand. As requested, I'm attaching a scan of the sections of Clemency's letter that I sent to the Kaplans. There's more, but since the additional material isn't relevant to you or the concerns you raise, I'd prefer to keep it confidential. (I guess I still feel protective of C, even after all this time.)

I told Mallory's family that the letter had only just come to light. It's possible I have made a bad situation worse with no good reason. C was very unwell when she wrote to me. All the same, I've come to regret not paying closer attention to what she was trying to say.

I don't know if Clemency was right about what you did or didn't see. But you were there that night, after all. 'Make of that what you will.'

T

The attached document was a scan of a photocopy. I found a quiet corte and sat down on the steps of a wellhead to scroll through it.

The sections of content to either side of the relevant paragraphs had been blacked out. Although it was hard to read on a phone, the tight cursive handwriting was surprisingly neat. It did not suggest the frantic scribblings of a lunatic.

Be kind to yourself, that's what everyone keeps saying. Be kind.

I'm not to blame, they assure me. There's nothing I could have done – or do – differently. It's not my fault my poor body keeps cannibalising itself and spitting out dead babies like so many gobbets of rank meat.

Don't blame yourself. That's what Nate had the fucking nerve to say, after the tenth one, the one in Rome. We were stuck in that hospital waiting room for hours, past midnight and beyond, him holding my hand in his guilty sweating paw. He confessed everything, in the end. Sobbed like the babies we never had.

And here's the thing: I really *don't* blame myself. I'm innocent, I get it. Plenty of blame to go round elsewhere: God, fate, luck, biology ... the limits of medical science. Yet people still insist it's Definitely Not My Fault. Which, let's be honest, is enough to make anyone paranoid. Just like they kept telling me how it was an accident, a tragic mistake, and that other child – the American girl – somebody else's poor dead baby – all splayed out and broken at the foot of the stairs ... not my fault either, they told me. Well, no. Obviously not. Doesn't mean I didn't feel the echo of violence, just like I could still feel the crusted blood drying between my legs.

Oh, they did a number on me, all right.

They thought – everyone thinks – that all my dead babies have rotted my brain, same as my womb. It's true I can't be sure of what I heard or saw. Still, I sensed the wrongness of it, like hate. And the gold cat, grinning in the shadows.

The trouble was, everyone was wearing a mask that night. But not me and not the dead child, who was never a real cat anyway, not like that slut with the tail and the claws. (Of course she was there. Of course he was with her. Make of that what you will. I'd tell you to ask the other one, Ada, about it, but she's the worst kind of bystander. One of those people who watches and waits, waits and watches, yet sees nothing at all.)

What I'm trying to say, I suppose, is that somehow they painted us over. Me and the dead girl. It was just like Nate said. The <u>pentimento</u>. And I understand, because I wanted to paint over me too. Cover up the broken lines, the wrong turns, the mistaken flesh. After Italy, it took a long time for me to be ready to strip the layers away.

I didn't want to admit that the first draft is sometimes the truest. Now it's too late. We're all painted in.

So it wasn't a confession. Quite the contrary, in fact.

My vision spotted as I read the letter for a second time, like it does just before you're going to black out. On the first reading,

I had raced through it so quickly I barely took in the words. On the third, I put the phone down and began to shudder. The world dissolved in a sickly, streaky blur.

Then my phone pinged again. Message from Lorcan. *Suki out. Are you on your way?*

I got to my feet, slowly and carefully. I waited for the ground to stop tilting. I smoothed down my hair. I put Lorcan's address into Google Maps and began to walk.

Venice was wearing her carnival robes. Now that the heat haze was gone, colour had returned to the city. Trees had regained a tawny autumnal shiver; almost before my eyes, the drab shades of stucco deepened to ochre and terracotta and peach. Here was a wince-bright glimpse of silver water; there, a sea-blue shadow cast by a bone-white wall. Glancing towards St Mark's Basin, I saw the prow of a giant cruise ship nudging into view. I wished it really was the monstrous alien space craft it resembled, and that it would suck the city's fragile jumble of domes and palaces and bell-towers up into its pristine maw, before spitting us out in one compact, ashy pellet. Dust to dust.

The apartment rented by Lorcan and Suki was a Renaissance suite overlooking the Grand Canal, just south of the Rialto. My hand hovered over the buzzer.

I looked at Tess's email again. She had replied from her work account; there was a mobile number as part of her e-signature. Before I could think better of it, I made the call.

She answered almost at once. 'I knew it would be you.'

'I just want to know one more thing,' I said. My voice was remarkably calm. 'You waited two years to share the letter. What changed?'

No answer, just a soft sort of click. Like somebody swallowing, hard.

'It's evident Clemency was losing her mind. She herself says she can't be sure of what, if anything, she heard and saw of Mallory's death. So what made you decide this was something the Kaplans should see?'

The pause was so long I thought Tess might have put the phone down and walked away. In the background, I heard a child calling. When she did eventually speak, she sounded immensely tired.

'Clemency did make one specific accusation, though it wasn't connected to Mallory's death. It was – well, it seemed very much part of the craziness. The vitriol. I did my best to put her ... allegation ... out of my mind. But then, a year or so ago, I discovered the allegation was true. And that changed things, because if Clemency was right about *that*, then it's possible she was right about other things. "The wrongness, like hate ..."' A ragged sigh. 'It's the wrongness I keep coming back to. In the end, I felt the Kaplans deserved to know.'

There was another long period of silence. 'I'm still not sure I did the right thing. In fact, I regret it more often than not.' Her voice was very soft. 'I hope digging this up isn't going to be something you'll regret too.'

The beamed entrance hall had traces of original frescos and a sweeping stone staircase that rose up two levels to the *piano nobile*.

I walked into a room spun from the purest shimmer. Pale silk brocade walls flecked with gold threads; swirling marble and plaster in ice-cream shades. Crystal chandeliers. Gilt mirrors. Terrazzo floors. And, at the end of the room, glazed doors opening onto a balcony over the Grand Canal. The irony of this did not escape me: here was what the Palazzo Monegario's theatrics had tried to conjure.

Annabelle and Lorcan were waiting for me in the middle of it.

The furnishings were mostly contemporary, in hushed neutral tones. Lorcan was slumped on one of the few antiques, a Regency sofa upholstered in primrose chinoiserie. Annabelle stood behind him, one hand resting on the frame. It had the same shining darkness as her hair. She was wearing a man's white shirt, sleeves pushed up and collar askew, and deceptively sloppy-looking jeans. Lorcan was similarly dressed but more authentically dishevelled.

'Quite some place you've got here,' I said.

'Yeah.' (*Yuh.*) Lorcan cleared his throat. 'It's Suki's first visit to Venice. Thought I'd push the boat out.'

I nodded. Then I sat down on a chair opposite them, placing my bag on the floor. It was impossible not to think of that earlier conference, ten years before. The cooling tea and murmured condolences. Grey faces in the grey dawn. I had thought myself so clever then. The *deus ex machina* descending from on high.

'So I found out why the Kaplans have started looking into Mallory's death. Clemency wrote a letter.'

Lorcan leaned forward. 'A confession?'

'No.' I paused: a cheap effect, admittedly. 'More of a muddled sort of accusation.'

'From beyond the grave? How extraordinary.' Annabelle's tone was mild.

'It was originally sent to your stepmother – ex-stepmother. Just before Clemency's suicide. Tess kept hold of it for some years, but then decided it contained material she felt others should see.'

I hesitated. I had intended to tell them about the postcard too, but perhaps at this point it would only muddy the waters. That could be dealt with later, if need be.

Annabelle had seen me hesitate. 'Is there something else?'

'Believe me, this is plenty.'

'Well, I'm all agog. By the way, I don't suppose you've got any gum?' Lightly and brightly, Annabelle walked over and reached into my handbag, picking up my phone almost before I'd registered she was there. 'Oh, Ada,' she said, smiling. 'Really. Will I have to check you for a wire, too?'

She turned off the recording feature and placed the phone on a side-table between us.

'Was this Harry Geffen's idea?'

I shook my head. My cheeks were hot. Despite myself, despite everything, I felt horribly embarrassed.

'Either way, if you're looking for leverage, I'm afraid you're going to be disappointed,' Annabelle said in the same kindly tones. 'Because the three of us are in this together. You made sure of that yourself. Right from the start.'

'I know. And now I also know that I made a terrible mistake.'

I was choked, again, by the humiliation of Clemency's words:

the worst kind of bystander. One of those people who watches and waits, waits and watches, yet sees nothing at all.

Yes, I'd been blind. Perhaps wilfully so. But of course my culpability ran much deeper than that. Clemency was wrong: I was never just a bystander. I was an accomplice. An accomplice to a crime I had entirely failed to recognise.

All this time, I'd thought Mallory was the stooge. The stand-in. Mallory, who I didn't think was interesting or important enough to be centre stage in anyone's drama, not even her own. Mallory, who had been the intended victim all along.

I'd sensed the aftershock of violence in the air, just as Clemency had. Clemency, who must have arrived on the scene only moments before me but had inferred the real wrongness at its heart.

Annabelle resettled herself on the sofa next to Lorcan. 'I presume all this drama is because you've seen the letter for yourself and have come to some colourful conclusions.'

'Tess sent me a copy, yes.'

'Well, we all know that if Clemency had written anything remotely incriminating, the Kaplans wouldn't be pussyfooting around with free pizza and boat trips. Nor would our step-mama have kept the goods in her knicker drawer for all this time. Let's face it: Clemency was bona fide cuckoo. I have no idea of what the poor woman chose to put in her assorted suicide notes, but even if she was alive, she'd be the least credible witness one could imagine.'

'That might be true. But she certainly had a way with words.' I turned to Lorcan. 'Aren't you going to say anything?'

'I was upstairs with the others,' he muttered. 'You know that. I only saw the body after Clemency phoned me.'

'Yeah, it never really came to alibis, did it?'

'Why should it?' said Annabelle, eyebrows arched. 'Mallory's fall appeared to be a simple accident. As you were so very keen to establish.'

'Which was lucky for you. I mean, if I'd come out to that courtyard just a few minutes earlier–'

'Lucky for *you*, actually. The conclusions you leapt to allowed you to leech off us for years.'

Her sudden viciousness took me by surprise. 'I–'

'Please,' she scoffed. 'You were absolutely *thrilled* to have found a way to insinuate yourself into our lives. Mallory's death was the golden opportunity you'd been looking for. You've been holding it over our heads ever since.'

'I don't – I never – I never asked for anything. That is, I never presumed …' How could I? I'd been the one to mastermind the cover-up, or so I'd thought. All I'd wanted was an acknowledgement of my importance in their lives. 'How can you–?'

'You were always there. Hovering. Always watching. Always *waiting*.' I flinched, despite myself. Annabelle had unwittingly echoed Clemency. 'Waiting for us to show how grateful we were.'

'I thought … I thought we were friends …' The words came out a shamed whisper. In that moment I hated myself even more than I hated her.

'We had some good times.' But Lorcan didn't meet my eye.

'We humoured you,' said Annabelle remorselessly. 'The irony is, you thought you were doing our family this great favour, when

308

all you did was needlessly complicate a very simple scenario. By rushing to assume Clemency's guilt, you created a pointless layer of intrigue that very nearly sent everything off the rails. God. As far as useful idiots go, you weren't even useful.'

'Ani. Don't be like that. It wasn't Ada's fault.'

Good cop, bad cop. I felt cornered, and perilously close to tears. How had this happened? I was supposed to be holding all the cards.

Annabelle got up abruptly and rubbed her arms. Her manner softened. 'No. I know that, really.' She began to pace about; thoughtfully, rather than in agitation. 'I have lived with this for a very long time, Ada, but it doesn't get easier.' Her mouth quirked. 'Because I'm not a psychopath, you know. This isn't something I've just … shrugged off. I think about that night every day. I know I did a wicked, horrible thing and – not that it makes any difference – I will always be sorry for it. For poor Mallory.'

Her acknowledgement of guilt was so matter-of-fact that at first I thought I'd heard her wrong. Until that moment, I hadn't been sure whether it was Annabelle or her brother who gave the fatal push.

'Ani,' said Lorcan again, more unhappily. 'Don't.'

Ani. Lorcan nearly always used her full name and nobody else, as far as I knew, employed the diminutive. It was disorientating to hear it now, especially as an entreaty.

'Please, Ani … We don't need to hear this.'

'Oh, but Ada certainly does. Though you've already worked most of it out, haven't you, Ada?'

I'd guessed from Clemency's letter and Tess's reticence, and I'd had my first inkling when I went up to Lorcan, after the memorial, only to see Nate turn around instead. The fatal misidentification had never been Mallory for Annabelle. It had been Lorcan for Nate.

Yet in the moment, my own discomfit was excruciating. I almost felt as if it was me who had been caught out.

But Annabelle's eyes were clear, her voice steady. 'When I think back to the girl I was at nineteen … I suppose plenty of people are a bit of a mess at that age. But I … I was this *wild animal*. Reeking with rage and self-loathing and bewilderment.' Another quirk of the mouth. 'Honestly, fucking my brother was only the half of it.'

Before my eyes, Lorcan flushed all over: from below the open neck of his shirt to the roots of his hair.

'It's not as uncommon as you'd like to think for siblings in our situation,' Annabelle continued. 'There's even a clinical acronym for it: GSA. Genetic Sexual Attraction. You could blame our parents for keeping us apart for so many years. When families live closely together, you see, they become desensitised to each other as sexual prospects.' She minutely adjusted the positioning of a vase. 'I've come to believe it's unhelpful to make too much of these things. Lorcan and I are only half-blood. It's not as if we ever *procreated*. So where was the actual harm?'

'Mallory,' I said creakily. 'Mallory was the harm.'

'Yes,' she conceded. 'That's true.'

'Mallory thought she saw you and Nate all over each other in the street in Rome. It was an easy mistake to make.' Nate and Lorcan were the same build and, at that time, had the same colouring. They had even had the same line in foxed shirts and tweedy jackets. 'Especially as you were sleeping with Nate too.'

More adjustment of the vase. Her concentration on it appeared to be total. 'I – I persuaded myself that Nate was the distraction I needed. A way out.'

'And to hell with his wife?' My voice was stronger now; I was starting to regain the initiative. But I still had to sit on my hands to disguise their trembling.

She put the vase down with a snap. 'I feel plenty of remorse for that period of my life, believe me. But the state of Nate's marriage was ultimately his responsibility, not mine.'

'That's how I finally realised you weren't with Nate that night, by the way. Clemency and Nate were in the hospital, because of her miscarriage. She said in her letter that they were stuck in a waiting room until midnight. He confessed the affair. So Nate couldn't have been the man Mallory saw you kissing ... But Mallory didn't know that. So why did she – why did she have to die?'

Annabelle looked away. 'Because I panicked.' Briefly, her face convulsed. 'That's the truth. All evening, I could see Mal was working up her courage for "a quiet word". Then I spied her talking to Clemency. I had no idea what Clemency was saying – it could have been about her hospital visit, for all I knew. Which, as you just pointed out, was effectively Nate's alibi for the kiss.'

Here was the real horror. Maybe, just maybe, I could have prevented all of this. I could have told Mallory to forget about what she'd seen, to have a drink and a dance and be happy for the night. Mallory would have listened to me. She had looked up to me, her parents said so. I could have offered reassurance, released her from her self-imposed moral obligations. Instead, I gave in to my worst impulses. I sent her off to Annabelle because I wanted to cause trouble.

But sending Mallory to Annabelle brought her another step closer towards the top of those stairs.

'In the moment,' Annabelle was saying, 'it seemed it would take so little for some version of the truth to get out. And I couldn't *bear* it. For people to think – to think us disgusting. Pitiful.' She shivered and began rubbing her arms again. 'Because that's how I thought of myself, back then. An overwhelming terror took hold of me. And Mallory – all it took was one impulsive shove. So childish, really. A playground push.'

I wondered about this. Annabelle must have told Mallory that, yes, she'd talk. Out on the stairs in the deserted courtyard. How spontaneous was any of it, really? I remembered how Annabelle had looked when she walked towards the body: her skin almost translucent, eyes cavernous.

'But I found Lorcan with the body. Not you.' I shook my head. 'I don't understand why you didn't just go for help as soon as you'd pushed her. It would've been so simple for you to tell everyone you were there when Mallory tripped.'

And how had Annabelle even got out of the courtyard? She couldn't have been hiding in the colonnade the whole time I was down there with Lorcan and Clemency: Lorenzo and I had met her in the lobby.

'Simple and sensible is easier said than done, in the seconds after you've committed murder,' said Annabelle crisply. 'I fully admit I wasn't thinking straight. I was on the phone to Lorcan when I heard Clemency screaming my name from inside. Given the state she was in, how much she hated me … my first instinct was to get out of sight.'

'So where did you go? Through the water gate?'

Despite everything, Lorcan gave a snort of laughter.

'No, Ada,' Annabelle said, with heavy patience. 'Not the canal. The door to the calle.'

That little door under the colonnade, the one which was used to put out the rubbish. I was embarrassed I'd forgotten about it. Annabelle must have slipped out to the alley and rejoined the party from the other entrance to the palazzo.

'So what did Clemency see?'

'You tell me. You're the one who read her letter.'

A gold cat, grinning in the shadows.

She'd spied the mask, before I stole it. And what else could she have witnessed? The final click of a door pulled shut. The crinkle of a collapsing rubbish-bag. A gasp of ragged breath. Or maybe it was no more than a hunch. We'd never know.

'Poor old Clem,' said Lorcan sadly. 'We were all so very emphatic, weren't we? Telling her over and over again what an unfortunate accident it had been.'

Clemency had been half-mad with grief and rage, never mind the grappa. *Baby … poor baby… poor baby girl.* She'd wept for Mallory while our eyes stayed dry. Lorcan had travelled with her in the ambulance to the hospital and stayed by her bedside all night. Whatever muddled ideas or uncertainties she had, Lorcan must have smoothed them away. Painted them over, as she said in her letter.

Yet something had come through the varnish, all the same. The wrongness, the hate.

'What's funny,' said Annabelle, quite easy now, 'is that the first thing Clemency did when she saw the body was to call Lorcan to say I was dead. He was already on his way down, of course. You got there a couple of minutes afterwards.' She shrugged. 'That was our only really bad luck in the evening. God.' She actually laughed. 'If it had been *anyone* else ...'

Lorcan gave a cracked little laugh. 'When you asked to meet with us the next morning, we were sure you had figured it out.'

Instead, I'd handed them an alternate cover story, with Clemency as the fall guy. I'd practically fed them their lines in my eagerness to have my theory proved right and my cunning applauded. I'd painted over Mallory too. Layer after layer after layer.

'But *you* were innocent,' I said to Lorcan. 'At least at first. Weren't you repulsed when you found out what your sister had done?'

'It was still a mistake,' he mumbled. 'Ani didn't mean to do it. What did you expect me to do? Turn her in?'

'Or maybe you were just grateful,' I continued, as if he hadn't spoken. 'Annabelle wasn't only taking steps to protect your reputations. She was protecting your inheritance. If your father had got wind of your dirty little secret, he'd have cut you off, double-quick. After all, he had a new son and heir on the way.'

Now Annabelle's lip curled. 'Seriously? You think this was about *money*?'

'I can't believe it was entirely irrelevant. Yes, you talk about shame and disgust and so on, but you said yourself you've come

314

to the conclusion that a spot of incest isn't so bad, in the grand scheme of things. I mean, even after Mallory was killed to protect your relationship, neither of you put a stop to it.' I was thinking back to Oliver's engagement party and nearly walking in on Lorcan in bed with some girl. I was now certain it had been Annabelle. Then there were the parts of Clemency's letter Tess didn't want to show me, and the 'wild' accusation she referred to that turned out to be true. 'You don't seem to have been especially careful not to get caught. I think Clemency guessed what you were up to, and I'm pretty sure your stepmother found out too. What happened? Did she also interrupt you *in flagrante*?'

Lorcan gave a small bleak smile. 'I did tell you we were monsters.'

'Yeah, well,' I said, and I was unable to hide my bitterness, 'you told me a lot of things.'

To manipulate and deflect, mostly. But there'd been some truth in there too. *I do love her, you know*, Lorcan had confessed to me, that drunken night soon after Clemency's suicide. *Truly. Madly. Ridiculously. All of that. I can't help myself, I suppose.* I'd thought he was talking about Petra. But it had never been about Petra. She was just another stand-in, another stooge. And so was Suki, out cluelessly shopping in the Salizada San Moisè.

And Annabelle? Annabelle had moved on. I'd seen how she had gazed up at Peter Masterton and how she held herself together now. I sensed it took effort, certainly; that for all these years she had probably been operating under a considerable level of strain. But it was Lorcan – crumpled, hunched, greenish where he'd earlier been red – who looked to be broken.

In truth, however, I didn't feel disgust at the idea of Annabelle and Lorcan together. I felt a certain squeamishness, but there was an underlying frisson, too. Then I saw Annabelle looking at me and realised she knew this, and was amused.

'Well, I think we've indulged your curiosity long enough,' she said. 'I can't imagine there's anything further to say. However unfortunate or offensive you might find the business, there's nothing that can be changed ... nothing that can be helped. I've had to come to terms with this. You should too.'

CHAPTER EIGHT

I stared at Annabelle. She was so perfectly a part of the room, the understated counterpoint to its silks and swirls and shimmer. Yet at that moment, she seemed like a mirage. A trick of light and dark. As if I could rub my eyes, and she'd vanish.

'You can't be serious,' I said. 'You can't expect me to just forget about this.'

'You think you're going to bring about some kind of *reckoning*? Please. It's obvious Clemency's letter is the ultimate red herring. Nobody has any proof of anything.'

'But Mr Kaplan – the whole family – they deserve to know. I'll tell them,' I said wildly. 'I'll tell them the truth and confess my part in it.'

'That would be unwise. It was your doing as much as anyone's that Mallory's death was dismissed as an accident. You obstructed the course of justice. You destroyed evidence and gave a false statement. These are serious crimes and you'd be held to account for them. First by the Kaplans, then by the authorities. Let's face it, you're hardly a more credible witness than Clemency. A proven liar … and a plagiarist.'

So Oliver had tattled. Well, good for him.

'I'll take the risk.' This could be my penance for everything. For sending Mallory to Annabelle at the party. For telling

Clemency about the gold cat mask. For putting the postcard of *The Birthday* into Nate's hands. All my meddling and my malice and my arrogance … I would pay for it, I would suffer and then I would be free. 'I'd get them to understand. Then the Kaplans could get the original investigation reopened–'

'Even in Italy, something as flimsy as this would never get to trial.'

I drew a shaky breath. 'All right. Maybe you're right. But maybe that doesn't even need to happen. Because I know Mr Kaplan would believe me. He'd believe Tess. Both of them already think something shady was going on. And Kaplan's influential and ruthless and rich – as rich as you two, or very nearly. He wouldn't let this rest. He'd pursue a civil action. He'd send anonymous smears to the press. He'd throw private investigators at you and everyone in your lives. He'd never, *ever* let this drop.'

Lorcan made a small choking sound. It spurred me.

'Now, you could say he was mad, bad, whatever. You could threaten to sue for defamation – maybe you'd be successful. But the stink would still follow you around, always. People would smell it. People would *wonder*.' I looked at Lorcan. 'You plan to go into politics?' Then at Annabelle. 'You want to be in a *Vanity Fair* power couple? Kaplan would fuck that up. He'd fuck *you* up. And I'd help him do it.'

It was *their* turn to be outplayed, *their* turn to be humiliated. All this time, they'd been sneering at me behind my back. Despising and resenting me for stumbling into the grease-slick of their crimes. Not any more. My fury was virtuous and white hot in my veins.

At long last, my words had their desired effect. Annabelle was looking at me as calmly as before, but this time I could see the tension behind it. The steadiness of her gaze was being held up with tightened muscles, like a weight.

'You think exposing us would bring the Kaplans closure.' She was striving for archness; instead, her voice sounded thin and stretched. 'You think it would heal their pain. Bring peace to their family. Reconcile them to their loss. Do you honestly believe the truth would set them free?'

'I'd like to find out.'

Annabelle made a small stifled sound, halfway between a laugh and a sob. She silenced herself by pressing two fingers against her mouth.

Lorcan looked up. Underneath its glaze of damp, his face looked all bones. 'So who are you doing this for, Ada? For Mallory?'

'Mal–'

He shook his head. 'You *despised* her. You did everything you could to avoid her company. You barely knew anything about her.'

'That was another of my mistakes.'

And just for a moment, Mallory was there, standing before me, as she had in the maze in the Villa Pisani all those years before. *Ada – hey, Ada. Wait up.* Smiling, hopeful, sweat stained.

And I had turned my back and run from her, deeper into the maze.

Grief poured through me like water.

'No,' Annabelle said. 'No. I don't believe it. Mallory is not your

319

motivation. I think you're mostly doing this for yourself. You feel betrayed, and you want the guilty to suffer.' Her voice was hoarse. I could see the too-rapid rise and fall of her chest; she had to pause before going on. 'Which is more than fair. I know I don't deserve to be truly happy or free. And I'm not, if that makes you feel any better. But that doesn't mean I intend to let one stupid, selfish act of madness, committed when I was nineteen, destroy the rest of my life and drag my brother down with me.'

'That shouldn't be up to you.'

'All right. All right.' Annabelle closed her eyes. At first it felt like a reprieve, though there was nothing peaceful about the silence. 'Your godmother, Delilah Grant, died recently,' she finally said. 'Did she leave you anything in her will?'

'I – uh – some – some personal items.' And a couple of thousand pounds. It was how I'd been able to afford my Venetian holiday. How the hell did they know about Delilah? 'I don't see what this has got to do with anything.'

'It means,' Lorcan mumbled, staring down at the floor, 'that if you suddenly came into a large sum of money, there'd be a plausible explanation for it.'

I laughed incredulously. 'Oh no. No, no, no, no, no, *no*.'

'Yes,' said Annabelle. She was almost herself again. Almost. 'If you're honest with yourself, you'll admit your quest for justice can't possibly end well, for anyone. There will only be more ugliness, more confusion and pain. If there was any way I could make up to Mallory's family for what I did, then I would have already done it. Believe me. However, I – or rather we – could still make things up to you.'

'By *buying me off?*' Like I was the hired help in need of a sweetener to incentivise loyalty. Or some law-enforcement grunt getting paid to look the other way.

Lorcan lifted his head up from his hands. He looked, and sounded, exhausted. 'What do you want, Ada?'

'It's not about what I want. It's about what Mallory, and her family–'

'It's always been about what you wanted,' Annabelle retorted. 'A way in. That's all Lorcan and I ever meant to you. Right from the start.'

'No,' said Lorcan. 'That's not quite right. Ada always wanted a way *back*.'

I closed my eyes. I was immensely tired too.

'A way back home.'

I don't even know which one of them said it.

When I opened my eyes again, they were both looking at me, composure restored. They were as grave yet serene as a pair of saints.

'Your father's family home is for sale,' said Annabelle. 'It's been on the market for over two years. A deal recently fell through; we spoke to the agent yesterday evening. The current owner is very anxious to sell and would accept a reasonable offer.' She gave one of her small, cool smiles. 'And, really, the cost is extraordinarily reasonable. About the same as a nice two-bed flat in London's Zone Two. You'd probably need a maintenance fund to cover basic running costs and living expenses, mind you. Large houses can be money pits – especially on a publishing salary.'

I got up from my seat. I was shaking all over. So this was their

321

trump card. How long had they been holding it in reserve? Had they, in fact, always been preparing for this moment?

Had I, too?

'I don't want to hear any more.'

But Annabelle continued – gently, remorselessly. 'Setting up a trust would be the obvious solution. A good financial advisor and lawyer could work something out. There hasn't been time to research all the details, admittedly. But I imagine the most straightforward arrangement would be to secure the necessary paperwork – a legal guarantee of some kind – from you in return.'

Now it was my turn to make a small choking sound.

'Do you really want to go back to the drab little life you've made? Denying your true self isn't a virtue. You know what you're capable of, with the right help. Oliver tripped you up once but he won't do so again. I can guarantee it. Because this time will be different. There will finally be no more lies between us.'

She was so dark and shining. So damn sure of herself. And yet, I'd seen her tremble. I could make her bleed.

'There's nothing you can do for Mal,' said Lorcan, very quietly. 'Nothing you can do for her family, or for Clemency either. It's too late. It's too late for me, and it's too late for Ani; we can't atone for any of this or ever leave it behind. But it's not too late for you. The final favour ... If there has to be someone who wins, somebody who walks away from the whole miserable mess towards something better, why shouldn't it be you?'

He fell silent. Both he and Annabelle were silent, and still.

They should be punished. All their lives, they'd been untouchable. Now they must face their reckoning – for the evil they had done to Mallory and their sins against Clemency too. And for everything they had done to me. For manipulating me. For lying to me. For failing to love me, when I had loved them. Whatever the price, it was worth paying.

But I shouldn't ever have needed them. I shouldn't ever have had to work for their favour. I had been exiled, and from that point on my decisions had been corrupted. I could lay all blame elsewhere, so that my homecoming would be more than a return. It would be my restoration. Whatever the price, it was worth paying.

Annabelle said this was my chance to be my true self.

Which choice would lead me there?

For the first time in what felt like a long while I became aware of sounds from the outside world: engines revving, water churning, throaty laughs and bellows … the clang of bells. The soaring space of the room was closing in on me. I needed air.

I groped my way out; not to the stairs, but through the glazed doors at the end of the *salone*, overlooking the Grand Canal.

On this brink, there was only more dazzle.

I heard more bells. I breathed in deeply; I looked for my answer.

There was nothing but light's cruel smattered wink on water, everywhere.

EPILOGUE

Smoke furled and heat rippled. It was a glorious day.

The bonfire I was making was purely symbolic. I suppose that's why I've always been attracted to Catholicism – it's the sense of ritual. As well as the art, of course. And these days, with so many online galleries offering print on demand, you can order any image you want at the click of a button.

Even though they were only postcards, I felt an iconoclast's thrill at setting fire to art.

The Birthday

Lilith

The Falsehood

The Ship of Fools

The Painter's Studio

I still had mixed feelings about the last one. Tipping off Mr Kaplan had been unconscionably reckless. At the time, all I'd wanted was a few discreet enquiries to be made, just enough to rattle Lorcan and Annabelle. Make 'em sweat. That was why I'd sent them the postcards in the first place – not so much to discredit Oliver, but to bind the three of us even closer. The Liar, the Fool and the Slut.

It's true I'd underestimated the gravity of my own crimes. But with Clemency dead, I thought we were safe, however much covert scrutiny we'd be under. I could never have guessed what Clemency's letter contained or how high the stakes really were. Playing the *deus ex machina* is an unpredictable game.

As it happens, that's the opening line of the novel I'm working on. A touch grandiloquent, perhaps ... but I like to think it would make Daddy smile. Even though I don't have to worry about Oliver any more, I've mostly set Anthony Howell's notes aside. I suppose you could say that I've found my voice.

The Triumph of Death ... *Rape of Proserpina* ... *Pietà* ... Gods and goddesses. Angels and demons. The saved and the damned. More beauty, twisting in the flame.

The house's sun-baked walls are warm against my back; a yellow rose foams by the entrance gates. They're open, ready for the arrival of my friends.

Art is a lie that leads us to the truth. So said Picasso. So say I.

And now truth and lies are smoke and ashes. Beyond all, my hills hold their blue silence.

Acknowledgements

In the course of writing a book about privilege, I've called in a lot of favours of my own. My greatest debt is to Sue Armstrong at C&W, who understood the book I was trying to write even better than myself. I'd like to thank her, along with the talented Sarah Hodgson and the team at Corvus, for doing so much to set Ada on the right (wrong) path.

Thank you to my early readers, especially Julia Churchill and Catherine Cooper, for their invaluable feedback, to Emma Dunne for her meticulous copy-editing, and to Christopher Wilkins and Dan Lyndon-Cohen for allowing me to pick their brains. And to Rosella Mamoli Zorzi and Marino Zorzi, who will – I hope – forgive me for finding murderous inspiration in the Merati.

And, lastly, Ali. Thank you for giving me the space and time to write, along with so much else.

Read on for an exclusive early extract from Laura Vaughan's brilliant, suspenseful new novel

Let's Pretend

PART ONE

CHAPTER ONE

'You know what I blame?' growled Nina. 'Me-sodding-Too. All the men are running scared. Even the shameless ones. I mean, it's all very well for the A-listers to come over all snooty about the casting couch. *They* can afford it.'

I was used to Nina mouthing off after failed auditions, so I just laughed and passed her the joint.

Nina and I first met at the age of ten, at a call-back for a yogurt commercial that neither of us got. Twenty-two years later and we're still bonding over our mutual rejections.

'Christ – if only I'd known my casting-couch power peaked at sixteen. In those days, they'd be happy with just a handsie, too.'

'Ew.'

'You're just jealous cos none of the dirty old men wanted *you*. They tagged you for an uptight little madam, and they were right.'

I blew her a kiss. It's never a good idea to rise to Nina's baits. Even as a kid, Nina was the edgy one, accessorising her own quirky niche with big nerd glasses and a shit-eating grin. I've never known how seriously I should take her tales of juvenile debauchery – then or now. But the Momager, for all her faults, kept me on a tight leash. Nina's mum is a drunk.

3

This is one of the many reasons the Momager's never approved of our friendship. 'Shop-soiled' was how she once described Nina, when she was still a teen. Nina didn't seem to bother with puberty, mind you, going straight from quirky-cute to *va-va-voom*. On her good days, she has a louche, jolie-laide sexiness that makes other girls seem insipid. I'm sometimes surprised it hasn't served her better.

The fact is, Nina Gill's spot on the 'Where Are They Now?' rankings is several places below mine. She gets by on the back of her residuals, supplemented by experimental theatre gigs and the occasional art-house movie, usually involving nudity.

'You and me should do a porno,' she said another time. 'We'd clean up. Little Miss Snowflake and the Disney Slut.' And later, 'We're two sides of the same fucked-up coin, baby.'

There are two things you should know about me. One is that I was briefly famous when I was four. The other is that I had a nose job when I was fifteen. These things are not, of course, unrelated.

To a great many people, Lily Thane is synonymous with Little Lucie, the winsome orphan who made a wish on a snowflake. ('All I want for Christmas is a daddy of my own!') Nobody expected *Snow Angels* to become a hit. It was a low-budget Brit romcom, with a cast of unknowns and an incongruous magical twist. But twenty-eight years later it's still on repeat every festive season, having somehow earned the status of a Holiday Classic. There I am, a tousle-haired, rosy-cheeked moppet, gazing upwards as the first cellulose snowflakes begin to fall. Forever frozen in my four-year-old glory.

I was only on screen for twenty minutes. The focus of the movie was the romance between nerdy Tim Randolf and sassy older sexpot Honey Evans. But even now, people will clock my name and ask me about it. ('So, what's Sir Tim *really* like?' 'Did they let you keep one of the snow mice?' 'Were you frightened of the icicle goblins?') The thing is, for a lot of people, that film looms larger in their childhood memories than it does in mine. I mean, c'mon, how much do *you* remember of what you were doing age four?

Off the back of *Snow Angels*, I had three more small film roles and a run of commercials and voice-over work. But the brutal truth is that a kid who is absolutely adorable at, say, four may not be the least bit adorable or even attractive once they've outgrown their dimples. Aged fifteen, I'd been pathetically relieved to acquire visible cheekbones. Alas, the loss of puppy fat came with a price: my nose was now distractingly prominent. Or so I thought.

When *Snow Angels* came out, reviewers liked to mention that the scene-stealing child actor who played Lucie came from a 'theatrical dynasty'. It's true that Pa and his two siblings are all performers of sorts, and my cousin Dido has a couple of Olivier awards in her loo, but none of them are what you'd call household names. In fact, we can only boast of one bone fide National Treasure: my grandfather, Sir Terence Thane, formerly Terry Stubbs, the butcher's son from Ealing who scaled the thespian heights along with Sirs Larry, Ralph and John. His nose was almost as famous as his Lear, and was long and arched, with flared wings. We've all inherited a version of it. On the right sort of profile – Dido's, for example – it is both handsome and distinctive. On others, it's simply all-conquering.

Either way, getting rid of the nose wasn't the liberation I'd hoped for. The new model was narrow and straight, with a demurely rounded tip. It made my face look neater, sweeter but also oddly unfinished. Work picked up, at least at first, but my late teens and twenties were filled with pilots for series that never got sold, forgettable British crime dramas and my most recent gig, the American legal dramedy *Briefs*.

Otherwise, my film credits are mostly along the lines of Pretty Girl on Plane, Prostitute at Party and Crying Bridesmaid.

If I had kept my nose, would it all have been different?

Would I still have agreed to beard for Adam Harker?

What then?

Ah, what then.

When the PR blitz began, it made for a cute anecdote: 'We were childhood sweethearts!' Like everything else, this was essentially bollocks.

I first met Adam when I was twelve and we were both enrolled at stage school. Students called it the Fame Factory, as if mock disdain could cover up the rancid whiff of our ambition. My first few years there were not happy ones, on account of the puppy fat and the nose. Meanwhile, the only name Adam had made for himself was that of a cocky little shit. He was small and squat and acne spattered, yet possessed of unshakeable confidence. 'Ten years from now,' he used to say, 'all these talent-show losers will be dining out on how they went to school with me.'

Adam was a year older than me, so we only got to know each other when we were cast as brother and sister in a play about an upper-crust family at war over their inheritance. They were small parts in a fairly awful show that folded after a month, but as the only juveniles on set we spent a certain amount of time backstage together. We used to play card games and take the piss out of the director, as well as the Barbies 'n' Kens (Adam's term) back at school. Adam liked hearing about the Thanes, too. 'A pedigree like that's the real deal,' he told me once, with a solemnity that surprised me.

'Sure, he'll be a great *character* actor,' the Ken dolls sneered when rumours of Adam's on-stage charisma began to spread. Then he got his growth spurt, his skin cleared up and, for a while, his rise seemed as effortless as it was inevitable.

At the age of nineteen, after rave reviews for his part in ITV's World War I drama *The Last Hurrah*, Adam headed to LA. From there he bagged a BAFTA for playing Brad Pitt's troubled son in art-house flick *Silent Hour*, which was followed by a few small but well-received parts before being cast in *Wylderness*, billed as the biggest dystopian fantasy franchise since *Hunger Games*. The box-office returns were disappointing, however, and when they didn't film the third of the trilogy, Adam's trajectory began to stall. There were rumours of difficult behaviour, an on-set bust-up that halted production on a film that was later shelved. His prediction that he'd be the Fame Factory graduate we all name-dropped had come true only up to a point. Most people knew who he was, but indistinctly.

'Adam Harker's a meth head,' said Nina authoritatively, the same afternoon as her #MeToo rant. 'He got a bit too much into character during that Deep South family saga. Hasn't been able to shake the habit since.'

'Says who?'

'The make-up girl on the *Evening Standard* shoot. So there.'

Nina always claims the most successful stars are nursing the darkest secrets. Drugs, violence, paedophile rings … She's got a lot of contacts in showbiz-adjacent roles, so she's better informed than most. But I also happen to know she makes stuff up and sends it to the blind gossip sites just for shits and giggles. I can see the appeal. I mean, *I* want to believe it. It's certainly easier on the ego to assume the famous and beautiful are also the miserable and the damned.

'I wish you'd dig up some dirt on the Thanes.'

'Pfff. No one gives a crap about your family.' Nina looked mischievous. 'Though I did hear Dido's shagging a spear-carrier.'

'No!' I was delighted. My cousin Dido is three years older than me and the heir apparent to Sir Terry's luvvie legacy. People still rave about her Lady Macbeth, and her Hedda is almost as fawned over as her Antigone. My one comfort is that she's too much of a snob to take her talents mainstream.

Actually, that's not true. I also take comfort in the fact that Dido's husband is a dick. Hence the spear-carrier, presumably.

'You can ask her about it tonight,' said Nina. 'He's fresh out of RADA and hung like a donkey. Allegedly. Mind you, those Shakespearean codpieces can be very misleading.'

'Dinner. *Shit.*' We'd spent the afternoon in Nina's flat, getting stoned and watching Fred Astaire movies. It's Nina's thing when she's had a setback. Those big monochrome dance numbers are trippy at the best of times, like an Escher print come to life, but weed slows them down. It's very soothing. Too soothing on this occasion; I now had less than an hour to straighten out and get to Dido's. It was her standard invitation: 'Just a kitchen supper, *super* relaxed, *super* fun crowd.'

For Dido, 'fun' means worthy yet snide. Habitat for Humanity meets *Mean Girls*.

Dido and Nick live in a large house in Highgate. Patchily painted in Gothic hues, it's chilly and cluttered, with stacks of Nick's unpublished novels and Dido's scripts piled up everywhere. There's quite a lot of dog hair, too, courtesy of Hotspur. Hotspur is an Afghan hound. Hotspur looks very much like Dido, but of course nobody has ever dared point this out.

As I said, it's not an inviting house. The location of these famous kitchen suppers is in the basement; the fittings are unvarnished wood, and the crockery looks like it's been thrown together by depressed Scandinavian pre-schoolers. But the thing about my cousin is that she can *really* cook. In interviews, she'll say things like 'feasting people is how I show love' and it's not entirely bollocks. Dining chez Dido means platters of fragrant meats melting from the bone, lacy lacquers of chocolate and slicks of spiced butter, swirls of boozy cream. The hostess herself will barely touch this largesse. She'll pick at a slice of fruit or paring of cheese, all the while eating us up with her eyes.

After retrieving a key from under the usual plant pot, I slunk in late, red-eyed and dishevelled, hoping to find the party in full tipsy swing. But the eleven people gathered around the kitchen table looked disconcertingly alert. Except for Nick, perhaps, who was doing the rounds with a carafe. The sloshing way he poured suggested he'd had a head start on the rest of us.

'Darling Lily,' said Dido, arms flung wide. 'We're all so thrilled you could make it.'

I wasn't sure if this was a dig. It can be hard to tell with Dido. I think she honestly believes she's doing me a favour with her condescending suppers and cast-off clothing and unsolicited advice.

'And how gorgeous you look!' Definitely a dig, then.

Dido's studied carelessness on the domestic front extends to her own appearance. She favours mannish tailoring, oversize shirts and ugly shoes. ('Who does she think she is?' sniffs the Momager. 'A lesbian?') But Dido can carry it off. She lopes about on her endless legs, curtained by swirls of her endless hair, that famous nose jutting forth like the prow of a very sexy ship. The kind with billowing sails and lots of guns.

'Isn't she adorable?' Dido declared to a narrow bearded man sitting at the more shadowy end of the table. 'Gideon, have you met my adorable cousin? Lily, this is Gideon. He's a music journalist and *the* most fascinating man.'

She ushered me into the seat next to him. Within seconds, a loaded plate of food was steaming in front of me. The gloom of the basement was barely alleviated by a scattering of hurricane lamps, so it was hard to tell exactly what I was eating. The pot had left me ravenous in any case. Blindly, I forked in various richly spiced and scented mouthfuls, as introductions to assorted artistes and do-gooders were made.

Dido had recently finished a run of *Mary Stuart* at the National, and the conversation I'd interrupted was moving from Schiller to Goethe. 'Not a fan of Weimar classicism?' Gideon asked in a stage-whisper.

'It doesn't come up much in my line of work.' I was too busy shovelling in food to pay attention. There was butter on my chin and I didn't even care.

'Aren't you an actress too?'

'Ah, but Lily's in actual "showbiz",' Dido trilled from the other end of the table.

'Right.' I took a long swig from my glass. 'Here to represent the bread-and-circuses division of Thane, Inc.'

'Oh, so *you're* the child-star,' said somebody else.

'I took a lot of growth hormones before coming out tonight.'

Nobody laughed.

'I remember you from *Briefs*,' said the woman across from me, so graciously it was clear she thought she was throwing me a lifeline. 'Weren't you the bitchy one? With kleptomania? The Honourable Hermione Whatnot.'

'Hancock. Yeah. It was a … fun role.'

'One of my guilty pleasures. Mostly, I watched it for the power-dressing.'

It turned out she was a lawyer. Human rights, inevitably. She started to tell me – archly, but in great detail – all the ways that TV shows get the legal profession wrong.

'What *I* find off-putting about those glossy American dramas,' said Gideon, cutting in, 'is how they make up their leading ladies to look like drag queens.'

'Oh, I know.' Human Rights made a moue of distaste. 'False eyelashes and ridiculous hair extensions and all that contouring goop.'

'People get self-conscious with high-definition,' I said, sounding defensive in spite of myself.

'Why should they? Seems to me everyone on the telly these days is a perfect ten. Or eight, minimum. Take a girl like you.' Jovially, Gideon speared an asparagus from my plate.

'You don't need three inches of slap to look fuckable.'

I turned my chair towards Nick, who was on my other side and had contributed even less to the general conversation than I had. He's quite good looking, in a sneery sort of way, but tonight he looked more than usually morose. Maybe Nina was right and Dido *was* carrying on with some oversized codpiece. I supposed I should feel sorry for him. 'So tell me about the new book ...'

Nick had an agent for a while, but they parted ways over the direction of his latest effort, which was written in the voice of a drug dealer from the Bronx who believes he's the reincarnation of the Earl of Rochester. Writers and actors share the impulse to be as overweening as they're insecure; the difference is that actors, even failed ones, have a pathological need to win over their audience. Nick has never felt the need to ingratiate himself with anyone. Thanks to family money, he's under no pressure to produce a bestseller. Or any kind of seller, in fact.

'Ever thought about self-publishing?' I asked at the end of his monologue on the relationship between gansta-rap and seventeenth-century erotic poetry.

'*Vanity* publishing?'

'Well, not exactly. I mean if, like you say, traditional publishing's so corrupt ... and, you know, the model's broken, why not look elsewhere? You'd get total creative control. And that could be good. Right?'

'Honestly, Lily.' He looked at me coldly. 'Asking a novelist if they've thought about self-publishing is like asking an actress if they've considered porn.'

'It's hardly –'

Gideon leaned in. 'Maybe you should expand your range. A webcam girl who quotes Schiller ... Think about it.'

'Excuse me. I've just remembered there's somewhere I have to be.' I got up from my chair, which scraped dramatically against the floor, knocking into Hotspur in the process. Amidst the anguished yelping and flurry of dog hair, there was no hope of a swift exit. Dido insisted on escorting me to the door.

'Are you sure you have to dash? I know how good you are at putting a brave face on things but Uncle Lionel *did* mention you're at rather a loose end ...'

'Right. Luckily for me, your guests had some tips for getting into porn.'

'You funny creature! But you *will* let me know if there's anything I can do to help?' She was thrusting a Tupperware filled with leftovers at me, followed by an enormous woolly muffler thing. It was possibly one of Hotspur's blankets. 'Anything at all. Promise me.'

'How about an introduction to one of your casting-director chums?'

Dido actually blanched. 'I, ah, thought you didn't do theatre ...'

'I'm kidding! But thanks anyway. It was a lovely evening. Except for Gideon. He's a perv.'

She raised her brows. 'I'm sorry, darling. I thought you were too stoned to notice.'